Deborah is a North Carolina author. She has had many hobbies since age thirty-five when she was introduced to creativity: painting in many media, pottery, beading, weaving, knitting, rug hooking, quilting, miniature bonsai trees, and more. She plays piano and has recorded several albums and CDs.

She enjoyed making up stories to her children when they were young. Several years ago, she wanted to tell her story of struggles from her early life. So, she began her first novel, *Through It All,* which is a fictional biography. After completing that book, she found that she very much enjoyed writing stories and is currently working on her fifth novel.

Deborah Ann Reardon

FOLLOW THE LEADS

Thorne Davenport Series – Book Two

AUSTIN MACAULEY PUBLISHERS™

LONDON ∗ CAMBRIDGE ∗ NEW YORK ∗ SHARJAH

Ordering Information
Quantity sales: Special discounts are available on quantity purchases by corporations, associations, and others. For details, contact the publisher at the address below.

Publisher's Cataloging-in-Publication data
Reardon, Deborah Ann
Follow the Leads

ISBN 9798891552302 (Paperback)
ISBN 9798891552319 (ePub e-book)

Library of Congress Control Number: 2023921652

www.austinmacauley.com/us

First Published 2024
Austin Macauley Publishers LLC
40 Wall Street, 33rd Floor, Suite 3302
New York, NY 10005
USA

mail-usa@austinmacauley.com
+1 (646) 5125767

Prologue

Charlotte Observer
April 1979

Yesterday, a robbery occurred at Beacon's Jewelry Store on Belaire Avenue around 4:30 in the afternoon. The owner suffered a head injury and was admitted to the hospital for observation. No suspect has been found. The value of the stolen merchandise is currently unknown. If you have any information regarding this, please notify the local police department.

Chapter One

The Lillington police chief, Logan, yes, two names the same; everyone called him Chief Lolo. He didn't mind and, in fact, liked it. He was in his late fifties and had been the police chief for about three years this term, and two previous elections. The town was too small for a large police force, neither was there a lot of violence, only petty crimes. Everyone was satisfied with the job Chief Lolo did.

He was a short man, balding at the top. He wore glasses for up-close vision, and he was always misplacing them. Chief Lolo never missed a day of work. He and his wife Beth Logan lived near town. She was 51 years old, a petite woman with short dyed-black, curly hair, and worked as a cashier and hostess at the local seafood restaurant and knew most of the people in town. She and Ms. Maggie were friends, they both attended the First Presbyterian church. They didn't think of themselves as gossip, just that they shared the things they knew about people so that they could keep up with the latest happenings in town.

Chief Lolo and his deputy, Marshall Goss, went to have lunch together at the seafood restaurant. Marshall was a tall, clean-cut, blond-haired guy in his late twenties, unmarried. He kept his uniform pristine and his shoes shined. Mr. Templeton, the realtor, walked in with his secretary, Stacy. As they were escorted to their table by Beth Logan, Mr. Templeton said, "Good evening, Chief, Deputy Goss."

The chief nodded and the deputy acknowledged them with a wave while taking a longer look at Stacy.

After they walked away, Goss said in a low voice, "That Stacy is a fine-looking woman. Wonder why she's not married."

Chief chewed his French fries and said, "Maybe she's in love with her married boss," and raised his eyebrows in a quizzical expression.

"You reckon?"

"Who knows?"

They finished their meal, paid the ticket, and went back to the police station.

The phone was ringing when they got inside. Deputy Goss answered, "Police station, Deputy Goss speaking." He listened for a few minutes, hung up, and turned to the chief.

Chief Lolo asked impatiently, "What was that about?"

"A neighbor of Eli Gruber's. She said that she hadn't seen him for a few days and thought we might want to look into it."

The chief said, "Well, I guess we can go check it out. We don't have anything better to do." He grabbed his hat, walked toward the door, and turned to Deputy Goss. "Come on, let's go. He's probably out of town or something. Sometimes I wonder about nosy people. I guess it will occupy our afternoon, at least for a little bit."

They arrived at Mr. Gruber's house. Mr. Gruber's Toyota Corolla was parked on the street in front of his house. They rang the doorbell, then knocked. No answer. They walked around to the back of the house, nothing appeared unusual. They went back to their cruiser.

"Well, I guess we need to look into this further," said Deputy Goss. "You know, we could break the door down or call a locksmith."

Chief said, "Let's not get carried away just yet Goss."

They drove back to the police station.

* * *

When Chief Logan got home that night, he had Eli Gruber on his mind. His wife, Beth, asked, "Something bothering you, Logan?"

"We got a call today from a woman, a neighbor of Eli Gruber and she said she hasn't seen him for a few days and wanted us to check it out. I took Deputy Goss with me. Everything looked OK, nothing suspicious. His car was parked on the street, but no one came to the door when we knocked."

Beth asked, "What do you think it might be?"

"Not sure. Of course, it could be several things. He may have been out with a friend, or he took a trip. Anyway, we'll wait and see if anything turns up."

Chapter Two

The next day, Beth Logan went to see Ms. Maggie at Barton's Drugstore. She waited for a couple of customers to checkout and leave, then she walked up to Ms. Maggie at the counter. No one knew the actual age of Ms. Maggie, but she had worked at Barton's Drugstore forever and knew everything about everybody in town. After the usual friendly greeting, Beth said, "Maggie, have you seen Mr. Gruber lately?"

Ms. Maggie put her long, wrinkled index finger on her chin and thought. "Come to think of it, no, he hasn't been in this week. He usually comes in every Monday, sometimes Thursdays." She shook her head. "No, can't say I have. Why do you ask?"

Beth continued in a secretive tone. "Well, yesterday Logan told me that a neighbor of Mr. Gruber's called and said she hadn't seen him for a while and wanted Logan to check it out."

Ms. Maggie's interest perked. "Did they check it out? What did they find?"

"Yes, Logan and Deputy Goss went to Mr. Gruber's house, but nothing was suspicious. They knocked but no one answered the door."

Ms. Maggie said, "They need to keep checking. I mean, something could be wrong."

"Logan said he could be out with a friend, or maybe he took a trip somewhere." Both ladies were quiet with their own imaginings.

Finally, Ms. Maggie asked, "Did you need to get anything today, Beth?"

"No, I just came by to tell you about Mr. Gruber."

Beth turned to leave, and Ms. Maggie said, "I'll let you know if I hear anything."

Beth replied, "And I'll keep you posted as I find out things."

Chapter Three

Carly was dressed in sweats with her shoulder-length blond hair pulled back in a ponytail. She was preparing tacos for supper. Thorne entered the house, hung his jacket and shoulder holster in the closet, and walked into the kitchen.

"Hello, my beautiful Mrs. Davenport! How has your day been?" and as always, he hugged and kissed her. Poohdinkle, their two-year-old Yorkie Mix, greeted Thorne with a wagging tail until he kissed Carly, then she barked a warning. As usual, Thorne said, "Dinkle, don't you know by now I'm a good guy?"

Carly said, "I think Dinkle wants a kiss and hug too." Thorne reached down and rubbed Dinkle's head. Dinkle wagged her tail in appreciation. Carly loved Thorne's relationship with Dinkle. Even more, she loved his good-looking, rugged appearance and how his eyes still twinkled when he smiled.

Thorne Davenport and Carly Jansen had married in September and had spent their honeymoon in Sugar Mountain, a ski resort in Western North Carolina. Thorne had planned this prior to the wedding because Carly had never seen the mountains during the autumn with the awesome array of colors. They stayed in a small cabin located a few miles from the Appalachian Trail and took the long way home along the Blue Ridge Parkway. Thorne had lived in Dunn close to his office but after their marriage, he moved into Carly's house in Flat Branch.

"Hope you're hungry. We're having tacos."

Thorne said, "One of my favorites, as long as they are homemade. And yes, I'm starved. I didn't take time to eat lunch today."

Sitting down to eat, Carly asked, "Sounds like you had a busy day."

"It was not that busy. I did have one person call with a major problem."

Carly looked at him. "Oh yeah, what about?"

Thorne said seriously, "This woman wanted to know if I could find her cat."

Carly said with a serious expression, "I hope you took her case." Then she couldn't help but smile.

Thorne said, "I figured that she would not want to pay my hourly fee. And, no, I told her that I didn't do that sort of thing. Otherwise, things were as usual."

Carly said, "Tomorrow I have an appointment to take Poohdinkle to get her rabies shot and a yearly checkup. I thought I would stop by the diner and see how Nellie's doing."

"Tell her I said hello."

Chapter Four

Mr. Arthur Templeton arrived at his real estate office late morning after a meeting of the Lillington Town Council. He was in his middle fifties, tall, professionally styled gray-streaked black hair, a dignified posture, lean figure enhanced by his tailor-made gray suit, starched dark gray shirt, navy tie, platinum tie pin, and cuff links. He had recently relocated from the main real estate office in Raleigh believing that being the manager would give him the prestige that he didn't have as being one of many agents in an office. The previous manager, Mr. Baker, and his secretary, Sally, both retired in September.

Mr. Templeton and his wife, Alice, after being married since college, were filing for divorce. Alice was not at all into the social events and committees that Mr. Templeton's position required. Even though they had no children, she stayed at home. Stacy Wainwright, on the other hand, had always dressed fashionably and had her hair stylized at the beauty shop. So, when Mr. Templeton heard about the opportunity for relocating, he talked with Stacy one night when they met secretly, and they both decided to relocate to Lillington.

Templeton walked into his main office. "Hello, Stacy." Stacy had been his secretary for over ten years in the home office in Raleigh.

"Hello, Mr. Templeton. Here's your mail." When he took it, their hands touched with obvious tenderness, and they looked at each other. He wanted to lean down and kiss her but knew that a client could walk in. "I'll get your coffee," she said.

"That would be fine, Stacy."

She took his coffee to his office and asked, "How was your council meeting?"

"The usual. Mayor Ashby's main concern was the increase in crime over the past month or so. He was rather firm with Chief Logan about planning how to handle it." He began looking through his mail. "I have an appointment with a client at 1 o'clock, Vernon Ward. Send him back to my office when he arrives, please."

"Certainly."

She closed his door and went back to her desk.

***

Mr. Vernon Ward arrived at the realty office promptly at 1:00 that afternoon.

Stacy said, "Hello, you must be Mr. Ward."

"Yes, I have an appointment with Mr. Templeton." He looked around and said to Stacy, "You're new here, I see. I heard that Mr. Baker and Sally had both retired."

"Yes, sir." Stacy buzzed Mr. Templeton's office. "Mr. Ward is here." She said to Mr. Ward, "He asked that you go right in."

Mr. Ward pursed his lips. "The place looks quite different, nicer furniture, love the paintings." Stacy assumed, by Mr. Ward's appearance, that he wasn't in the market to buy, maybe rent. He was an older man, dressed in jeans, a flannel shirt, and tennis shoes.

He walked to Mr. Templeton's office. Templeton stood, reached out to shake Mr. Ward's hand, and said, "Come in, Mr. Ward. Have a seat. How can I help you today?"

Mr. Ward said. "I heard that Mr. Baker had retired. I bought my house from him years ago. Nice man." He paused, cleared his throat. "You've done an impressive job decorating the place."

Templeton replied, "Thank you. Stacy, my secretary, gets all the credit."

Mr. Ward said, "I need to find a place to rent. My daughter and her son are moving here. My home isn't large enough for them to be comfortable. I would like for the house to be in a good school district. She can't afford a luxury home, but she needs at least two bedrooms."

Mr. Templeton reached on the shelf behind his desk for the property listings. After looking over it, he said, "I have a couple of places that I think would meet your needs."

Mr. Ward cleared his throat again. "How much is the rent each month?"

"One is $350, and the other is $375. Of course, there is a one-month deposit upon signing the rental agreement."

"That sounds doable. I'll take care of the deposit. When can I see them?"

Mr. Templeton looked at his calendar to make sure he didn't have any appointments later that afternoon. "Right now, if that's good for you."

"Sure, fine."

On the way out of the office, Templeton said to Stacy, "We're going to look at a couple of rental properties. I should be back around 3:30 or so."

When they got into Templeton's BMW, he said, "You said your daughter is moving here?"

"Yes. My daughter, Jennifer. She has one son, Kenny. He's in the fifth grade. That's why I asked about the school district."

Templeton said, "Both of these houses are in the Harnett Primary School district, a good school from what I hear."

"That's good to know."

Mr. Ward decided on the house on N. Park Avenue, two bedrooms and the small yard wouldn't be too much for Jennifer to care for.

Templeton asked, "How old is your daughter? When will she be moving in?"

"She's thirty-two. She currently lives near Charlotte and will be here later this month and will stay with me until she can move in the first of November."

They went back to the realty office and Mr. Ward paid the deposit of $350 and signed the one-year rental agreement to begin November first.

Mr. Templeton said, "Since the house is empty, she can move in when she arrives. That would be no problem."

"I really appreciate that. Kenny can get enrolled in school and they can get settled sooner." He stood to leave. "I'll let you know when they arrive and are moving in."

"Fine. And thanks for coming in. It's been a pleasure. I look forward to meeting them."

Stacy said as Mr. Ward came out of the office. "Did you find what you liked?"

Mr. Ward paused near her desk. "Yes, sure did." He turned toward the door and, looking back, he added, "My daughter and her son will be moving here later this month. I'll be bringing them by to meet Mr. Templeton."

Stacy smiled. "I look forward to meeting them. Have a good day, Mr. Ward."

Mr. Templeton brought the contract papers and payment to Stacy. He said, "His daughter and her son are moving here. I didn't ask any questions, of course, but I wonder what the situation is."

Stacy said, "I wondered the same thing."

Chapter Five

When Chief Logan got to the police station the next day, he said to Deputy Goss, "Marshall, call down to Mr. Templeton's office and ask if Eli Gruber rents his house from him, or if he owns it."

"You want me to ask Stacy?" Goss asked.

"That'll be fine."

When the phone rang, Stacy answered, "Templeton Realty, this is Stacy."

Goss cleared his throat. "Hey, hello, ah, is this Stacy?"

"Yes, I'm Stacy, Mr. Templeton's secretary. How may I help you?"

"We wanted to find out, Chief Lolo and me, if Mr. Templeton rented a house to Eli Gruber."

"Yes, in fact, we do. Why do you ask?"

Goss put his hand over the receiver and looked at the chief. "Chief, do you want me to tell her why we wanna know?"

The chief shook his head, yes.

"I'm Deputy Marshall Goss. Chief Lolo got a call yesterday from a neighbor of Mr. Gruber's and thought there might be something wrong because she hadn't seen him in a few days. We went to check it out and no one was home, but his car was there."

Stacy said, "Well, I don't know anything about that. His rent is paid up to date. Otherwise, we don't know much about him."

Goss said, "Well, thanks for your help. Goodbye." He turned to the chief. "She said they don't know anything."

The chief thought a minute. "I think we need to go back to Gruber's house and look around a little more. Call her back and ask if they have a key that we can use to go inside."

They left, retrieved the house key from the realtor, and on the way to Eli Gruber's house, Deputy Goss asked, "What if he is inside, dead?"

"Don't go thinking the worst, Goss. We'll see when we get there." They drove the rest of the way in silence.

Chapter Six

The next morning, after Thorne left for his office, Carly and Dinkle left to visit with Nellie before going to Doc Skinner's office. Nellie Garrett was in her mid-seventies and had worked at the Green Hornet Grill in Bunnlevel since it opened.

The previous owner, Ed Madry, had died and in his Will, he had left the diner to Nellie. She hired a bookkeeper; otherwise, she kept doing her usual jobs as cook, waitress, and cashier. The diner was her home. She and Carly were best friends. She was from Ohio, had two sons who lived in Florida, and she still drove an older model Chevrolet Impala which Carly thought fit Nellie's personality, sturdy, well made, lasting forever.

As usual, Nellie greeted Carly like she hadn't seen her in a long time. "Hey, Carly. Glad you could stop by. Want some coffee or breakfast?"

"No, just wanted to say hello. I have Dinkle in the car. She's going to Doc Skinner to get her rabies vaccination."

Nellie asked, "Well, how are things with ya'll?"

"Just great. Thorne's work is a little slow right now. In fact, you won't believe it, but yesterday he had a lady call to ask him to find her cat!"

Nellie laughed. "I sure would have liked to have heard that conversation."

"How are you doing, Nellie? Staying busy, I guess."

"Yes, same crowd still coming in. Lunchtime is the busiest."

"I gotta get going. Come see us sometime."

"I will. I thought I would let the newlyweds settle in first. Speaking of newlyweds, how was the honeymoon?"

"The mountains were awesome. I really enjoyed it." She opened the door. "Later, Nellie."

* * *

At Doc Skinner's office, Carly noticed that the Doc looked tired and older than before and wondered if he was well, but she didn't say anything. Ms. Maggie would know, she thought, and she would ask her the next time she had to go to Barton's Drugstore. Doc Skinner had been the town vet forever, and Ms. Maggie had operated the drugstore forever. That's the way it seemed in Lillington. Nothing ever changed.

Chapter Seven

When Carly and Dinkle returned home, Dinkle went to the sofa and slept for a long time. Carly decided to work on the fiction novel she was writing about Bonnie. She took out the folder and began reminiscing about how she had met Bonnie Hardin.

Nellie had hired Thorne Davenport to find out who Carly's birth parents were. Thorne had previously been a police officer in Richmond, Virginia, but with the justice system giving the bad guys a slap on the wrist and releasing them back into the world to commit more crimes, Thorne got frustrated with the job. He became a private investigator with a firm in Dunn. When the owner moved away, he bought the business and renamed it Davenport Investigations.

After the outcome of locating Carly's biological mother ended with such total and crushing rejection, Thorne felt leery of trying to find her biological father. That turned out better than imagined, however.

Earlier that spring, Carly had bought her house with the inheritance from her parents. When she moved in, she had found a box of journals and memorabilia in the attic and asked Thorne to try to find who the previous renters had been. He located Bonnie and Josh Hardin. They visited Bonnie in Miller's Creek and found that she had written the journals. When Carly was telling about the rejection of her birth mother and said her name, Kate Simmons Richardson, it turned out that Bonnie was Kate's sister.

They further discovered that Bonnie remembered a letter she had received from Kate years prior which mentioned the name of the man her sister was dating the summer before she left for college. Thorne located Joey and, to Thorne's relief, the results of that reunion were better than one could dream. Joey and Janice Saunders accepted both Carly and Thorne into their family. They planned and paid all expenses for Thorne's and Carly's wedding which was held at their home, on the beach at North Topsail Island, North Carolina in September.

When Thorne and Carly had returned the box of journals to Bonnie, Carly agreed that Bonnie's life story would be interesting for a fiction novel. Carly had gone to college for journalism, as writing novels was her goal. Bonnie agreed to tell her story to Carly, at first on tape. Later Bonnie's husband, Josh, a wildlife artist, and sculptor, was participating in a street festival in Dunn to sell his art, so Bonnie came to Carly's for the weekend to tell her life's story in person.

Carly now sat at her desk in her office and opened the file. There was so much to write. She became engrossed in the story as she typed. Dinkle appeared at the doorway and laid down like a good guard dog.

Chapter Eight

Since Carly didn't get to go to the drugstore when she was in town for Dinkle's visit at the vet, she decided to go today. At the drugstore, she entered, and Ms. Maggie greeted her, as usual.

When Carly went to checkout, Ms. Maggie asked, "Have you heard about Mr. Gruber?"

"No, what about him? I don't think I know him." Carly said.

"I guess you wouldn't. But, anyway, he's lived here for several years. Lives across town. Well, yesterday, Chief Logan's wife, Beth, you know her, right?" Carly shook her head. "Well, she came in and told me that Mr. Gruber is missing."

Carly asked, "How do they know?"

Maggie rang up Carly's purchases and said, "Beth said that the chief got a call from one of Mr. Gruber's neighbors who said that she hadn't seen him in a few days and wanted the police to check on him."

"I see." Carly paid.

Ms. Maggie gave her change and continued. "The chief and Deputy Goss went to his house, Mr. Gruber's, and he wasn't at home, but his car was there."

Carly knew how Ms. Maggie loved to tell the gossip in town. "Maybe he went somewhere with a friend or something."

"We'll see. Beth told me she would keep me in the loop."

"That's good." On her way to the door, Carly turned back. "Ms. Maggie, I was at Doc Skinner's yesterday. He looked a little under the weather. Have you heard anything about him?"

Ms. Maggie thought and said, "No, don't believe so. I sure hope he's OK."

"Me too." Carly said and left the store.

* * *

When Carly returned home, Dinkle greeted her at the door. She put her supplies away. "You ready to go outside for a while?" Dinkle wagged her tail and followed Carly to the back patio. Dinkle investigated all the smells in the yard and came back to sit quietly with Carly. She thought about what Ms. Maggie had told her and wondered if there was anything to it. Dinkle barked once. Carly saw a rabbit come to the edge of bushes along the back of her yard. She would talk to Thorne about what Ms. Maggie said tonight when he got home.

* * *

After supper, Thorne and Carly, and Dinkle were sitting in the living room discussing their day. Carly said, "I stopped by the drugstore today. Ms. Maggie was in one of her tell-all moods."

Thorne asked, "What was it this time, or should I say, who was it about?"

"She said that Chief Logan's wife came by and told her that Eli Gruber, a man in town, was missing, at least by a neighbor's report."

"Missing? How do they know that?"

"I guess they don't really know it. She said that one of Mr. Gruber's neighbors had called the police and told them that she hadn't seen him for a few days and thought that they should check on it."

Thorne, knowing the good and prompt responses of their police force, asked, "Did they do anything?"

"Ms. Maggie said they went to Mr. Gruber's house, his car was parked on the street, but nobody was home."

Thorne said in a faked, trembly voice, "Oooh, I bet something sinister is going on." He smiled.

"You know how Ms. Maggie is, and her friend, Beth Logan."

"Oh yes, I'm quite familiar with their goings-on. They can truly make a mountain out of a molehill."

Carly paused and asked, "Do you think you might need to look into it?"

Thorne answered, "They'll probably call me if they need to. Let's just wait and see." He got up to go get a glass of water. "Does Mr. Bennett at the paper know about it?"

"I'm not sure, probably not yet."

Thorne called out, "Can I get you anything?"

"No, I'm fine."

That night in bed, Thorne broke the silence and said, "Carly, I've been wanting to talk about something." Carly didn't say anything, just looked at him. He continued, "I know we haven't talked about it, but I've been thinking. Do you want to have children?"

Carly was surprised. She knew that years ago he had lost his wife, who was pregnant at the time in an automobile accident, and assumed that he might not want children. She quietly said, "I thought it would be difficult—"

Thorne interrupted. "I know what you might think. That was a terrible time in my life, but my life is different now and I want us to be a family."

Carly considered it a moment and softly said, "I would like that too, Thorne." Their intimacy was extra special, with more feelings of love than ever.

Chapter Nine

Chief Logan parked his police car across the street from Mr. Gruber's house. The neighbor on the other side of the street came out of her front door and waved at them. "Chief, Chief," she called. The chief stopped and turned to her. She asked, "Have you found out anything?"

"Not yet, Mam. We're still investigating." He motioned toward her house. "You go on back inside. You'll hear if we find out anything."

"Well, alright then." She turned and mumbled something the chief couldn't hear.

The chief and Goss walked up the sidewalk. Deputy Goss opened the front door with the key and stepped back to let the chief go inside first. "Dang, you smell that, Chief?"

The chief already had his nose covered with his handkerchief. They slowly walked through the house, one room at a time. Nothing until Goss got to the bedroom.

Deputy Goss exclaimed, "Oh my, oh my, oh no." He backed slowly out of the room.

The chief entered the room, walked over to the bed, and saw Eli Gruber. He was fully clothed, lying on his back, with his shoes on. He knew that Eli Gruber was not among the living. He turned to Goss and said, "Call Sledge, tell him that he has a customer." Tom Sledge was the county coroner. He was late in years, always wore clothes a size too large and wrinkled, with slumped posture, uncombed hair. He had never been married, and it was obvious in his appearance.

After gaining his wits, Deputy Goss went to use the phone in the kitchen and called the coroner, giving him the address. He waited for the chief, not wanting to see the body again. When the chief walked down the hall, Goss said, "The coroner will be here in a few."

They looked around the rest of the house to see if anything looked out of place but saw nothing suspicious.

* * *

Chief Lolo called Mr. Templeton when he got back to the police station. Stacy answered, "Templeton Realty, this is Stacy."

"Hey, Stacy, is Mr. Templeton in?" asked the chief.

"Yes sir. May I tell him who's calling?"

The chief thought, *Shouldn't she recognize my voice by now?* "It's Chief Logan."

"Hold on, I'll connect you." She buzzed Mr. Templeton's intercom and said, "Chief Logan is on the phone."

"Thanks, Stacy." Mr. Templeton clicked the button. "Chief Lolo, how in the world are you today? What can I do for you?"

"I'm good. I was calling to inform you that we found Mr. Gruber."

"Grand!" Mr. Templeton exclaimed.

"Well, sir, not so good. He's dead."

"Dead? What happened?"

Chief Logan explained, "We don't know. We're waiting on the coroner's report. We found him on his bed. No sign of trouble."

"How terrible."

"Yes sir, pretty bad. Anyway, I just wanted to let you know that your rental house will be available to rent but you might want to get a cleaning crew over there. The smell is pretty bad."

"We always do that. Several houses are in worse condition than others. Listen, I appreciate the heads-up. Hope you find out what happened."

"We definitely will." They hung up.

Mr. Templeton walked into Stacy's office on his way out and said, "Stacy, please call the cleaning crew. Eli Gruber was found dead, and his house is vacant and needs cleaning before we can rent it."

"Yes sir, I'll do it now." She picked up the phone as he left.

Chapter Ten

Carly awoke the next morning. Thorne had already left for work. She went to the kitchen, opened Dinkle's doggie door, and turned to make coffee. Thorne had already made it and left a note beside her coffee cup. "Mrs. Davenport, you have my heart and hopefully our little one. Have a great day."

Carly's heart swelled with warmth and gratitude. She felt like the most blessed person on earth. She went outside to have her coffee and to be with Dinkle. As they sat, she thought about the Eli Gruber situation. Maybe Mr. Bennett at the newspaper knew something about it. She had worked for Peter Bennett, the newspaper editor, ever since moving to Lillington after college. She would find out when she turned in her article for this week's publication. She looked at Dinkle and got up from her chair.

"Well Dinkle, I need to get busy on my book. Bonnie's story can't tell itself. Come on." Dinkle dutifully followed Carly back inside. Carly dressed and went to her office to continue writing her novel. Dinkle lay guard at her office door.

A little later, Carly took a break from writing. She had not yet read the newspaper this morning. She went out and picked up the paper from the front porch, poured a cup of tea, and sat at the kitchen table to read the paper. Sure enough, the front-page story read, "Dead man found, cause unknown." She continued reading.

Yesterday, about 4:00 in the afternoon, Chief Lolo and Deputy Goss arrived at the home of Eli Gruber and found him dead in his bed. The day prior, a neighbor of Mr. Gruber's had called the police, reporting that she hadn't seen him in a while and thought they needed to check it out. The cause of Mr. Gruber's death is undetermined currently. More on this story as it develops.

Carly immediately thought of Ms. Maggie and the chief's wife and how wild their imaginations could be. It should be interesting to hear. At least, now she knew that Mr. Bennett knew about it. Carly returned to her office to continue working on her manuscript. Dinkle lay guard at the door, as always.

Later in the morning, Carly's phone rang. "Hello."

"Hey, Carly, this is Nellie." Carly knew who it was but let Nellie introduce herself.

"Hey, Nellie, what's up?"

"Did you see the paper this morning?"

"I sure did. So bad about Mr. Gruber. Did you know him?"

"He came into the diner occasionally, mostly at lunchtime. Always ordered the same thing, cheese toast and the soup of the day."

Carly was amazed at how Nellie could remember such things.

"I guess the coroner will be able to find out what happened," Carly said.

"Maybe, who knows with ole man Sledge."

Carly asked, "The coroner?"

"Yes, Tom Sledge. Old as the hills, half deaf, and who knows if he has the brains to figure these things out."

Carly said, "Well, let's hope so. Mr. Gruber probably died of natural causes."

"Yeah, maybe. But with the crime picking up around here, it could be anything, a robbery or worse, a murder. Thorne may need to get involved." Nellie said, sounding a little excited. "It's about lunchtime, so I better let you go. Just wanted to check and see if you knew about this."

"I appreciate it, Nellie. You take care. Bye."

* * *

That afternoon, Donna Brewer, Carly's neighbor, came by. Dinkle announced her arrival. Donna and Carly sat in the living room, and Dinkle on the sofa beside Carly. Dinkle liked to hear all the latest conversations. After small chitchat, she said, "I guess you saw the paper this morning."

"Yes, I did." Carly answered. "Can I get you something to drink? Tea or coffee?"

Donna answered, "No, I can't stay. Charlie is going on a rally this weekend and I have to get his things packed."

"Will he be gone all weekend?" Carly asked.

"They usually are. I get a little time to myself when he goes off for a weekend. I can catch up on my reading and things."

Carly said, "You know, you can always visit if you get bored."

"I know and that's sweet of you to offer. I just wanted to let you know."

"You know you can call us if you need anything."

"Thank you." Donna left.

Carly looked at Dinkle. "You know, Dink, it looks like I'm not going to make much progress on my manuscript today. What shall we do?"

Dinkle barked twice. Carly wasn't sure how to interpret that. She walked to the patio doors. Most of her flowers in the flower garden had quit blooming and were dying out for the winter. The gardenia bush, however, was still green and looking healthy. So, she didn't need to weed her garden. Her phone rang again.

"Hello."

"Hi Carly. This is Bonnie. Are you busy?"

"Oh, hey Bonnie. It's been a while. And no, I'm not busy. In fact, I was just talking to Dinkle about what we could do today. How are things with you?"

"They're fine."

Carly asked, "How's Josh? Is he still going to street festivals to sell his art?"

"As always, working away on his sculptures. It's amazing how he can form a bird or owl or hawk, or anything for that matter, with his hands and then paint it so very realistically. His creatures and faces even have a personality, I think."

"Yes, he is truly fortunate to have such a creative talent. I treasure the little chickadee sculpture that Thorne bought for me when he was at the Dunn festival. It looks like he could fly any minute. I have it on the bookshelf where I keep my favorite collection of things."

Bonnie asked, "Did you have a good time on your honeymoon?"

Carly replied, "Yes. The mountains are gorgeous, the view from the cabin where we stayed was like a dream world."

"Where did you go?" asked Bonnie.

"In a place called Sugar Mountain, a ski resort in the western part of the state."

Bonnie asked, "That's about an hour from us. Did you go skiing?"

Carly laughed, "Me? Oh no, I prefer standing on my own two feet. In fact, I've never been able to roller-skate."

Bonnie laughed and said, "Me either. I'm with you on that."

Carly asked, "How's the kids?"

"They're doing good. Melanie's ex-husband, Billy, passed in his sleep. His health wasn't that good, from what I understand. It was such a sad thing. Even though they had been divorced for several years, it still hurt. It is so sad for her two kids. I went to the memorial service. Otherwise, everything is going good with them. I talked to them at least once a week, sometimes more. How is your husband?"

Carly answered, "His work is a little slow these days. A funny thing, the other day a lady called and wanted to hire him to find her cat."

"Now that sounds like a serious case," Bonnie exclaimed.

Carly said, "Bonnie, I'm so glad you came to our wedding. The handmade quilt you made for our wedding gift is something I will cherish forever. Thorne loves it too. It gives our home a very cozy feeling. Your being at the wedding meant so much to me. And thank your boys for me too."

Bonnie said, "I'm glad. We wouldn't have missed your wedding. Joey and Janice did a beautiful job arranging everything. I'm just so glad to have you and Thorne in my family. Have you started on the book? I don't mean to bug you about it."

"Yes, I've been working on it. It's been a little slow lately. Seems like I get a lot of interruptions."

"I better let you go, Carly. I just wanted to see how things are with ya'll. We'll talk soon, OK?" They hung up.

Chapter Eleven

Chief Logan drove to the see Tom Sledge, the coroner. The old building needed some paint and a few other repairs. He walked up on the porch, rang the bell. Mr. Sledge answered. "Hello, Chief Lolo. What brings you by?"

Chief thought, *Oh my, what a dufus, he should dang well know why I'm here.* "I'm just here to find out what you know about Eli Gruber's death."

Mr. Sledge ambled across the room to his desk. The chief followed. "Well, it's hard to tell. I didn't see any signs of trauma, no cuts, or gunshots, no marks around the neck. It could be something in his blood and tissue tests. I'll have to wait and hear what the lab tests show."

"I see," said the chief. "Well, you be sure to let me know those results as soon as you find out."

"Right, right, sure will, Chief."

The chief returned to the police station. When he entered, Deputy Goss asked, "Did you find out anything from Mr. Sledge?"

The chief said, "As usual, the old codger doesn't know the first thing about being a coroner. And, no, nothing he could see. Waiting on lab tests results."

Deputy Goss said, "That could take a while."

"I know. Meanwhile, there's nothing we can do. Just wait." He mumbled to himself, "Except get a new coroner." He walked down the hall to his office.

Chapter Twelve

Friday night, after supper, Thorne and Carly watched the 6:00 ABC nightly news on WTVD Raleigh-Durham. They were curious if anything about Eli Gruber would be on the news. Nothing. Carly said, "It seems like a newsworthy story to me."

"They may not know about it. Chief Logan would have to let them know, I guess."

Carly said, "Yes, but it was already in the Harnett County News."

"I see your point. Maybe tomorrow."

Carly said, "I didn't accomplish much on my manuscript today. I started but then Bonnie called. She just wanted to see how we were and if we had a good honeymoon. I told her how amazing the views were in the mountains."

Thorne asked, "How are she and Josh?"

"All sounds good. I thanked her for coming to our wedding and for the quilt. She asked about the book. I told her it's slow-going but coming along."

They sat quietly for a while. Carly remembered. "Oh, another thing, Donna, you know our neighbor, came by. She said that her husband, Charlie, was going to a bike rally this weekend. I told her that since she would be by herself that she was welcome to visit. She sounded like she enjoys the solitude. So, we'll see."

Carly got up, held Dinkle, kissed her on the head. Waving her paw, she looked at Thorne, "Night, night Daddy." and took Dinkle to her bed.

* * *

The next morning, having coffee in the kitchen, while Carly prepared eggs and bacon, and toast for breakfast, Thorne said, "I brought home some paperwork I need to get finished this weekend."

Carly replied, "I thought you always did that at the office."

"I do. But I couldn't stand to be away from my wonderful wife this weekend, you know, so I can kiss her occasionally."

"Oh yeah? And who would this wonderful wife of yours be?"

Thorne got up from the chair, walked over to the stove, put his arms around Carly, and kissed her on the neck. "Why you, my dear."

"You are a funny man." Carly put the food on their plates. She said, "I hope to get more of my book written."

"Great," Thorne said. "I'll know where to find you at any time."

* * *

Later that afternoon, Thorne walked out to his car. He noticed several cars down the road at Donna Brewer's house. It was late. When he went back inside, he said to Carly, "Donna must be having some church friends over. There's several cars at her house."

"Really? She didn't mention anything about that to me when she was here yesterday." Carly looked out the window. She saw a police car drive by. "Thorne, there's a police car going to Donna's house. Wonder what's wrong?"

Thorne walked over to the window. "Maybe the church folks are fighting." He smiled. They watched a while longer.

Carly said, "It's late. I'll go over there in the morning and see if there is anything I can do."

Thorne reached around her and said, "In the meantime, my love, I have an idea of something we can do."

Carly said, "Let me put Dinkle in her kennel and you can tell me all about it."

Thorne laughed. "I think I'd rather show you."

Afterwards, they both thought, maybe tonight a baby was made.

Chapter Thirteen

Sunday morning, Carly wanted to go see Donna early. She knew that Donna went to church around 10 a.m. She said to Thorne, "I'm going to walk over to Donna's. I'll be back shortly."

Thorne said, "OK, call me on my cell phone if there is anything you need from me." Dinkle barked goodbye to Carly.

"I will."

Carly saw that there were still two cars in Donna's driveway. She walked up and rang the doorbell. A lady whom Carly had never seen answered the door. "Yes, may I help you?"

Carly said, "Hello. I'm Carly from down the street. I noticed visitors here last night and then the police chief's car. I wanted to make sure everything was OK with Donna."

"Come in, my dear. It's awful, just terrible." She cried.

"What? What happened?" asked Carly, concerned.

"It's Charlie. Poor man. Oh, I just can't believe it. Then again, we've always worried about him riding that motorcycle." Carly waited. The woman continued. "Late yesterday, he had an accident on that bike of his."

"Where?" asked Carly.

"I'm not sure exactly. Chief Lolo came by to tell Donna about it. It happened somewhere near Boone, you know where they were having that bike rally that he goes to every year."

"Is he OK?"

"Oh, no, my dear. He's in critical condition at a hospital somewhere near there. Poor Donna, she can't go there. She certainly can't drive that far, especially in her condition." The woman suddenly thought, "I'm sorry, I didn't introduce myself. I'm Marilou, Marilou Bell. I go to the same church as Donna."

"Nice to meet you. I can call my husband to see if he can drive Donna to the hospital."

"Don't bother. I'm sure she doesn't want to put you out."

"No problem. I'm sure he won't mind at all." She called Thorne.

He answered, "Carly, how are things?"

"It's Charlie. He's been hurt in a bike accident and is in the hospital near Boone. He's in critical condition. Donna is in no condition to drive there and, evidently, there isn't anyone to take her."

Thorne immediately said, "I'll be glad to drive her, you know that."

"Let me find out more information first. I'll call you back or see you at home." They hung up.

Marilou came back into the living room. She said, "He's at the Watauga Medical Center in Boone. Did you call your husband?"

"Yes, and he will be more than glad to drive Donna there, anytime she is ready."

"I'll talk to her and let you know, if that's OK," Marilou said.

"Let me give my number to you. Please tell Donna that I'm so sorry and I hope Charlie will be alright."

"I certainly will."

When Carly returned home, Dinkle was waiting at the door. Thorne reported, "You know, Dinkle can hear your footsteps all the way down the street. How is Donna?"

"I only spoke to a lady from her church who was staying with her, I assume. I didn't get to see Donna. I guess she's too upset. They will call us if Donna decides to accept your offer to drive her to Boone."

Carly and Thorne spent the rest of Sunday relaxing.

Carly said, "Even though I didn't know Donna that well, I feel so sorry for her. I think she and Charlie have been married most of their lives."

Thorne said, "I guess she's not going to call."

"She probably feels like she would be imposing on us. Her friends from her church all seem to be elderly people. Maybe they will transport Charlie back here to the hospital."

"May be."

Carly said, "I wish there were something I could do. Everything is being taken care of by her friends. If we don't hear anything today, I may go back tomorrow to check on things."

* * *

Later that evening, the doorbell rang. Thorne answered. The older woman looked at him and said, "Hello, you must be the husband. I'm Marilou, Marilou Bell. I met your wife yesterday at Donna's house."

Thorne opened the door and stepped back. "Yes, of course. Please come in Ms. Bell."

"Just call me Marilou," she said, walking into the living room.

Carly appeared from down the hall. "Hello, Ms. Bell. Come in, please have a seat. How is Donna?"

Marilou slumped her shoulders. "That's why I've come. The hospital called this afternoon. Charlie passed."

"Oh, no," replied Carly, and she walked to the sofa where Ms. Bell had sat.

"I guess it's for the best. He was in such bad condition, according to the people at the hospital. Anyway, they are transporting him here to O'Quinn's Funeral Home. I think he's going to be cremated. I tell you Donna is beside herself. She is so upset that she didn't get to see him and say goodbye."

"I imagine so," said Carly. Thorne quietly slipped from the room. Carly continued, "Can I get you anything, Ms. Bell?"

"No, thank you. I'm fine. I need to get home and tend to things. There's not much else I can do at Donna's. One of her other friends came over to spend a couple of days with her."

Carly said, "That's good. I'm glad she's not alone."

Marilou said, "What's so bad is that Donna has no idea about the finances, the bills, the payments, anything really. Charlie took care of everything, as far I know. I just don't know what she will do, how she will manage."

Carly tried to reassure Ms. Bell. "I'm sure things will work out. I'm sure there are many women who have been left in that situation."

"I know. I just hope it works out." Ms. Bell stood up and said, "I need to get home. Again, I thank you for your concern and especially your husband's willingness to drive Donna to the hospital."

"You're certainly welcome. That's what neighbors are for." Carly walked Ms. Bell to the door. "You take care."

When Carly closed the door, she turned, and Thorne came out of the kitchen. "What a sad fix that lady's in. It's hard to believe that this day and time there are women who are clueless about things like that."

Carly said, "I guess you were eavesdropping?"

He smiled. "Who, me?"

Chapter Fourteen

On Monday morning, the cleaning crew arrived at Eli Gruber's house to prepare it for new renters. They dusted, vacuumed, cleaned out the cabinets in the kitchen and bathroom, packed up books and odds and ends. There were several boxes to pack from the bedroom, clothes, shoes, and linens. When they were emptying the closet, one of the workers, Max, pulled a box from the top shelf. He said to the other worker, "Hey, James, look at this."

James walked over. "Nice box. Open it, see what's inside."

Max said, "It's locked, no key. Have you seen a key lying around anywhere?"

James replied, "Nope."

They took turns examining the box, shaking it, turning it over. James said, "Maybe we could pry it open with a knife or something."

Max smirked. "You know better than that. Mr. Templeton would have our hides."

James agreed. "Yeah, you're right. I guess we can take it by his office when we finish here."

Max and James finished. Took the trash to their truck, closed, and locked the house door. Max put the box between them on the front seat. They entered the real estate office. Stacy greeted them. "How was it, much of a mess?"

Max replied, "Not really. It didn't take us long to get it presentable. The painters are going to do the inside work tomorrow, I believe."

James walked up to Stacy's desk and held out the box. "We found this in the man's closet. It's locked and no key was found. I figured Mr. Templeton would want to give it to some of the man's relatives."

Max chimed in, "Could be something important in there."

Stacy took the box. "Thanks, fellows. I'll see that he gets it."

"We'll see you next time." James and Max left.

She held the box in her hands. It wasn't heavy, something rattled inside when she gently shook it. It was a small box. The wood reminded her of her grandmother's dresser. The clasps and hinges were not cheap metal.

Chapter Fifteen

Ever since the council meeting, Chief Lolo had been in a grumpy mood. He didn't have much to say and when he did say something, it was short and to the point. When he walked out of his office, he told Deputy Goss to call the coroner to see if the lab test results had come back.

Deputy Goss called Mr. Sledge.

"Hello, coroner's office."

"Mr. Sledge, Chief Lolo, I mean Chief Logan, asked me to call you about the lab tests results for Eli Gruber."

Mr. Sledge fiddled with some papers. "Yes, yes, I have them here somewhere." Deputy Goss waited. Finally, the coroner spoke, "Here they are. Let's see now." The phone was quiet while he looked over the report.

Finally, Deputy Goss asked, "What did they say?"

"Ah, it says here minimal alcohol content, some sign of decreased oxygen in the blood, which could indicate suffocation. Conclusion: cause of death undetermined."

"Suffocation? How?"

"Now, I wouldn't know that exactly. Just suffocation. He could have choked on his own spit, or somebody put a pillow over his head. How am I supposed to know that?"

Deputy asked, "You didn't see any signs of suffocation when you did the autopsy?"

"Well," the coroner paused, "There were some blood vessels, you know small hemorrhage-like spots in his eyes. I figured he was a big drinker, you know, red nose, blood-shot eyes. Didn't think much about it, really."

"Would that be a sign of suffocation?" asked the deputy.

"Could be, yes sir, could be."

"OK, thanks. I'll tell the chief." They hung up.

Deputy Goss went to the chief's office. "Chief, the coroner says the lab report showed cause to be undetermined, but a suggestion of possible suffocation. When I questioned him about his autopsy findings, he admitted there had been blood spots in Mr. Gruber's eyes, but at the time, Mr. Sledge thought it was probably due to drinking."

The chief shook his head, "Thanks, Goss." When Goss left the room, the chief said to himself, "Like I said, we need a new coroner."

He called Deputy Goss back in the room and asked, "How about next of kin? Has he found anybody yet?"

Deputy looked down at the floor. "I didn't ask him about that."

Loudly the chief said, "Well, call him back and find out, will you?"

"Yes, sir."

The coroner answered and Deputy Goss said, "Mr. Sledge, it's me again, Deputy Goss. The chief wants to know if you have located any relatives of Mr. Gruber's yet."

"No, in fact, there doesn't seem to be any. I called the local clinic to find out anything about his medical condition. They said that he came in about once a year just for a general checkup. No problems, though."

"Thanks. I'll tell the chief." They hung up.

The chief came out of his office and asked, "Well, anything?"

"Mr. Sledge said that he couldn't locate any relatives. But he did call the clinic and found out that Mr. Gruber didn't have any medical issues, just yearly checkups. All was fine, they said."

Chief Logan mumbled to himself as he left the office, *what to do, what to do*.

Chapter Sixteen

When Mr. Templeton returned to the office, Stacy told him that the cleaners had finished their job at Eli Gruber's house. She added, "They boxed up the clothes and other belongings and put them in the storage facility for the relatives. However, they did find one interesting thing and brought it to you." She reached for the box on the shelf and handed it to Mr. Templeton. "This box, they said they found it in the closet at his house. It's locked and they couldn't find a key and thought they ought to turn it in to you."

"Good men. I'll take it to my office." He took the box, turned it over in his hands. "Nice box. Looks expensive. I'm not sure what kind of wood it's made from, but it pretty."

Stacy said, "I thought so too. I wonder what's in it."

"Maybe we can find out." He went into his office and closed the door.

The front door opened, and Stacy recognized Mr. Ward.

"Hello, Mr. Ward. How are you?"

Mr. Ward walked up to her desk, with his daughter and her son following. "This is my daughter, Jennifer Owens, and her son, Kenny. I brought them to meet Mr. Templeton if he's in and has a minute."

Stacy replied, "Have a seat and I'll check." She buzzed Mr. Templeton's office and informed him that Mr. Ward was there.

"Tell him I'll be right out."

Stacy said, "Mr. Ward, Mr. Templeton will be out in a minute."

"OK, thank you, Mam." Mr. Ward replied. They took a seat to wait.

Mr. Ward stood up when Mr. Templeton walked into the room. He put out his hand. "Sorry to bother you, but I wanted you to meet my daughter, Jennifer, and her son, Kenny."

Mr. Templeton shook Mr. Ward's hand, looked at the daughter, and said, "It's nice to meet you. Your dad is a fine man, and he has taken care of everything. I'm sure he's filled you in on the details."

Jennifer answered, "Yes sir."

Kenny had not stood but sat slumped in the chair. It was clear that he didn't want any part of this situation. When Mr. Templeton said hello, Kenny just flipped his hand up in greeting.

Mr. Ward said, "That's all we wanted to do, introduce you and let you know they will be moving in this week. We'll let you get back to work."

As they walked to the door, Mr. Templeton said, "Be sure to let me know if you need anything. Any problem, just call and let my secretary know."

"Will do." Mr. Ward and Jennifer walked out, with Kenny shuffling behind.

Stacy said, after they had left, "I don't know about them. What do you think?"

Her boss shrugged. "Hard to tell. But we'll see. The boy seems unhappy, to say the least. It seems obvious that they are running or hiding from something or someone."

Stacy shook her head. Mr. Templeton went back to his office. He looked at the box on his desk and thought, *No relatives, good health, suffocation. This situation needs investigating, I do believe.* He decided to call Chief Logan.

"Police station, Deputy Goss speaking."

"I would like to speak with Chief Logan. I'm Mr. Templeton from Templeton Realty."

"Hold one minute, please." Deputy Goss walked to the chief's office and told him.

The chief picked up the phone. "Hello, Mr. Templeton. Is there a problem?"

Mr. Templeton answered, "Yes and no, Chief. It's regarding Eli Gruber. When the cleaners were there preparing the house for rental, besides the usual, they found a small, locked box, no key was found. I was thinking that it should be given to someone in his family."

Chief said, "The only problem with that is that there is no family, according to the coroner." He considered his alternatives. "You say it's locked, and no key?"

"That's correct."

The chief said, "You know there seems to be a lot of questions about this whole situation. Why don't I come by your office and pick up the box, or you can bring it here, whatever is convenient for you?"

"Sounds good. I certainly have no use for it. I'll leave it with my secretary, and you can come by when you get a chance. As you know, our office closes for lunch, but at any other time, we should be here."

"Will do," said the chief. They hung up.

Chapter Seventeen

For the article in the newspaper, Carly decided to write about the increase in crime, rather than a feel-good human-interest story. It was becoming worrisome, especially since the suspicious death of Mr. Gruber. After finishing her article, she looked at the guard dog lying in the doorway of her office. "All done, Dinkle. I'm going to get it turned in early this week. I hope Mr. Bennett likes it."

Dinkle looked at her as if to say, "Silly, you know he will, he always does."

When Carly returned home after turning her article into Mr. Bennett, she saw Donna walking toward her house. "Hello, Donna," she called out. She waited until Donna was beside her and they went inside.

At the entrance, Donna said, "It's getting a little chilly out," and took her sweater from around her shoulders.

Carly agreed, "Yes, it is. You can put your sweater on the back of that chair," pointing to the living room area. "Come on in the kitchen. Some hot tea would be nice, how about you?"

"That would be nice. Seems the cold affects me more as I get older."

Carly asked, "How have you been?"

"That's why I came to see you. You have been such a good neighbor. I wanted to let you know that I'll be moving."

"Moving? Where?" Carly asked as she put the teapot on the stove.

"Since Charlie—" Donna pulled a tissue from her skirt pocket and wiped her eyes, "since Charlie passed, I've been at a loss as to what to do. I mean, he took care of everything. I don't have the slightest idea of what to do about anything. Of course, I can cook and take care of myself, but the house, the bills, the checking account, all of it, I'm completely lost."

"It must be very difficult for you, Donna," Carly said.

"More than difficult. It's impossible." She wiped her nose.

Carly placed the teacup on the table. "Here. Have some tea. It will warm you inside."

"Thank you, Carly."

"Let's go in the living room, where it is more comfortable."

After they settled, Carly asked, "Where are you going to move to?"

"All my family is in West Virginia. I don't know if I ever told you I'm from there. Anyway, my sister and her husband are coming to get me. Their children are grown, and they have plenty of room in their house. I feel like I'm imposing, but I really don't have a choice."

Carly said, "I'm sure you won't be imposing. You and your sister will be good company for each other." Carly sipped her tea. "When are you leaving?"

"My sister will call me when they decide, but it should be in the next week. First, I need to go see Mr. Templeton about selling the house. I'll leave most of the furniture and appliances, just take my personal things and some special keepsakes."

Carly asked, "Do you need any help with packing or anything?"

"No, no. I've just about finished," Donna said and stood to take her cup to the kitchen. "I need to get back."

Carly said, "Why don't you stay for supper?" Dinkle froze and stood still at the command word 'stay'. Carly laughed, "Oh Dinkle, you are such a sweetie. Come." Dinkle followed her into the kitchen.

Donna said, "I have quite a bit of food still that the ladies brought over when they heard about Charlie." She wiped her eyes again. "I know you have things to do. I'll let you get back to it." As she turned to the door, she remembered and said, "I almost forgot, but please tell Thorne how much I appreciate his offer to drive me to Boone. It truly was above and beyond, as they say."

Carly followed her to the door. "Thorne is just a great guy through and through. He cares about people. I'll tell him what you said." Carly watched Donna walk back down the road.

Closing the door, she said to Dinkle, "I wonder if I'm ever going to get that novel written, Dink. There seem to be so many interruptions and, you know, I moved to this place to have some solitude." Dinkle barked twice, interpreted as 'I know'. She walked back to her office. Dinkle once again took her guard post.

* * *

That afternoon, Donna went to see Mr. Templeton about selling her home. She located the address and parked her car.

When she entered, Stacy greeted her, "Hello."

Donna walked over to Stacy's desk. "My name is Donna Brewer. I'm here to see Mr. Templeton about selling my house."

"Yes Mam, have a seat and I'll let him know you are here."

After Stacy buzzed her boss, he left his office and entered the front room, walked over to Donna, "Ms. Brewer, I'm Author Templeton. Nice to see you. Come into my office."

Donna followed him. He closed the door. "Have a seat." He walked around his desk to his chair, sat down, and said, "How I can be of service?"

Donna answered, "I'm here to see about selling my house. You see, my husband passed away recently." She paused, took a tissue from her purse. "I'm going to move to my sister's house in West Virginia."

Mr. Templeton leaned forward on his desk. "I'm sorry for your loss. I remember seeing the write-up in the newspaper."

"You see, I am not able to keep up with everything. Charlie took care of the finances and all."

"I see." He paused and continued, "Did your husband have a Last Will and Testament?"

Donna said, "no, he didn't." She wiped her eyes.

Mr. Templeton could see that this was a difficult thing for Ms. Brewer to do. He said, "You probably aren't aware, but the laws in North Carolina State that without a Will, there has to be a two-year probate, a waiting period before any properties can be sold."

Donna became more anxious. "Oh no, I can't wait two years. What am I going to do?"

Mr. Templeton wanted to ease her mind. "One solution, since you are moving away, would be to list your home as rental property. That way, there will be income for the two years it is in probate, after which time you can continue to rent it or decide to sell it."

Donna considered what he had said. "That sounds better. I'm leaving most all the furniture and appliances. I'm mainly taking my personal items."

"That wouldn't be any problem. A furnished home usually rents faster than one unfurnished. We can fill out the necessary paperwork while you are here if you like. When did you say you are leaving?"

"In a week or so." Donna then asked, "You will take care of the house and the property. I mean, I would hate for it to be damaged."

"Yes, Mam, we would make sure of that. And, if by chance anything was damaged or in need of repair, we would take care of that as well. Any costs would, of course, come out of the rental payments."

"I understand and yes, I would like to do the paperwork now, if it is convenient for you."

Templeton picked up his phone and called Stacy. "Would you please bring in the rental agreement forms for Mrs. Brewer to sign?"

Donna signed the papers and felt relieved. On her way home, she stopped by Carly's house.

Carly and Dinkle answered the door. "Hello again, Donna. Come in."

Donna replied, "No, I can't stay. I wanted to stop by and tell you that I went to see Mr. Templeton, a nice man, about selling my house. He told me about probate law that prevents me from selling it for two years. So, he will be renting it. I wanted to tell you so that you would know what to expect."

Carly replied, "I really appreciate that. Are you sure you won't come in and visit a while?"

"Thank you, but no. I need to get back." Dinkle barked once, 'bye'.

Chapter Eighteen

Jennifer Owens and her son, Kenny, had settled in their new home on Park Avenue. Jennifer, with the help of her father, Mr. Vernon Ward, had taken a job as a receptionist at an engineering firm.

The morning Kenny was to enroll in school was more of a struggle than it previously had been. He stomped around his room, throwing clothes on the floor.

Jennifer stood at the door to his room. "Kenny, why does it always have to be this way? You know that you have to go to school."

He blurted, "I hate school. I hate it. I hate the people. I hate the teachers. I hate the people on the bus." He plopped down on his bed.

Jennifer walked closer, wanting to calm him, and reaching out her hand, he jerked away. "Just leave me alone."

"Kenny, if you skip school, the truant officer could put me in jail for three years? What would you do then?" Leaving the room, she said, "The bus will be here in 15 minutes."

Kenny grudgingly dressed, lumbered out the door. Jennifer wanted to tell him to have a good day but knew it wouldn't do any good. She just hoped he made it through the day without any major incidents.

* * *

Chief Lolo went by the realtor's office to pick up the locked box found at Eli Gruber's house. When he got back to the police station, Deputy Goss saw it and said, "That looks expensive."

"Yes, I think it probably cost a pretty penny," said the chief and he took the box into his office and put it on his desk. He turned it a few times, shook it lightly, examining it. He called out, "Goss!"

Deputy Goss entered the chief's office. "Yes, Chief. What is it?"

The chief said, "Have a seat." The deputy sat in the wooden chair across from the chief. "You know, I've been thinking. Gruber didn't have any relatives. The cause of his death is not known. I was thinking about calling in a private detective to look into things."

"That sounds like a good idea," said Deputy Goss.

"What's the name of that woman who works at the newspaper, you know, she writes those weekly articles?"

"Carly Davenport, used to be Carly Jansen until she married."

The chief thought, "What's her husband's name? Isn't he a private eye?"

"I believe so. I've heard Ms. Maggie at the drugstore speak of him."

"Good, see if you can get me a phone number for his work, OK?"

"Will do, Chief."

Chief Lolo called the office of Davenport Investigations. The phone rang, the message machine answered. The chief began, "Mr. Davenport, this is Police Chief Logan in Lillington. I would like to speak with you about a situation we have here. If you would call me, I would appreciate it." He gave him his phone number and hung up. He left his office to go to lunch. On his way out, he said to Deputy Goss, "I put in a call to the PI. If he calls, tell him I'll be back after lunch, and I will try him again."

"Sure enough, Chief."

Chapter Nineteen

It wasn't until the next day when Thorne returned from Raleigh that he got the message from Chief Logan. Instead of calling, he decided to go by the police station on his way to his office. When he entered, Deputy Goss greeted him. "Good morning. May I help you?"

"Good morning. I'm Thorne Davenport. Chief Logan called me yesterday. I was out of town. Thought I would come by instead of calling. Is he in?"

"Yes sir. Have a seat and I'll tell him you are here."

The chief came from his office, walked over to Thorne, "Good morning, Mr. Davenport. You could have called to save yourself a trip."

"No bother. My office is in Dunn, and I figured you might want to see me, so I stopped in on my way to work."

"Mighty considerate of you. Come on in my office. Would you like some coffee?"

"I'm fine, had breakfast before leaving home." Thorne sat in the wooden chair across the chief's desk. He asked, "What is it that you wanted to talk to me about?"

The chief sat in his chair, clasped his hands together on his desk, and began. "I guess I need to start at the beginning. Last week, I can't remember what day exactly. Anyhow, a lady called and reported that she hadn't seen her neighbor for a few days and wanted us to check it out. The neighbor is, or was, a man named Eli Gruber. He wasn't that well known in town. Deputy Goss, and I, rode out to his house and nothing appeared suspicious. His car was parked on the street, so we figured he went off with a friend or something."

"That night it stayed on my mind so, the next morning, we contacted the realtor's office to find out if he rented from them, which he did, so we picked up the key to his house. When we got there, things looked the same, but inside we found Mr. Gruber dead on his bed. I let the realtor know that the house was now vacant but that he needed to get a cleaning crew before trying to rent it to anyone else."

He paused, "Are you sure I can't get you some coffee?" Thorne shook his head. "Well, the coroner said there was no obvious cause of death, he sent his usual samples to the lab for testing. The final report was that the cause of death was undetermined, but suffocation was a possibility. Something to that effect."

Thorne interrupted. "Chief Logan, I'm not sure what you want me to do in this situation."

"Let me finish. I like to give all the details, so you'll get the idea." He cleared his throat, leaned forward on his desk, and continued. "The cleaning crew did their job, and they found a small, locked box in the house, which they turned over to their employer, Mr. Templeton, the relator. When he found out that Mr. Gruber didn't have any relatives and things seemed a little suspicious, he called me, and I went to his office and retrieved the box." He reached to the floor beneath his desk and pulled out the box and handed it to Thorne.

Thorne looked it over. "This looks to be a rather expensive box. And you say no key was found?"

"That's right. We figured that there are some relatives somewhere and you could find them. It also wouldn't hurt if you looked into the whole situation. I mean, with his questionable death. He was lying on his bed fully clothed. Weird."

Thorne sat the box on the chief's desk. "I would agree."

The chief said, "About your fee. Just give the bill to me and I will present it at the next council meeting. I'm sure it won't be a problem since we don't have a detective on our staff and this situation needs to be resolved."

Thorne said, "That will be fine. The first thing I need to do is look at his house, and then talk to the coroner."

"Yes, of course. My deputy will give you the addresses and whatever else you need. I might add, don't expect a whole lot of help from our coroner, Mr. Sledge. When you meet him, you'll see what I'm talking about." The chief reached in his pocket and handed Eli's house key to Thorne. He looked at the box. "And I guess you can take that box, maybe get a locksmith or something. It's too expensive to use a screwdriver on."

Thorne smiled, "I agree." He stood, shook hands with the chief. "I assumed the house is still vacant."

The chief replied, "I'm sure it is."

"And Chief, everybody calls me Thorne." Both men smiled.

Thorne got the necessary information from Deputy Goss, thanked him, and left the office.

Thorne didn't have anything pressing to do at his office and decided to pay a visit to the coroner, Mr. Sledge. When he found the address, a house needing repair, he parked, got out of his car, walked to the porch, and knocked. A man wearing crumpled clothes answered. "Yes?" the man said.

"Hello, sir, I'm here to see the coroner, Tom Sledge. Is he in?"

The coroner opened the door wider and said, "That would be me. Who did you think I was, the butler?" He didn't smile.

Thorne thought, *No wonder the chief didn't describe him to me*. He entered the house. It was apparent that Mr. Sledge lived here by the furnishings, as well as performed his autopsies here by the smell.

The coroner stopped in the hallway and turned to Thorne. "What did you say your name was again?"

"I'm Thorne Davenport, a private investigator. Chief Logan asked me to investigate the death of Eli Gruber. I understand that you performed his autopsy."

Mr. Sledge thought, *Oh yes, I did, didn't really find anything though*. He turned to the living room area. "You want to sit down?"

Thorne sat in a chair that he hoped didn't break with his weight. "The chief said something about suffocation."

"I didn't find any obvious reason for his death, so I sent some tissue and blood to the lab. They didn't find much either, a little alcohol in his system. They said something about his oxygen level and even though the conclusion was undetermined, they questioned suffocation. I told Chief Lolo that I had seen some petechia in the eyes but figured that he might have been a heavy drinker."

"I see," said Thorne. "Do you think I could get a copy of the autopsy and lab results as well as the death certificate?"

"Of course. I have extra copies on my desk. I made them for the family but couldn't find any relatives." Sledge went to his office area across the room, opened a file drawer, and pulled out the folder with the documents. He handed Thorne what he had requested. "Here you go."

Thorne got up and said, "I appreciate your time and your help. Have a good day." The coroner didn't respond and walked with Thorne to the door.

When Thorne left, he drove to Eli Gruber's house.

Chapter Twenty

Around lunchtime, at the drugstore, Ms. Maggie and Beth Logan were discussing the latest news. Beth said, "Logan said he was going to call in an investigator to look into that Eli Gruber's death since the findings were suspicious. Also, the people who went to clean up the house found a small, locked box, which they turned over to the realtor, Mr. Templeton."

Ms. Maggie asked, "When will he contact the investigator?"

"He called Davenport Investigations yesterday, left a message, so hopefully the detective will call him back today. I'll find out more tonight, I'm sure."

The door to the drugstore opened. Both Ms. Maggie and Beth Logan turned to see who it was. Jennifer Owens walked in, and Ms. Maggie said, "Hello. Come on in. Let me know if you need any help with anything."

Jennifer nodded and said, "Thank you." She walked to the cashier counter with her purchases. Beth stepped back, then walked to a nearby counter, not so far that she couldn't hear, of course.

Ms. Maggie began clicking the number keys on the ancient register and asked, "Don't believe I've seen you in here before. Are you new to the town?"

"Yes, Mam," Jennifer replied in a soft voice.

Ms. Maggie said, "Well, I'm glad you found our store. Where abouts do you live?"

"On Park Avenue. My father found the house for me."

"Your father?"

"Yes, Vernon Ward."

"Do you have any children?"

Jennifer thought, *What a nosy woman.* "A son, Kenny. He's in the fifth grade, enrolled in Harnett Primary School."

Jennifer paid and took her change. Ms. Maggie put her receipt in her bag. "Where did you move from?"

Jennifer ignored the question, took her bag, and said, "Thank you." And walked toward the door.

"I hope to see you again soon," Ms. Maggie called to her.

After Jennifer left, Beth walked back up to the counter. With raised eyebrows, she asked, "What do you think is up with her?"

Ms. Maggie tapped her chin with her long, bony finger. "I don't know but I'm sure there's a story there."

Beth said, "I better get going."

"You call me if you find out anything about the Eli Gruber situation."

"I will, and you let me know if you find out anything about the stranger in town." Beth left the drugstore.

Chapter Twenty-One

Thorne parked on the street across from the address of Eli Gruber's house. When he got out of his car, he noticed the neighbor peering out her living room window. *She must be the one who called the chief*, he thought.

He walked across the street, down the crumbling sidewalk to Eli Gruber's porch, which needed repair. Using the key that Chief Logan had given him, he entered the house. First thought, *too clean. Why don't people call me before the cleaning? I'm sure I won't find any evidence now.* He slowly walked through each room. No personal items, only normal, necessary furniture, a sofa with two end tables, two chairs, a center rug under the coffee table, a cabinet with a built-in small television bolted to the shelf, book shelving on one side.

In the kitchen, clean and neat, normal appliances, sparse supply of dishes in the top cabinets, and pots and pans in the lower cabinets. No food supplies. The rest of the house was the same, only necessities for the house to be a furnished rental. When he got to the bedroom, again, clean, nothing out of place, all ready for a new occupant. He went to the back door and saw that a window to the left of the door was slightly open.

He examined it further, went outside to check and he noticed that the screen was missing. He saw no footprints nearby in the small backyard. A rusted, dilapidated swing set with a sliding board was near the back of the yard. He thought, *They'll have to do something about that if children move in.*

Thorne walked around to the front of the house toward his car. He saw the neighbor standing on her porch. She walked down her steps to meet him. She waved her hand and said, "Can I ask what you are doing here?"

Thorne said, "And you are?"

"Ms. Wiggins, Ms. Emma Wiggins."

"Hello, Ms. Wiggins. I'm a private investigator. I was contacted by the chief of police, Chief Logan, to investigate Mr. Gruber's death."

"Well, it's just terrible. I can tell you that. The man was no trouble. He went to work, came home, and made no trouble. Last year, he helped get my car started. The battery was dead."

"Did you know him well?" asked Thorne.

"No, I don't think anyone did. Of course, we would wave when we saw each other."

"Did he have a lot of visitors?"

Ms. Wiggins paused. "Not really. Occasionally, a man would visit. He wore a uniform, but I couldn't make out where he worked or anything. He didn't ever drive a company vehicle, just his car."

"What kind of car, do you recall?" Thorne asked.

"Lord, no, I don't know a thing about cars. I've had my Buick for so many years, I can't even remember when I got it."

Thorne figured this was all she could tell, so he said, "I need to get to another appointment. It was nice to meet you and I appreciate your help."

Ms. Wiggins opened her mouth to speak, but Thorne had already turned to his car. She walked back inside her house.

* * *

It wasn't quitting time, but Thorne decided to call it a day. When he pulled into the driveway at home, walked to the door, Dinkle started barking. When Thorne entered, Dinkle's tail was wagging. Thorne reached down and rubbed her head. "Where's your mama?" he asked Dinkle.

Dinkle answered but Thorne had yet to be able to interpret her barks as well as Carly.

Carly called out, "Hey, Thorne, I'll be there in a minute. I'm cleaning the bathroom."

He walked down the hall, stood in the bathroom door. "Can I help?" As he pretended to roll up his sleeves.

Carly laughed. "Yes, I left the toilet for you to clean."

Thorne frowned. Carly finished wiping down the counter, dried her hands. She went to Thorne, and they hugged. "How was your day?"

"Different, and busy. I'll tell you about it later. How about yours?"

Carly said, as they walked back to the kitchen, "I was able to work on my novel for a good amount of time."

"I'm glad."

The evening was cool. Thorne, Carly, and Dinkle sat on the patio after supper.

Thorne began, "I forgot to tell you but yesterday when I got back to my office, I had received a message from Chief Logan. So, on my way to work this morning, I decided to stop by the police station before I went to work. The chief gave me a detailed account of the situation, which I guess didn't hurt. Seems Eli Gruber was found dead in the home that he rented, and the cause was questionable. That's the man Ms. Maggie told you might be missing, right?"

Carly shook her head yes. "But that's not the real reason he decided to call me. The cleaning people found a small, expensive box in the house. Since the box was locked, and no key found, they turned it over to the realtor, Mr. Templeton, who in turn gave it to the chief. Seems nobody wanted to damage the box because it looks expensive. That added to the suspicious death and the fact that the guy has no relatives, is why they called me to investigate."

"Wow," Carly exclaimed. "That's some story. Where will you begin?"

"I started today since I didn't have anything urgent to do at the office. I visited the coroner, a Mr. Sledge, and he's a story all by itself. Not much info from him. Then I drove out to Eli Gruber's house. That was a waste of time. The cleaners and the painters had been, so anything that might have been helpful had long been removed. On my way back to my car, the neighbor who initially had called the chief, came out to meet me. She asked me what I was doing at Mr. Gruber's house."

"Did she know anything helpful?"

"Not really. She said that she saw an occasional visitor, a man dressed in a uniform that she couldn't describe and who drove a car she couldn't describe. Other than that, nothing useful."

"What do you plan to do next?"

"I'm going to try to find out more about Eli Gruber, where he's from, any relatives, etcetera."

Carly started up from her chair. "It's getting a little cool. You want to go back in?"

Dinkle was already at the patio door. Carly said, "She's already cold. I guess it's time to get out her little winter jacket."

Thorne followed them inside. Carly picked up Dinkle, looked at Thorne and waved Dinkle's paw, "night-night Daddy," and took her to the kennel.

Too tired, they didn't try to make a baby that night. Thorne just held Carly in his arms.

Chapter Twenty-Two

Thorne left home the next morning and took the locked box to a locksmith in Dunn, close to his office. He walked in and the owner, Jim Steele, was behind the counter. He greeted Thorne. "Nice box you have there, Thorne." He had helped Thorne over the years with various types of locks.

"Yes, I think it is. That's why I didn't take a hammer to it." He laughed.

The owner, frowning, said, "Goodness no. What a shame that would be."

Thorne placed the box on the counter and asked, "Do you think that you can make a key for it?"

"You know better than to ask. Of course, no problem. Have you got time? I'll do it while you wait."

"That would be very helpful." Thorne stood waiting at the counter, as there wasn't a waiting area with chairs.

After about twenty minutes, Mr. Steele came from the back room. "All done, my man." He handed the box to Thorne.

Thorne asked how much he owed, paid the owner, and left with the box and key in hand. He thought, *I wonder if he opened it. No, I'm sure he did.*

Thorne drove to his office, took the box inside, and put it on his desk. The phone rang, wrong number. He sat in his chair, opened the box, and began examining the contents. Not much, several loose coins, I.D. bracelet with a scratched, unreadable inscription, and on the bottom was a photograph. He didn't know what Eli Gruber looked like, so he would have to find out the identity of these two guys. They were similar in appearance, one a little younger. They had their arms around each other's shoulders and were smiling. The black-and-white photograph was old, a little bent around the edges, and slightly yellowed. He placed everything back inside the box, closed the lid, and pocketed the key.

He called Chief Logan. When Deputy Goss answered, he forwarded his call to the chief, who answered, "Chief Logan here."

"Chief, this is Thorne. Just one question for now. Do you know how old Eli Gruber was or where he moved from?"

Chief Logan sat back in his chair, rubbing his chin. "Let's see here, best I can recollect, I believe the realtor, Mr. Templeton, said he was in his fifties, give or take. But I wouldn't know, never seen the man except, of course, when he was dead, and I couldn't tell at that time. Don't know where he lived before."

Thorne said, "I appreciate the info. Talk later." They hung up.

Thorne opened the box once again, took out the contents to see if there was a hidden compartment and, sure enough, a small flap covered with velvet lay snuggly in the bottom. He took his letter opener and pried it up, lifted it out. On the very bottom of the box, there was a worn, folded piece of paper. It appeared to have been torn from a newspaper. It had yellowed with age. Some words were missing letters. The article read:

Charlotte Observer, April 1979

Yesterday, a robbery occurred at Beacon's Jewelry Store on Belaire Avenue around 4:30 in the afternoon. The owner suffered a head injury and was admitted to the hospital for observation. No suspect has been found. The value of the stolen merchandise is currently unknown. If you have any information regarding this, please notify the local police department.

Thorne could just make out the words, as the paper was well-worn in the creases. He felt relieved and thought, *Alright, somewhere to start.*

He wrapped the newspaper clipping in plastic and put them in the folder that held the rest of the information about the case. He would go to Charlotte tomorrow. He knew it was his birthday, but he couldn't put off this investigation.

It was around 6 p.m. when he arrived home. Carly met him at the door. In preparation for the surprise she had planned, Carly had put Dinkle to bed early. She knew Ms. Maggie was allergic to dogs. Thorne hung his jacket and holster in the closet. He exclaimed, "What a day. What a day. Where's Dinkle?"

Carly followed and sat with him on the sofa and said, "I put her in her kennel for the night."

"I guess I'll have to give you Dinkle's share of kisses and hugs."

Carly said, "Tell me about your day. I have some soup warming on the stove."

Thorne said, "You know that dog would die protecting you. I mean, she's not scared of anything. I believe she would attack a bear, if need be, to keep you safe."

"I believe that. I need to protect her from herself. She's something special." Carly leaned forward and asked, "Are you hungry?"

"Starved, but almost too tired to eat." Thorne began. "My day. It's hard to know where to start." He rolled up the sleeves of his shirt. The doorbell rang. Carly got up to answer it. Thorne leaned his head back against the sofa.

"SURPRISE! SURPRISE! HAPPY BIRTHDAY!" came voices from the hall. Thorne jolted from his rest and stood up. There stood Nellie, Ms. Maggie, and Doc Skinner, all with those silly pointed birthday hats, blowing on those noisy blowing party favors. Although tired, Thorne came to life. With a big smile of total surprise, he greeted everyone. He said with his arms out. "Come in, come in. Have a seat." Carly took everyone's coats.

They all gathered in the living room. Carly came in from the kitchen carrying a birthday cake with forty-five blazing candles on it. They all sang happy birthday to him. Thorne blew out the candles. He looked at Carly and said, "I guess you know what I wished for," and kissed her. She knew she had wished for the same thing.

It was a pleasant time, small talk while they munched on hors d'oeuvres. Everyone left around 7:30. Thorne looked at Carly. "How in this world did you manage to pull that off?"

"It wasn't easy being married to the world's greatest detective." In the kitchen, while they put things away, Thorne said, "That was so sweet of you to do that. Totally unnecessary and for sure, unexpected, but still sweet, and thoughtful." He pulled her to him, wrapped in each other's arms, kissed tenderly. He said, "My wish could possibly be fulfilled but I need your help."

Carly smiled and led him to their bedroom.

* * *

While eating breakfast the next morning, Thorne told Carly about his need to go to Charlotte. "I may be gone a few days. I didn't get a chance to tell you everything last night because something interrupted us. Anyway, I took the box to my locksmith guy. I opened it back at my office. In it, I found a few items that may be related to the case. There was a newspaper article about a robbery in 1979. The article was written in the Charlotte Observer. So, I felt I could start there with my investigation.”

“That’s wonderful. I know you will get to the bottom of it. I’m going to miss you so much. But it will give me a chance to work on my novel. I’ve had so many interruptions so far; I haven’t made a lot of progress. I’m sure Dinkle and I can find something to keep us occupied.”

Thorne added, “I’ll call you with my hotel information when I get there. Of course, I have my cell phone if you need me. In fact, I have it if you don’t need me, but just want me.” He smiled and kissed her on the cheek.

Chapter Twenty-Three

Later that week, Jennifer was at her work at the engineer's office. Her cell phone rang. "Hello," she answered.

"Ms. Owens?"

Jennifer didn't recognize the voice. "Yes, this is she." Her mind immediately thought of Kenny.

"This is Ms. Kennedy. I'm the assistant principal at your son's school. Would it be possible to talk with you in my office this week?"

Jennifer thought, and said, "Yes, if I could make it on my lunch hour."

"Good," Ms. Kennedy replied. "How about tomorrow around 12:30?"

"OK, I'll be there. Can you tell me what this is about?"

"Your son, of course. I think he's headed for trouble if something doesn't change. I would just like to talk to you about the situation."

"OK, fine. I'll be there tomorrow." They hung up.

Jennifer had a difficult time concentrating on her job for the rest of that day. When she arrived home, Kenny was on the sofa, watching television. She walked over, turned off the TV, looked at Kenny and said, "The school's assistant principal called me today." Kenny rolled his eyes and slouched further on the sofa. Jennifer continued, "Do you know what it's about?" She waited. No answer. Jennifer said, "I would like a little heads up, so I'm not blindsided when I meet with her tomorrow."

Kenny quickly leaned forward. "Tomorrow? Why the big rush? I ain't done anything wrong. I don't know what the big fuss is about."

"Well, there's something. I wish you would tell me. Has anyone said anything bad to you or treated you badly?"

Kenny shook his head. Jennifer walked out of the living room and went into the kitchen to prepare supper. She called to Kenny that supper was ready. He walked in and sat down. Jennifer said, "Well, I guess I'll find out what this is all about tomorrow."

The next day at lunchtime, Jennifer arrived at the school and sat in the front office waiting to see the assistant principal, Ms. Kennedy. She came out of her office a short time later. She was a short, stout woman, in her forties, no makeup, hair in a bun, no jewelry. She had on a black pantsuit with a white blouse. Unsmiling, she looked at Jennifer as if to say, well, come in!

Jennifer walked into Ms. Kennedy's office. Feeling nervous, she said, "I hope Kenny hasn't been a problem." *Wishful thinking*, she thought.

Ms. Kennedy sat behind her desk, motioned to the chair across it for Jennifer to take a seat. She began, "Ms. Owens, I called you here hoping to avoid an escalation of the situation." She didn't take a breath but continued. "It seems that your son needs an attitude adjustment. We here at the school cannot tolerate his current behavior. He is belligerent toward his teachers, mocking and irritating to his fellow classmates, and continues to disrupt his classes with inappropriate remarks. My question is, what do you plan to do about it?"

Jennifer's mouth was dry, her words gone. Then she managed to say, "I'm trying. In fact, I've been trying. I don't know what to do, to tell you the truth."

"Well," continued Ms. Kennedy, "you had better do something. I'm afraid your son is headed for delinquency if things do not change." She got up from her chair. "I appreciate your coming to see me. I hope you can figure things out, for Kenny's sake, of course."

Jennifer got up and thanked her for her concern and left the school. She returned to work, but she felt like crying, or screaming, or dying. She was at a loss. She had tried being sweet, demanding, encouraging, pushy, gentle. What else could she do?

At home that night, she tried talking with Kenny calmly. He didn't make any comments while she explained her feelings about the meeting she had with Ms. Kennedy.

Finally, Kenny jumped up from the sofa and blurted out, "If Dad was still here, he would understand!" He ran to his room and slammed the door.

Jennifer leaned back on the sofa, tears trickling down her cheeks. Too numb to think.

Chapter Twenty-Four

After Thorne left for Charlotte, Carly and Dinkle sat out on the patio. Carly planned her time while Thorne would be away these few days. She could spend the mornings writing Bonnie's story, do errands in the early afternoon, and write more after Dinkle went to bed. She and Dinkle went back inside, the phone was ringing. Carly thought, *Oh no, not Grand Central again.* She answered, "Hello."

"Carly, this is Donna. I'm sorry to bother you. I just wanted to let you know that I have arrived at my sister's house in West Virginia, and things are going well."

"I'm so glad to hear that, Donna. It is so thoughtful of you. To let me know."

Donna replied, "I think this is the best. Listen, I'll let you get back to what you were doing. Tell Thorne I said hello."

"I will." They hung up.

Carly spent much of that day writing her novel.

* * *

Thorne arrived in Charlotte just before lunch and checked into a Holiday Inn. He asked the desk clerk about a good place to have lunch. He gave him a couple of choices. Thorne picked the one closest to the library. He would start his search there.

When he got to the library, he inquired about microfiche from newspapers starting around 1979. He sat down at the desk table, took out his notepad, and began his search. It didn't take long to find the article about the robbery in 1979. He searched for follow-up articles but didn't find any. The news was about the weather, hurricane predictions, and such.

He then searched for the name Eli Gruber. He came upon an article, *Frank S. Gruber, Obituary.* He opened it, scanned through it, and found Eli's name mentioned as a surviving son of the man, along with another son, Joshua Gruber. Thorne felt encouraged and noted this on his notepad. It was late afternoon and his eyes felt like they were popping out of their sockets, so he printed out the articles, paid the clerk for them, and left to return to his hotel.

He ordered a chef's salad with fries, and lemonade from room service. After finishing his meal, he called Carly.

She answered on the fourth ring. "Hello."

Thorne tried to change his voice to sound more formal. "Could I possibly speak with Mrs. Thorne Davenport, please?"

Carly laughed aloud. "Oh, Thorne, you are a silly man. You don't think I would recognize your voice regardless of how you changed it?"

He laughed too. "Oh well, I tried. What has my beautiful, loving wife and her faithful ferocious guard dog been up to today?"

Carly answered, "I've accomplished more than I even hoped on my novel. It was a quiet day. Donna called first thing to let me know she had arrived and was doing well. She said to say hey to you. That's about it. How about you? Anything?"

Thorne explained his research. "While I'm thinking about it, I'm staying at the Holiday Inn in room 112. Let me give you the number."

Carly said, "I can look it up. Tell me more about your research."

"It turned out much better than I anticipated. I found the newspaper article about the robbery, same as the one in the box. However, there was no follow-up. But, on further looking, I found an obituary of Eli Gruber's father. And better yet, Eli has a brother, at least he did at the time of his father's death. Tomorrow I will check the county records to find any properties in their names."

"That sounds wonderful and promising."

"I agree. I'm bushed though. My eyes, if nothing else, need a good night's sleep."

"I'll let you go. I miss you, Thorne."

"Thorne misses you too. Sleep well and tell Dinkle to take care of things." They hung up.

Chapter Twenty-Five

Carly awoke the next morning. She missed Thorne so much. He had become such a wonderful part of her life. The house felt empty. She dressed and she and Dinkle had a lazy morning. After feeding Dinkle, she had a piece of toast with orange juice. She felt a little nauseated. She took Dinkle outside, it was too cool to spend time outside. Afterward, she started work on her novel, Dinkle guarding the office door.

She had difficulty concentrating and decided to visit Nellie at the diner for lunch. It had been a while. She informed Dinkle of her plan and said she would be back soon.

At the diner, the lunch crowd had not yet begun. Nellie was wiping off a table. She saw Carly's car and put the sponge down and walked to the door and opened it before Carly got to it. "My girl! It's so good to see you. You are radiant, my dear. Come in. Come in."

"It's good to see you, Nellie." Both took a seat at a table near the counter.

Nellie began, "I have thought about you every day, wondering how things are, and everything. The lunch crowd won't be here for a little while, so fill me in."

Carly said, "Everything couldn't be better. I wouldn't know where to start. But the latest, is I've been able to get quite a bit accomplished on my novel, which I'm pleased to say."

Nellie asked, "Your novel is still based on your biological aunt, right?"

"Yes, it's fiction, of course, but it is based on her life's story."

"I got so excited to see you I forgot to be a waitress." She laughed. "Can I get you anything?"

"No, I'm fine."

"How is Mr. husband detective Thorne these days?"

Carly answered, "He has started on a possible murder investigation and is in Charlotte for a few days."

"Yes, the Gruber murder. A few customers have talked about it, mainly that nobody knows anything."

"My detective husband Thorne will figure it all out, I'm positive."

The door to the diner opened. Nellie said, "Oh me, the lunch crowd is starting. I guess I shouldn't complain. That's what keeps me in business." She got up.

Carly said, "I better get back to Dinkle. Take care, Nellie. I'll see you soon."

Nellie said, "Be sure not to wait too long. I miss seeing you."

Carly arrived home and was greeted by Dinkle. She said, "Dink, I think I'll take a little nap. I feel tired." Dinkle barked. Carly answered, "OK, if you insist." So, she went to the sofa, pulled the knitted Afghan over her. Dinkle snuggled at her feet.

Chapter Twenty-Six

At lunchtime, Beth Logan entered Barton's Drugstore. Ms. Maggie was anxious to hear the latest. Beth looked around to be sure there were no customers and said, "Good, nobody here."

Ms. Maggie says, "You would think that the lunchtime would be busy, but I guess folks eat lunch and wait until they leave work to drop in to buy things. Anyway, what's new?"

Beth leaned on the counter and began, "I hope you don't mind, but I brought my lunch. I have a book club meeting at 1 o'clock." She opened the paper bag and pulled out a chicken salad and lettuce sandwich. She looked at Ms. Maggie and asked, "Would you like half? I can't eat the whole thing." Ms. Maggie declined. Beth continued, "That Investigator Davenport came by Logan's office. He's going to investigate Eli's murder. Logan gave him that little locked box also, thinking it might contain something useful. That's all I know about it. I'm sure the investigator will keep Logan informed."

Ms. Maggie, watching Beth devour the entire sandwich, said, "Davenport, is his first name Thorne?"

Beth answered, "I don't know. Why?"

"Well, you know Carly, used to be Carly Jansen, works at the newspaper office for Mr. Bennett. She got married in September to a private investigator named Thorne. I'm pretty sure his last name is Davenport. I bet that's him. Next time she comes in, I'll find out."

Beth crumpled up her sandwich wrapping and paper bag and handed it to Ms. Maggie to put in the trash. She said, "I almost forgot. You know that woman that came in here last time I was here? Well, I think her son is a troublemaker. I'm not sure about the details, but I heard that there was some trouble at school the other day."

Ms. Maggie said, "I haven't heard anything about that."

On her way out the door, "Don't worry, I'll keep you posted." She left to attend her book club.

Chapter Twenty-Seven

When Jennifer awoke the next morning and Kenny had left for school, she called her dad before going to work.

"Hello," answered her father, Vernon Ward.

"Hey, Dad. Have you got a minute?"

"For you, always. What's up?"

She sat in the kitchen chair. "It's Kenny. He's acting out in school. You know I thought a relocation and new school would help, but I think he's getting worse. I've tried talking to him and he just gets an attitude. The assistant principal at the school called me and I met her at the school yesterday. I have to say not a very pleasant person. She said that something had to be done," she paused. "I'm at my wit's end."

Her dad said. "Maybe I could have a talk with him. Do you think that would help?"

"At this point, I will try anything. Last night when I was telling him he had to behave, he yelled and said if his dad were here, things wouldn't be this way and that his dad would understand."

Mr. Ward tried to calm his daughter. "Listen, sweetheart, it's not the end of the world. I'll come by this weekend, or you can come here, and I'll have a chat with him. We could plan a fishing trip or something together. Now don't you worry too much. We'll figure this out. OK?"

Jennifer had tears in her eyes. Her dad had always been on her shoulder to cry on and he always did his best to help. "OK, Dad. Thank you. I guess I better get to work. We'll talk later."

"OK, Jenn. You call me anytime. You are everything to me, you know that." They hung up.

Jennifer freshened her makeup and left for work.

Chapter Twenty-Eight

Thorne left the county record of Deeds' office. He couldn't find any record of property for Eli Gruber, nor Joshua Gruber. He did find an old deed in the name of Frank S. Gruber, which had since then been resold a couple of times.

He drove to the address. It was in an older section of town. The neighborhood appeared well-kept. No kids' toys or bikes in the yards. Mostly older model cars in the driveways. He parked his car in front of the house he was looking for. He walked to the door and knocked.

A young woman, blond hair, jeans, smacking gum, and with a baby on her hip answered the door. "Yeah, can I help you?"

Thorne said, "Mam, I'm Thorne Davenport, a private investigator. I'm looking for some information about a previous owner of this house."

"I wouldn't know nothing about that. We just moved here about a year ago from Kentucky. We rent, we don't own it." She changed the baby to the other hip. She added, "You might want to talk to the old lady across the street. She's old as the hills and I think she's lived here since the beginning of time."

Thorne said, "I appreciate your help. Take care."

Since it was lunchtime, Thorne drove around the area and found a small diner, like Nellie's. He stopped in and ordered a cheeseburger, fries, and a large lemonade. He made notes in his notepad. Afterward, he drove back to the neighborhood to see the old-as-the-hills lady across the street. He thought, *Hopefully, she won't be suffering from dementia. Maybe I've found my Ms. Maggie.*

When he knocked on the door, an older teenaged, neatly dressed boy answered. "Yes sir. Are you here to see my granny?"

Thorne said, "Yes, if she is available."

The boy said, "She's gone to the grocery store with my mom, and they just left, should be back in about an hour. You can sit on the porch and wait if you want to."

Thorne thought, then pulled a card from his breast pocket and handed it to the teenager. "Here's my card. I can come back tomorrow if that would be OK."

The boy asked, "What's this about Mister?"

"You can tell her that I would like to ask her some questions about the man that lived across the street," he pointed to the house.

"I'm sure it'll be fine. My Granny knows everybody around here."

Thorne thanked him and left. It was too early to go back to the hotel, so he drove around the city and found some quaint shops. One of them looked interesting, an antique shop. He parked, put money in a meter, and went inside. He wanted to find just the right gift for Carly. After looking around, he found the perfect bracelet. Her birthstone was a diamond. The platinum bracelet had one sapphire stone and a diamond on each side. Very elegant and perfect, thought Thorne. The elderly gentleman came over, "May I help you, sir?"

Thorne pointed to the bracelet through the glass case. "What can you tell me about that bracelet?"

The clerk pulled the bracelet from the case and put it on a velvet cloth on the glass top. He said, "Fine, fine. A fine piece, designed around the 1920s, the art déco period. The electric-blue sapphire has a European-cut diamond on each side. Quite exquisite."

Thorne asked, "How much are you asking?"

The clerk cleared his throat and said, "This piece sells for $750. It's an elegant treasure."

Thorne thought for a minute. He was quite sure Carly would love it and be surprised. He asked, "Will you gift wrap it?"

"Of course, sir, most definitely. The lady that gets this may just fall in love with you." He smiled and put the bracelet in a leather, velvet-lined case.

Thorne paid and left to go to his hotel. He wanted to go home and give it to Carly immediately but knew he had to do his job tomorrow. *Hopefully, the little ole lady will be my Ms. Maggie.*

After he finished his supper that he ordered from room service, he called Carly. She told him about her day, and he told about his progress and his plan for tomorrow.

Carly said, "I really hope that lady will give you lots of answers. I love you and I really miss you."

“Same here, Mrs. Davenport. And give the Dinkle a pat for me.” They hung up. Thorne didn't mention the gift, he wanted to see her reaction.

Chapter Twenty-Nine

Kenny Owens sat in the school office with a fellow classmate, Bucky Winthrop. The two boys were about the same height and weight. They had been fighting in the boys' bathroom when the football coach walked in and broke it up. The coach escorted both to the office.

The assistant principal called the police station.

"Police station, Deputy Goss speaking."

Ms. Kennedy said, "Deputy, I'm Ms. Kennedy, assistant principal at Harnett Primary School. I have two boys in my office whom I believe need to be taught a lesson. One of them is a real troublemaker. He and another student were in a fight this morning."

The deputy asked, "Is anyone seriously hurt?"

Ms. Kennedy answered, "No, the coach broke it up before any serious damage could be inflicted. I just think it would be helpful if the chief came and put a little scare into them. Do you think he could do that?"

"I don't see why not. I'll give him your message."

Ms. Kennedy thanked him, and they hung up. She walked out to the front room and said to the boys, "Your parents will be here shortly. I have called the police. You are in deep trouble this time. You wait here until I call you." She turned and walked back to her office. The boys sat slumped in their chairs, waiting impatiently.

After about half an hour, Chief Lolo walked into the school office, removes his hat, nods to the secretary, and walks over to the boys. Standing in front of them, he says, "Well now, I hear you two boys have had a little tussle. What's that all about, huh?"

Neither boy spoke. The chief continued, "Let me give you a little hint about the situation. In our town, we don't tolerate bad guys and you boys seemed to be headed in that direction if things don't change." The boys still sat slumped with their heads hung down. He continued, "You can begin by sitting up in your chair and looking at me." Both boys slowly sat upright and looked at the chief. "Now, that's much better."

Ms. Kennedy walked out of her office and came over to the chief. "Hello, Chief. I'm Ms. Kennedy. I'm the person who called your office. Bucky here has never really caused any trouble, but I can't say the same for Kenny. He is new to our school and has been a problem since day one. Something needs to be done."

The chief shook his head. "I think we can handle this."

Bucky's dad, dressed casually, walked in the office and over to the chief. He looked at Bucky. "What has happened?" he asked.

Ms. Kennedy started to speak but the chief interrupted, "Seems there has been a little misunderstanding, but I think we can get this all straightened out. I don't believe these boys are aware of the consequences of their actions."

Bucky's dad said, "Can I take my son home now?" The chief looked at Ms. Kennedy, who nodded yes.

The chief said to Bucky, "I hope I don't see you in any kind of trouble in the future, young man."

The boy said, "Yes, sir." He and his father left the school.

The chief sat in a chair beside Kenny. "Anything you want to talk about, son?"

Kenny quickly said, "I'm not your son!" Jennifer came into the office, saw the chief with her son, and walked over to them. She tried to control her shaking hands.

Chief Logan turned to her. "You must be Kenny's mother. I'm Chief Logan."

Jennifer greeted him, "Yes, I'm Jennifer Owens."

She looked at her son. "What now, Kenny?"

Kenny said, "We had a misunderstanding and I hit him."

"Hit who?" asked Jennifer.

"This guy, Bucky."

Jennifer looked around. "Where is he?"

Kenny said, "His dad came to pick him up," with emphasis on 'Dad'.

The chief had an idea of what this was about. He had seen it before in kids whose parents separated. He said to Jennifer, "Mam, may I talk to you for a minute in the hall?"

Jennifer followed the chief. Out in the hallway, he turned to her and said, "We've seen this situation quite a lot. I have a suggestion if you would be interested."

Jennifer quickly answered, "Very much, anything. I'm at a loss as to what to do."

The chief said, "We have a counselor in town, and she is extremely good with kids, especially ones with anger issues. I may be wrong, but I get a sense that Kenny is angry about something."

Jennifer shook her head, "Yes, his father and I are getting a divorce and Kenny doesn't understand. He's been acting out ever since. We moved here thinking that new surroundings, new school, and neighbors would help. So far, not so."

Chief asked, "Where did you live previously?"

She said, "outside of Charlotte. My dad, Vernon Ward, lives here and he helped find us a house to rent here."

The chief asked, "Where do you work?"

"I'm a secretary at the Knott Engineering office."

"Yes, I know of them." After a moment, he asked, "Do you think you would be interested in Kenny seeing a counselor?"

"I'm willing to try most anything," she said.

The chief got out his notepad and wrote down the counselor's name and gave it to Jennifer. "I guess you can take the boy now. Ms. Kennedy did say that if anything further trouble happens, Kenny will be suspended."

"I understand." Jennifer went back into the school office and motioned for Kenny to come with her. He slowly got up and walked out the door with her.

The chief went back to speak with Ms. Kennedy. He stood in the doorway to her office. When she looked up from her desk, he said, "I believe we have this on the way to being resolved. I gave Kenny's mother the name of Sarah Longstreet. Hopefully, she will set up an appointment for him to see her."

Ms. Kennedy said, "Thank you, Chief. I certainly hope so."

The chief left and returned to the police station. When he got inside, Deputy Goss asked, "What happened?"

The chief gave him a rundown. He said, "I hope his mother gets him some help or else there's going to be real trouble in that boy's future, I'm afraid."

While driving home, Jennifer made a change of plans. She would take Kenny to her dad's house to see if he could stay the weekend.

Chapter Thirty

The next morning, Carly opened Dinkle's doggie door. She was still in her pajamas. She didn't feel hungry, so had a glass of juice. She put on sweatpants and a pullover and got her newspaper off the front porch. Dinkle came back inside and she closed the doggie door. She placed the newspaper on the coffee table in the living room to read later.

In his motel room, Thorne shaved, showered, and dressed in his gray slacks and blue blazer, as it was chilly this morning. He stopped at the small diner again for breakfast and called Carly.

She answered and Thorne said, "Good morning, my dear."

"Good morning to you."

Thorne asked, "Got any plans for today?"

"No, not really, just writing more. I need to outline a few ideas I have and make an outline of what I've written so far."

"Sounds like work,"

Carly said, "I know, but necessary. What about you? I guess you're going to see Emily Struthers today?"

"Yes. I'm hoping she will know everything about everybody, and I can make some headway on the case."

Carly heard noises in the background and asked, "Where are you?"

Thorne answered, "I'm at this little diner that I found yesterday. The food's surprisingly good. I'm just having breakfast. Got a feeling this might be a long day."

"Enjoy, and I hope you get all the information you need."

"Me too. Have a good day." They hung up.

Thorne finished his breakfast and drove to Ms. Struthers' house. He parked and walked up the walkway. The house appeared to be freshly painted, a nice blue, with white shutters. The wooden porch was painted battleship gray. There were three tall-back white wooden rockers on the porch, along with a swing hanging from the ceiling.

When he knocked, a petite elderly lady answered, smiled, and said, "You must be Mr. Davenport."

"Yes, Mam, I am." He showed her his I.D.

"Please come in." She opened the door wider for him to enter. "We'll sit in the living room if that's OK with you." He followed her. She said, "Please have a seat." She was dressed in a shirtwaist dress, hose with back seams, and black leather shoes with thick heels. Her white hair was in a braided bun pinned with pearl pins. She wore a flower-patterned apron.

Thorne sat in the blue velvet upholstered Victorian chair next to the fireplace. The room was packed full of whatnots, doodads, framed photos, pillows along the sofa, all the furnishings were Victorian style. As he looked around the room, he said, "You have quite a collection."

"Yes, I do. All these beautiful things were given to me over the years. They are from my children, my grandchildren, and my great-grandchildren." She walked over to the mantel and took down a framed photo, walked over to Thorne, and said, "This is my entire family, except for my dear husband, Benjamin; he passed 20 years ago. He had a heart attack while shoveling snow. We were able to get everyone together two years ago for Thanksgiving and my daughter hired the photographer to take our picture. It is a real treasure to me."

She pointed to a young boy in the photo and said, "This is my oldest great-grandson, Luke, the one you met yesterday. A fine young man, if I do say so myself. His mother, my granddaughter, comes to take me to the grocers when I need to go, about once a week. Such a dear she is." She walked over and placed the photo back on the mantel and continued, "I don't drive anymore, you know. My reaction time is not as good as it once was."

Thorne said, "Yes, Luke was very polite and friendly. It's very thoughtful of his mother to help you out. Ms. Struthers, I—"

She interrupted as she walked back across the living room, "I have made tea. I hope you like tea. I have delicious crumpets also. You know crumpets originated in the Victorian Era. That's what the people in England call them. That's why I call them crumpets. People here just call them tea cookies. That's almost sacrilegious, don't you think?"

Thorne thought, *This is going to be long, very long day.* He answered, "Yes Mam, tea and crumpets sound delightful."

She said as she hurried past him to the kitchen, "It will only take me a minute, you just sit and make yourself comfortable."

Thorne again thought, *I hope I get to talk. I think I found four of Ms. Maggie's rolled up into one. I guess she's lonely.*

Ms. Struthers returned with the tea and crumpets, held the tray for Thorne to take his. He took a sip. "This is very good. Thank you." He sat his cup and saucer on the table beside his chair. As she sat on the sofa, he said, "Ms. Struthers, I would like to ask you some questions about a man who used to live across the street from you back in 1979."

Ms. Struthers got a thoughtful expression on her face. "Let me see, 1979," she repeated.

"Yes, Mam, his name was Frank Gruber." Thorne waited while she turned her thoughts to that time.

She said, "Frank Gruber. Yes, I remember the Grubers. Sad situation, that one."

Thorne asked, "Can you give me some background on what you remember?"

She continued, "After Ben and I were married, we moved into this house. It was in good repair, only needed painting and repair of the wood on the porch. Otherwise, we were able to move in after the realtor did all the paperwork. The Grubers moved in shortly after that. I don't remember the date exactly. I do remember there was him and his wife, and they had two boys. What were their names? Let's see, one was named Elijah, they called Eli; the other was Joshua; no nickname for him, I guess."

She sipped her tea. "I saw the boys get on the school bus every weekday. I can't remember where the wife worked but I know she did because she left home at the same time Monday through Friday. For quite some time when they first moved here, Mr. Gruber also went to work, I can't remember where though. I believe he was in his forties when his wife died. I don't know if she died or just left. Sad time for those two boys. Seemed they were home alone a lot of the time. Mr. Gruber would go off and sometimes not come home for a day or two. I kept an eye on the boys, from here, of course, didn't want to seem like a nosy neighbor, you understand."

Thorne nodded his head, took a sip of tea. He reached in his jacket pocket and took out a notepad, thinking, *this is going to be a detailed history, better take notes.*

Ms. Struthers continued. "Seemed like everything was normal up until Mrs. Gruber died or left. Everything changed after that. Occasionally, I would see two men visit. They looked like questionable characters, I thought. They looked up to no good if you ask me. Of course, I have no idea who they were or anything else about them. But they would show up late on Friday or Saturday night driving a big black car. They would stay a little while, then leave. You know, as I think about it, when they were younger than those two boys didn't spend a lot of time playing outside, like most kids."

She looked at Thorne and asked, "May I get you some more tea and crumpets?"

"No Mam, I'm fine. That was delicious, thank you. Do you remember when they moved away?"

She gently wiped her mouth with a lace handkerchief. "Before that, I need to continue my story. The boys had grown up. Sometime later, Joshua got married and moved away, I don't know where. The reason I know that is because one Saturday there was a car in front of the house with 'Just Married' painted on the back window. Can't remember too much about Eli. Later, I believe it was around 1980 or so, Ben and I were awakened by a siren. We got up and saw an ambulance and police car at the Gruber's house. They put Mr. Gruber in the ambulance. One of the police officers saw our light on, I guess, and came over to ask us if we saw anything. We told him that we were sleeping until the sirens woke us up."

She again gently wiped her mouth with her lace handkerchief. "Anyway, Mr. Gruber never returned home. I assume he died in the hospital. Come to find out later, he had been shot. Awful, just awful, especially for those two boys who were men by that time, of course. Also, I might add, the whole incident was very scary for our neighborhood. Ben and I had several conversations about moving, but, of course, we never did. Since then, there haven't been any problems. The house is a rental now, I believe. People come and go. I haven't gotten to know any of them very well. I think they see me as a little ole feeble lady, which I am not."

Thorne replied, "No, Mam, I agree with you. If you don't mind me asking, how old are you?"

She stood up and proudly said, "I'll be 94 my next birthday, spry, fit as a fiddle, thank the good Lord."

Thorne could sense a sermon coming on. He said, "Ms. Struthers, you have been so extremely helpful. I really appreciate your taking the time to talk to me. And the tea and crumpets were superb." He stood. "Is there anyone else in the neighborhood who may have known the Grubers?"

Ms. Struthers answered, "Oh my no. These houses have all turned into rentals, mostly young folks."

Thorne said, "You have my card. Please call me if anything else helpful about the Grubers comes to mind. If I don't answer, just leave a message and I'll call you back."

Ms. Struthers said, "I would very much like it if you would join me for lunch. It's about that time."

He answered, "I have a few more people to see so I need to be on my way."

"I understand. Let me see you to the door." Thorne held back a smile. He thanked her again and left.

He felt encouraged by the information that Ms. Struthers had told him. He needed to plan a next step. He stopped at the first pizza parlor he saw, had a small supreme pizza and a beer. He thought about calling Carly but didn't want to interrupt her if she was working on her novel. He would wait until later this evening.

* * *

Since it was early in the afternoon, he stopped at the police station to inquire about the shooting of Frank Gruber in 1979. He knew it was a long shot, but he may just get lucky. He arrived and the desk sergeant took his information and made a call. After hanging up, the sergeant told Thorne, "Sir, the detective that handled that case has since retired."

Thorne asked, "Would it be possible for me to get a copy of the file?"

The sergeant made another call to the records department. He hung up and said, "You can have a seat. It will only be a few minutes. They'll bring you a copy of the reports."

Thorne took a seat and waited. Shortly, a young woman brought the file to the sergeant who handed it to Thorne and said, "Here you go, Mr. Davenport." Thorne took it and thanked him. When he got to his car, he opened the file. The report was brief, so was the investigation. No witnesses, no evidence, no suspects. He thought, *Well, that was a dead end.*

He drove back to his hotel, called the DMV, and requested the record for Joshua Gruber. He had no address or other information. The secretary took his information and credit card information to cover the fee and said, "Mr. Davenport, you should receive the report in a few days. Is there anything else I can help you with?"

"No and thanks, I appreciate your help."

He looked at his watch and thought, *it's early so I can leave now and be home in time for supper.* He was looking forward to giving Carly the bracelet he had purchased from the antique store. He packed his few belongings and checked out of the hotel.

While driving, his cell phone rang. Ms. Struthers said, "Is this Mr. Davenport?"

"Yes, it is. Hello, Ms. Struthers."

She began, "You said to call you if I thought of anything that I forgot to tell you. Well, I just remembered that sometime after Mr. Gruber died, I did see Eli once or twice. One afternoon, a new Lincoln Continental parked in the driveway and Eli got out of the driver's side. The reason I know what kind of car it was, is because my husband, Ben, told me. He said that it was an expensive car."

"Ms. Struthers, this is helpful. I thank you so much."

Thorne called Carly.

"Hello," she answered. Carly didn't want to tell Thorne that she hadn't felt very energetic and said, "I was outside with Dinkle, just came inside. My day was slow, not much progress on the book. I guess some days the creative juices get sluggish. Dinkle and I took a nap earlier on the sofa. Did you see the neighbor lady?"

"Yes. Ms. Struthers was quite helpful. More important, I see right now I must return home immediately before I'm replaced by a vicious guard dog." They laughed. "I'll fill you in on the details when I get home, which won't be long. I'm pretty much finished around here and couldn't stand being in a hotel away from you any longer. I'll be there around supper. Do you want me to pick up something?"

Carly said, "I'm not all that hungry. I can make a salad, and there's sandwich meat."

Thorne said, "Sounds perfect. I'll see you around 5:00 or so." They hung up.

Chapter Thirty-One

Jennifer pulled the car into her father's driveway. She looked at Kenny. "I hope you will behave while you're here, Kenny. Your papa loves us very much and he has done so much to help us."

Kenny shrugged his shoulders.

Jennifer reached to open her door. "Come on, let's go."

Mr. Ward opened the front door as they walked up the sidewalk and said, "My two favorite people in the world! Come in."

Jennifer and her dad hugged in the doorway. "Hey, Dad, I appreciate your help."

Mr. Ward replied, "All I can do is try. Hopefully, it will be beneficial, but you never know."

Kenny finally slowly made his way up the steps. Mr. Ward said, "My boy, look at you, my you've grown. You're bigger than your ole papa." He smiled and padded Kenny on the shoulder.

Kenny quietly said, "Hey, Papa."

"Come on in. I'm so happy that we can spend some time together."

Jennifer walked into the den and sat down. Her dad and Kenny sat in chairs opposite her. Mr. Ward said to Jennifer, "I've got a good supper on the stove, I hope you can stay and eat."

Jennifer answered, "We just came from the school and didn't take the time to go home and pack anything for Kenny's stay. I wanted to make sure that it was OK with you first. I'll go home and get his clothes packed for the weekend and be back in time for supper."

"Wonderful." He sat up in his chair, leaning forward slightly, and said, "Now, want to tell me what this is all about?" He looked at Jennifer and then at Kenny. No one spoke.

Jennifer said, "Kenny, do you want to tell him or should I?"

Kenny shrugged again. Mr. Ward said to him, "It would be the polite thing to do to answer a question when someone asks you something, Kenny."

Kenny looked at his mother. "You tell him."

"Fine." She looked at her dad and began. "Kenny has an attitude problem. I don't know exactly why, but he has temper problems. He got into a fight with a boy at his school today. The chief of police was there when I arrived, which alarmed me, to say the least. I feel like I'm at my wit's end. I don't know how to help. The chief suggested that it may help if Kenny saw a counselor. When we were on our way home, I thought of the best counselor I've ever known and here we are."

Mr. Ward said, "Well, I wouldn't go as far as all that. I just look forward to spending time with Kenny. It's been a long time and we need to get reacquainted, you might say."

Jennifer stood, looked at Kenny, and said, "I'll go pack your things and be back in time for supper." She looked at her dad. "Dad, do you need anything? Can I bring anything for supper?"

Her dad stood, "No honey, just you and a healthy appetite." He walked her to the door, hugged goodbye. He stood at the door for a moment pondering, *What do I do now? I hope I can come up with some magic words. Help me, God.*

Mr. Ward walked back into the living room and said, "Kenny, are you hungry? You want a snack before supper?"

Kenny asked, "What 'cha got?"

Mr. Ward said, "Come on in the kitchen. We'll see what we can find." He took out chocolate chip cookies and sliced cheese, poured two glasses of milk. They sat at the table, not talking while they had their snack. Kenny had quite an appetite. Mr. Ward chuckled and said, "Now I know why you're so much bigger than me." Kenny nodded his head.

After the snack, Mr. Ward checked the pot of soup, stirred it, replaced the lid. "You want to help set the table?" he asked Kenny.

Kenny said, "Sure." Mr. Ward pointed to the cabinet where the bowls were. "Bowls are on the first shelf. Silverware is in that second drawer from the sink."

Kenny set out three place settings with paper towels for napkins, like he did at home.

Mr. Ward said, "Let's go outside. I love to sit by the little creek and toss pebbles. I have a jacket you can use if you like."

Kenny said he was fine, and they walked down to the creek that ran along the back of Mr. Ward's property.

Kenny spoke up. "This is neat. Any fish in it?"

"Afraid not. The level changes too drastically for fish to stay around. Speaking of fish, the lake at the end of this creek has nice catfish. How about we give it a try tomorrow? Would you like that? I have enough rods. We could dig for some worms for bait."

Kenny thought and answered, "I guess."

Mr. Ward stood up and said, "It's about time for your mother to be here for supper. You come on in when you're ready."

He walked back to the house just as Jennifer pulled into the driveway. When she got inside and noticed that Kenny wasn't there, she asked, "Where's Kenny?"

"Oh, we took a little stroll down to the creek and I told him that he could come along when he wanted."

"I'll go call him," she said.

"No, no, just let him be. He'll come in his own time," her dad assured her.

They sat, Mr. Ward put the soup on the table, and each filled their bowls. Jennifer tasted and said, "This is so good, as always, Dad." She ate a little more and asked, "What do you think? Do you think you can help him?"

"I have no idea, but I certainly can try. We'll going fishing down at the lake tomorrow. We'll just wait and see how it goes."

After finishing their soup, Jennifer had to get home, so she kissed and hugged her dad. "Thanks again, Dad. It means a lot." She left.

Chapter Thirty-Two

Carly met Thorne at the door and, of course, Dinkle did her dance when they kissed. Thorne rubbed Dinkle on the head. He took off his jacket and shoulder holster, hung them in the hall closet, and they went into the kitchen. "I see they have put a for rent sign in Donna's yard."

Carly began, "Really, I hadn't noticed. Now, tell me, I've been anxious to hear how your meeting with Ms. Struthers went." She began fixing the salad.

"She was a cute little old lady. Full of energy and information. Her memory is not about to be failing her. You ought to see her house. She has a trillion whatnots and doodads, all from her children, grandchildren, and great-grandchildren, she informed me."

Carly interrupted, "How old is she?"

"She says she's ninety-four. One thing, she hasn't slowed up except that she doesn't drive anymore because her reaction time is not what it once was. Her house is decorated totally in Victorian furniture, lamps, and rugs. It was a pleasure meeting her. Her husband died about twenty years ago and she never remarried."

"How does she get around if she doesn't drive?"

"Her granddaughter takes her to the grocery store, and I imagine anywhere else she needs to go. I met the granddaughter's son, Luke, the first day I stopped by. Nice young man, very polite and helpful."

Carly interrupted, "What did she remember about the Grubers?"

"Quite a bit. Seems they had two boys. Oh wait, let me go back. As I said before, I first went to the library to find the article about the jewelry store robbery, which I did, along with the obituary about Frank Gruber. So, getting his address led me to Ms. Struthers. Yesterday she wasn't home, so today I spent most of the morning with her. She remembered many details. The man was married with two sons. The husband and wife worked, and the boys went to school."

"At some point, the wife/mother died or left, don't know the circumstances. But afterwards, seems Mr. Gruber was different. He didn't work, had a couple of strange characters visit late on weekends who drove a big black car."

Carly said, "That doesn't sound good."

"I agree. Sometime during all this, Joshua had married. My, how time flies, right? One night, Ms. Struthers and her husband were awakened by sirens. The police and an ambulance were at the Gruber's house. She found out that the father died in the hospital. She also said that he had been shot."

"That's scary."

Thorne continued, "That's what Ms. Struthers said too. She didn't see Eli after that. However, she called me when I was on my way home to tell me she recalled Eli coming to the house one time and he was driving a new 1979 Lincoln Continental."

Carly asked, "Do you think all this has something to do with the jewelry store robbery back then?"

Thorne said, "Could be. After I left Ms. Struthers' house, I went by the police station to see if there was a file or any kind of report about it. They gave me a copy of the reports, but they were not helpful. No witnesses, no suspects, no arrests."

Carly said, "What now? All that information but it leads nowhere."

"I knew I had to find the brother, Joshua. He may know the details. I couldn't find any property listed in his name, so I contacted the DMV, and they are sending me the vehicle information and address. I should get it next week, hopefully."

Carly put the salad in Thorne's bowl, got the dressing out for him. He asked, "Aren't you eating anything?"

"I've just felt a little under the weather today, mostly tired. I think Bonnie's story is getting to me, so I'm going to stop working on it for a couple of days. I felt a little queasy and I may go by the drugstore tomorrow and ask Ms. Maggie about something that would help."

Thorne offered, "I'll be glad to pick it up and you can rest."

"Thanks, but I need to deliver my article to Mr. Bennett. I'm going to ask him if he has heard from Harry. He'll be back soon and resume writing the weekly interest articles. I really want to spend most of my time on writing Bonnie's story."

Thorne got up and cleared the table. They went to the living room. The evening sun was setting. Thorne said, "I'll be right back. I need to get my suitcase out of the car. I was so excited to see Dinkle, I forgot to get it." He smiled.

"Dinkle? What about me?" Carly laughed.

He returned and took his suitcase to the bedroom, opened it, and took out the wrapped box with the bracelet inside. He went back to the living room. "That quilt on the bed that Bonnie gave us for our wedding is one beautiful piece of work."

Carly says, "I love it. Makes the room so cozy."

Thorne held out the box and sat beside her. "I got a little something for my beautiful bride."

Carly's eyes twinkled. "Me?"

Thorne laughed. "Well, I believe you are my one and only."

She took the gift. "The wrapping is exquisite." She opened the leather box lined with velvet. Thorne thought her eyes were going to pop out. She held the bracelet up, placed it over her wrist, and reached to Thorne to fasten it. She didn't speak.

Thorne finally asked, "Well, do you like it?"

Carly reached for him, hugged, and kissed him. "I've never, never seen anything so gorgeous, so precious, so, so, I can't describe what I feel."

Thorne laughed, "If you're going to write novels, you might want to learn how to express feelings."

They sat quietly for a while. Dinkle didn't show much appreciation for Carly's new bracelet. Carly said, "I think I'll turn in early. Maybe tomorrow I'll feel better."

Thorne said, "I think I know what your problem was today."

Carly asked, "What?"

"You missed me and needed me," he said.

She smiled, "You are correct." She let Dinkle wave goodnight to Thorne and took her to her kennel for the night. She kissed Thorne on her way back to the bedroom.

Thorne said, "I'll be there in a while. I want to make some notes while they are fresh in my mind."

He took off his shoes, retrieved his notepad and pen from his briefcase, and sat at the kitchen table to make a concise list of what he knew so far. He began to list facts:

1. *The Grubers moved in shortly after Ms. Struthers, no date.*
2. *Wife worked, unknown place.*
3. *Frank Gruber worked until his wife left or died; he was in his forties.*
4. *Boys home alone often. Frank would stay gone days at the time.*
5. *After the death of wife, occasionally two men of questionable character would show up late on Friday or Saturday nights. Drove a big black car.*
6. *Joshua married and moved away.*
7. *No memory of Eli after that.*
8. *Around 1980, ambulance and police; Gruber had been shot and later died in the hospital.*
9. *Sometime later, Eli parked a new 1979 Lincoln Continental in the driveway.*

He put the papers in his briefcase, turned off the lights, and went to bed.

Chapter Thirty-Three

Saturday morning, Kenny came into the kitchen. His papa had already prepared breakfast. "Morning, sleepyhead," he said as Kenny sat at the table.

"Morning, Papa."

"I hope you're hungry. I have fixed an omelet, scrambled eggs, and sausage, onions, and mushrooms." He poured himself coffee and poured milk for Kenny.

"How'd you sleep?"

"Fine."

"You ready to catch a big one today?"

Kenny shrugged. They ate their breakfast without talking.

Mr. Ward said, "You clear the table while I get the fishing tackle together, OK?"

"Sure," Kenny said.

Kenny met him at the back door. They put on their coats and toboggans. They grabbed the fishing rods, tackle box, and bait. Papa said, "I had some worms left from my lasting fishing trip, so we don't need to dig any." They walked through the back of the property, through a sparse tree line to the creek, and followed it to the lake. "Just a little further, I've got my special fishing spot all set up."

Papa saw that Kenny looked puzzled about baiting the hook. He asked, "You ever baited a hook?"

Kenny answered, "I've never been fishing."

Papa said, "Here, let me show you. You watch me bait mine." Papa then showed Kenny how to cast his rod. Kenny failed the first few times, and his worm came off. Papa watched him bait his hook again and try once more. A success.

It wasn't too long before Kenny's rod bent. Papa said, "Reel him in!" He walked over to Kenny and helped him. "Nice one," he said. "Let me show you how to take catfish off the hook. They are scary creatures. You see that barbed fin on top and on each side? It will hurt like the dickens if you get stuck. Believe me, I know." He showed Kenny how to grab the fish and remove the hook. "I'll be glad to help you next time. I don't want you getting hurt."

Kenny said, "Thanks, Papa."

Mr. Ward thought, *Well that was a change; maybe we're getting somewhere.*

They fished a while longer. Papa spoke up and said, "You know Kenny, one thing I've figured out in life and that is that every single decision, little or big, you make in life has the potential to affect your entire life. Sometimes for the better, sometimes not."

Kenny didn't say anything. They fished a while longer and caught enough for supper. They gathered up their stringer of fish and headed back home to Papa's.

Kenny said, "That was fun. Do you think we can go again tomorrow?"

Papa laughed. "If you like, that would be good. We will have to dig worms for our next great fishing expedition, however."

Papa showed Kenny how to skin a catfish with the knife and pliers. "The skin is tough on these suckers," he said. Kenny managed to skin one and Papa the rest. They cleaned up the cutting board, washing it down with the water hose. "Let's get supper started, how about it." He washed off the fish and said, "Let's cook outside. Nothing tastes better than fish fried on an open fire."

Kenny seemed to be interested in all his papa was doing. He was glad there hadn't been a sermon about his behavior. He thought about how nice it would be to have a dad like his papa.

They entered the kitchen, Mr. Ward said, "You can slice a couple of potatoes and one of those small onions," and pointed to the cabinet where they were kept. "I'll go out and start the fire."

Kenny was amazed at the things his papa knew about. As they ate, Papa talked about his life as a boy growing up on a farm, his parents, and brothers. He told a little about his time in the navy, and his falling in love with his wife, Nadine. He said, "That was one of the happiest days of my life, except, of course, when your momma was born. How Nadine did love that child; me too. She was something special. The saddest day of my life was when Nadine got the cancer. Those couple of years were so painful. Sometimes I would lie in bed and let the tears flow."

Kenny interrupted, "You cried?"

"Sure did. I couldn't bear to see the love of my life suffering so much. That was many years ago but sometimes it feels like yesterday." He cleared his throat, poked a stick in the fire. After a long while, Papa said, "Looks like the fire is about out. You ready to go inside?"

"Yes, sir." They sprayed the dying fire with the water hose. When they got inside, Kenny said, "I'll do the dishes."

"That would be fine. I sure have enjoyed your being here. Gets lonesome sometimes." He poured himself another cup of coffee and sat at the table to keep Kenny company while he did the dishes.

Kenny quietly spoke, "I wish my dad was like you, Papa." He turned to look at his papa, who had slumped in his chair, mouth open, arms hanging by his side. Kenny panicked, didn't dry his hands, walked over, and cried, "Papa! Papa!" He ran to the phone hanging on the wall in the kitchen and dialed 911, gave them the information. He got a wet paper towel and put it on his papa's head. "Papa, please, don't go away," he pleaded in a whisper. Then he thought, *I better call Momma.*

Jennifer answered the phone on the second ring, hoping Kenny wasn't in trouble when she saw that it was her dad calling. "What's wrong?" she answered.

"Mom! Mom! It's Papa. I think he's dying. He's just slumped over in his chair at the table!" He was out of breath as he told it to his mother.

Jennifer said, "I'll be right there. Did you call 911?"

"Yes. Hurry, Mom. I don't know what to do!" They hung up and Kenny went back to his papa. His papa was slowly opening his eyes. They were glazed and out of focus. Kenny said, "Papa! Papa! Can you hear me? It's Kenny. I called the ambulance, and they are coming. Mom's coming too." He wet another paper towel and held it against his papa's head. Tears came to his eyes. He was really scared. He had never experienced anything like this. He whispered, "Please don't die Papa. I need you. I want you to be here with me."

The ambulance arrived and shortly after, Jennifer came running through the house. The EMTs had her dad on a stretcher, ready to transport him to the hospital. She said, "What is it? What happened? Can you tell me? Did he have a heart attack?"

The EMT woman said to her, "Try to be calm, miss. Are you related to Mr. Ward?"

"Yes, yes. I'm his daughter and this is my son, Kenny." She looked at Kenny and said, "Come on, Kenny. We'll go to the hospital."

They arrived and the nurse at the desk said, "I understand your worry, but please have a seat. The doctor will come and give you an update when they have finished their exam."

Jennifer and Kenny walked over to the nearest chairs and sat, not speaking, just fearfully and hopefully waiting.

A while later, the doctor came out, walked over to Jennifer and Kenny. "Ms. Ward? I'm Dr. Brown."

"I'm Jennifer Owens. I'm Mr. Ward's daughter."

"Yes, Mam. Ms. Owens, I've examined your father and for his age, he's in good condition. We need to run some more tests and he will be staying with us for a day or two."

Jennifer wiped her eyes. "Is he going to be OK? He didn't have a heart attack?"

The doctor answered, "Like I said, we need to run more tests. If he did, it was a light one." He looked toward the nurse's station. "Do they have your phone number?"

Jennifer answered, "Yes, I gave them all the information. Can we see him?"

The doctor said, "I don't see why not. Just see the nurse and she will show you to his room."

"OK, thank you, Dr. Brown."

Jennifer and Kenny walked to Mr. Ward's room. He had a monitor attached to his chest and arm. He saw them come into the room. "Sorry about all this," he quietly said.

Jennifer walked to the side of his bed. Kenny stood at the foot of the bed. "Oh, Dad, you scared us half to death. Are you feeling better?"

He looked at her and then at Kenny. He said, "Kenny, I guess I interrupted your washing dishes," and smiled.

Kenny said, "I completely forgot about the dishes, Papa. I'm just glad you are better."

"Don't you worry. Takes more than a little funny heartbeat to get me down." Mr. Ward closed his eyes. "I think I'll take a little nap."

Jennifer kissed him on his cheek and motioned for Kenny to follow her out of the room. As they walked back to the waiting room, Jennifer said, "I need to go to Papa's house and get him some things, since he's going to be here a day or two."

Kenny said, "I can stay here while you do that."

"No, I need you to come with me. They will call us if Dad needs us."

When they walked past the nurse's station, they heard an elderly woman asking about Vernon Ward. Jennifer paused and when the lady turned around, Jennifer said to her, "Hello, I'm Mr. Ward's daughter, Jennifer. Do you know my dad?"

Edna Cooper said, "I'm Edna Cooper. I live next door to Vernon. He talks about you all the time. He said that you were moving here. It's nice to meet you." She looked at Kenny and said, "You must be Kenny."

"Yes, Mam."

Ms. Cooper asked, "How is he?"

Jennifer told her what the doctor had said. "We visited him. He looks tired and is taking a nap. Kenny and I were just going to his house to pack the things he needs. The doctor said he needs more tests and will be here a day or two."

Ms. Cooper said, "I'll just wait out here. I'm sure they will call you if need be." Ms. Cooper was in her sixties, a little on the stout side, short graying hair, and dressed in slacks and a pullover, with tennis shoes. She wore jewelry that looked expensive.

Jennifer reached into her purse, took out a pen and notepad, and wrote her phone number on it. Handing it to Ms. Cooper, she said, "Here's my phone number. We won't be gone long but should he need us, please call me."

"I will and I'll be here when you get back."

In the car, Kenny said, "Mom, Papa's going to need somebody to stay with him until he's all better. I can do that."

Jennifer thought about her job and said, "You have school, Kenny. I have my job and I'm not sure if they would allow me to take off for an unknown amount of time." She thought about Ms. Cooper and said, "Ms. Cooper evidently knows your papa pretty well, so maybe she can keep a check on him. I'll ask her when we get back."

They arrived at Mr. Ward's house. When inside, Kenny said, "Mom, I'm going to finish the dishes while you get Papa's things together. I wouldn't want him to come home to a mess."

Jennifer smiled to herself. "That is very thoughtful of you. It shouldn't take me long." She could see that her dad had influenced Kenny in a good way. *Hopefully, it will last*, she thought.

Jennifer and Kenny returned to the hospital and entered the ER waiting area. They walked over to where Ms. Cooper was sitting. Jennifer asked, "Any news?"

Ms. Cooper said, "No, I haven't heard anything."

Jennifer put the suitcase for her dad beside the chair and sat next to Ms. Cooper. Kenny surprisingly asked, "Mom, can I get you and Ms. Cooper anything? Coffee or a snack out of the vending machine?"

Ms. Cooper shook her head. Jennifer couldn't believe her ears. She reached into her wallet and handed five dollars to Kenny and said, "I'm fine, Kenny. Get something for yourself."

* * *

That weekend, Carly had felt tired. Thorne did a little paperwork but waited on Carly so she could rest. Dinkle, of course, tried to help too.

Carly was lying on the sofa and Thorne said, "Carly, I really think you ought to see the doctor. It's not normal for you to be this tired."

"I agree. I'll call on Monday and make an appointment. With Thanksgiving coming up, it might be a while before they can see me. We'll see."

Chapter Thirty-Four

Thorne awoke Monday morning and Carly was already up. He got up and went into the kitchen, where she was sitting at the kitchen table. He put his arms around her shoulders. "Couldn't you sleep? Anything wrong?"

Carly said, "I may be coming down with a bug. I just don't feel perky. I fixed some peppermint tea if you want some."

Thorne said, "I'll pick up something on my way to work. You're going to call the doctor today, right?"

Carly replied, "It's about time for my yearly checkup, so I may schedule that appointment. No hurry. It may be just something I ate that didn't agree with me. I'm going to turn in my article today, then I'll drop by the drugstore and get some Pepto-Bismol or something."

Thorne kissed her on the forehead. "You do feel a little warm. Do you want me to stay home and drive you to town?"

"Of course not, I'll be fine. Will you let Dinkle out of her kennel?"

Thorne went to Dinkle, "Hello, girl. You need to take care of your momma today. She isn't feeling too perky." Dinkle wagged her tail and headed for the doggie door. Thorne opened it and looked at Carly. "Are you sure you don't want me to drive you?" She shook her head.

Thorne showered, dressed, let Dinkle back inside, and left for work.

Carly delivered her article to Mr. Bennett. She felt like she wanted a steak, so she walked across the street to Womble's Meat Market. Mr. Matthews greeted her. "Well, hello Carly. How have you been? It's been a while."

"I'm fine, Mr. Matthews. I just feel like having steak tonight for supper."

She picked out her cut of beef and asked, "How's Scott?"

"Fine, fine. You know he's getting married. Nice girl too."

Carly said, "No, I hadn't heard about that." She paid Mr. Matthews and said, "Tell Scott that I said hello and congratulations on his engagement."

"I will. You come back soon."

Carly walked across the street to Barton's Drugstore. The bell tinkled when she walked in. Ms. Maggie was reading the newspaper behind the counter, looked up, and greeted Carly.

"My, my, Carly, you're out early this morning."

Carly walked up to the counter. "I had to turn in my newspaper article to Mr. Bennett."

Ms. Maggie said, "I'm really enjoying your articles. They have real feeling."

"Thank you. I've enjoyed writing them." She paused, and said, "Ms. Maggie, what do you recommend for a queasy stomach? I can't remember what my mother gave me."

Ms. Maggie put her long, wrinkled finger over her lips, thinking, and said, "I remember the old folks used to make ginger or peppermint tea. Never tried it but you can look back there and see what Mr. Edwards recommends. You know he's turning out to be a good pharmacist. People like him. Of course, we all miss Mr. Perkins since he moved away."

Carly remembered that she had both peppermint and fresh ginger at home and said, "I think I'll just give ginger a try. I have some at home. Thanks Ms. Maggie. You have a good day."

Ms. Maggie quickly asked, "Carly, how's Thorne coming along on the Gruber case? Anything new?"

Carly kindly wiggled her index finger toward Ms. Maggie and said, "Now, Ms. Maggie, you know I can't talk about Thorne's work. It's all confidential stuff."

Ms. Maggie looked frustrated. "I didn't mean to be nosy or anything. I'm just concerned, that's all."

"I know, Ms. Maggie. I'll let you know as soon as I can. You take care." She left the store.

* * *

When Thorne got home that evening, he said, "Something smells good."

Carly said, "I stopped by Womble's today and got us a sirloin steak for supper. I've made the salad, so we can eat shortly." Thorne sat at the table while Carly filled him in on her day. "I asked Mr. Matthews about Scott and he said that he was engaged. That was a surprise. Anyway, I stopped by to see

Ms. Maggie and she told me that she heard peppermint or ginger was good for an upset stomach. I made some tea with ginger when I got home and, sure enough, it helped.”

“Good, I’m glad you’re feeling better.”

Carly smiled and said, “Ms. Maggie, you know that she is the real newspaper in town. She asked me about the Gruber case. I told her that it was confidential. I think she got a little frustrated about that.”

Thorne said, “I know how she is. She can’t help herself, I guess. Did you call the doctor?”

“No, but I will tomorrow, I promise. There’s a new pharmacist at the drugstore. Mr. Perkins moved away, and Steve Edwards took his place.”

They sat quietly in the living room. Dinkle lay on the floor beside Carly’s chair. Thorne was comfortable on the sofa.

The phone rang, Thorne got up and answered, “Hello.”

“Thorne, this is Bonnie.”

“Hey, Bonnie, how are you?”

“We’re fine. I know it’s late notice, but I was wondering if you and Carly would like to come to our house for Thanksgiving. All my kids have plans with their in-laws, so it will just be Josh, me, and Renee. I would love it if you would come.”

Thorne answered, “That’s nice of you, Bonnie. Hold on and let me ask Carly.” He turned and said to Carly, “It’s Bonnie. She and Josh are inviting us to their house for Thanksgiving.”

Carly quickly replied, “Yes, that would be great.”

Thorne put the phone back to his ear and said, “Carly is good with it. So, I guess it’s a date. What time do you want us to be there?”

Bonnie said, “Anytime, the earlier the better. Tell Carly she can keep me company in the kitchen. You and Josh can do whatever. Josh isn’t into watching football or parades.”

Thorne laughed, “Me either. It will just be good getting with family. So, we’ll see you mid to late morning that Thursday. Thanks for the invite.”

Bonnie said, “It might be good to start a new family tradition. Hopefully, my kids and their family can come one year. Tell Carly I can’t wait. Talk to you later.” They hung up.

Chapter Thirty-Five

Monday morning, not long after Mr. Templeton arrived at the realty office, a young man came in.

Stacy greeted him. "Good morning. May I help you?"

"Yes, I'm Mike Lawson. On my drive into town, I saw a house for rent in Flat Branch, a few miles out of town. It had your company name on the sign. I would like to find out more about it."

"Yes, sir. Let me tell Mr. Templeton that you are here. Please, have a seat." She rang Mr. Templeton, then said to Mr. Lawson, "You can go in," and pointed to his office door.

Mr. Templeton stood up, reached out, and shook Mike's hand. "Good morning, Mr. Lawson. My secretary says you are interested in the house we have listed in Flat Branch."

"Yes, sir. My wife, Shelly, and I will possibly be relocating from Raleigh. How many bedrooms are in the house?"

Mr. Templeton pulled the file. "There are three. The master bedroom has a bath. The house is quite spacious. Also, it is furnished. The lady who lived here moved away after her husband died."

Mike Lawson said, "Sorry to hear that. I would like to see it, hopefully this afternoon. I have an appointment this morning with Dr. Skinner."

Mr. Templeton said, "Doc Skinner? Our veterinarian?"

"Yes. He's thinking about retiring and I've applied for the position. After I meet with him this morning, hopefully I will be moving here."

Mr. Templeton said, "How about 1:30 this afternoon?"

Mike Lawson replied, "That sounds perfect. If, for some reason, I don't get the job, I'll stop by and let your secretary know."

"I would appreciate that. See you this afternoon."

Mike Lawson said goodbye to Stacy and drove to Doc Skinner's office. Doc Skinner walked from a room in the back when he heard the door open. "Hello, you must be Mr. Lawson."

"Yes sir. Mike Lawson. Here's a copy of my resume." They shook hands.

Doc Skinner took the folder and said, "Good to meet you, young man. Come on back to my office. I don't have any scheduled appointments for a while, so we can talk."

Doc Skinner told Mike about some of his patients and their owner's peculiarities. Mike listened attentively. Doc Skinner remarked, "I see that you went to North Carolina State University."

"Yes. Since graduating, I've worked in a veterinary clinic in Raleigh. My wife and I don't particularly care for the big city, and this will be the perfect opportunity for us. We have one two-year-old daughter, and my wife is pregnant."

"Family, a good thing. I lost my wife many years ago. We never had children. I'm getting on up in years and it's difficult for me to lift the heavier dogs and such."

Mike said, "I understand. On my way into town, I saw a house for rent in Flat Branch. Not to be presumptuous, I stopped by the realtor's office and, if you give me the job, I have an appointment to see it this afternoon."

Doc Skinner rubbed his chin. "Flat Branch." He thought and said, "That must be the house down the street from Carly and Thorne Davenport. Oh, Dinkle, that little fellow is something else. Spoiled rotten to the core." He laughed. Then said, "Carly is a swell girl. She works at the newspaper office and her husband, Thorne, he's a private eye."

"I look forward to meeting them."

Doc Skinner asked, "Do you have any pets?"

"No, with school and living in an apartment, it hasn't been possible. I hope to get a dog soon, so it can grow up with the kids."

"That's wonderful." After a bit of chitchat and questions, Doc Skinner said, "Well, young man, I think you'll make a fine doc in the town. When can you start?"

Mike thought and said, "I'll need to give a notice at my job, I believe only a week is required. There are several doctors in the clinic so that won't be a problem. How about two weeks from now, after Thanksgiving? Hopefully, we can move and get settled in by then."

"Sounds fine, Mike. I'll be telling my patients about you, so they won't be surprised. Maybe I can get Carly to put something in the paper about it."

Mike stood up, shook Doc Skinner's hand, and left. It was too early for his appointment to see the rental house, but it may be possible to see it now. He arrived at the realtors. When he walked in, Stacy saw him and looked at her watch. "Hello, Mr. Lawson."

Mike walked up to her desk and said, "I know it's early, but my interview didn't last as long as I thought. Would it be possible for me to see the house now?"

Mr. Templeton came out of his office and saw Mr. Lawson. "I was just on my way to lunch. Will you join me?"

Mike said, "If you don't mind, I'll just wait. I had a big breakfast and I'm not that hungry."

Mr. Templeton thought for a minute and said, "I tell you what, we could go see the house now and I'll grab something on the way back. There's the best diner between here and Flat Branch. The Green Hornet Grill in Bunnlevel. Nellie Garrett is a must for you to get to know, which I'm sure you will if you live in Flat Branch. Nellie is friends with your neighbors, Carly and Thorne Davenport."

After seeing the house, Mike told Mr. Templeton that he would rent it. On the way back, they stopped at the diner.

Nellie was checking out a customer. She looked up and said, "Welcome. Just take a seat anywhere. I'll be with you in a jiffy."

Mike liked her already. She came over and took their orders. Mr. Templeton told Mike a little about the town. They talked about Mike's vet career. Nellie was so busy with the lunch crowd that she didn't have time to stay and chat. They finished their lunch, went back to the real estate office, filled out the rental contract, and Mike headed back to Raleigh. He couldn't wait to tell Shelly about his day.

* * *

When Mike returned to their apartment, Shelly was anxious to hear about his day. He walked in and she met him at the door, saying, "How was it? Did you get the job?"

Mike kissed her on the cheek. "Yes, but something better than that."

She asked, "What?" and followed him into the kitchen. Jill was in her playpen in the living room. She added, "I've got supper ready. Chicken soup and crackers. I fed Jill earlier, so she's fine playing for a while." While she set the table and filled their bowls, she asked, "What is the town like?"

Mike said, "It's a quaint little place. Everybody seems friendly. On my way there, I saw a house for rent. It's about ten miles from where I'll be working but I liked it. So, I went to the realtor's office and inquired. Mr. Templeton, the realtor, took me to see it. I think it's perfect. It has three bedrooms and a nice size yard for Jill and, of course, the new little one."

Shelly said, "Wow, you accomplished a lot. What's the neighborhood like?"

Mike said, "It isn't really a neighborhood. It's out in the country, about ten miles from Lillington, a place called Flat Branch. There's a house not far down the road. According to the realtor, a nice couple lives there."

"How did it go with the doctor?"

Mike chuckled and said, "He's a trip, really. Pretty old but loves his customers. I couldn't tell if he was talking about the pets or the pet owners. He has a good-sized patient list." He finished his soup and sat back in his chair. "I rented the house. I know you will like it. It's furnished, so we don't have to go to the expense of buying a lot of things."

Shelly asked, "So, you took the job and rented the house?"

"Yep. I start my job in two weeks, after Thanksgiving. So, I guess we need to start packing."

"This is all so fast. I'll go to the U-Haul place tomorrow and get some boxes."

"Sounds good," Mike said.

Chapter Thirty-Six

Early the next morning, Beth Logan entered the drugstore. Ms. Maggie said, "My, you're out bright and early this morning."

Beth walked to the counter. "I know. I just couldn't wait to tell you."

Ms. Maggie leaned on the counter. "What?"

Beth said, "You know, the other day when that new woman came in, Jennifer, who had a son that I thought was a troublemaker?"

Ms. Maggie shook her head. Beth continued, "Well, it's worse than I thought. That Jennifer is not the best mother. She left her son, the troublemaker, at her father's house. She was going to leave him there; you know, abandon him. People are so irresponsible these days. Anyway, the poor father couldn't take the stress off it all and he had a heart attack."

Ms. Maggie gasped. "No, you're kidding."

Beth said, "No, it's true. He was admitted to the hospital. A neighbor lady came to see about him. I bet Jennifer is in a tizzy. What will she do now?"

Ms. Maggie said, "Jennifer should have thought about that. Her son, what's his name?"

Beth said, "Kenny."

Ms. Maggie continued, "Kenny, that's right. Jennifer should have known her father was too old to put up with her shenanigans. The poor thing."

Beth said, "I agree. She did it on purpose, I'm sure."

Ms. Maggie asked, "How is the dad? Did he die?"

Beth said, "No, he went back home. His neighbor, I'm sure, is the one who is going to look after him. I'm glad I never had children. They disappoint you so."

Ms. Maggie said, "I always wanted a family, but since I never got married, I guess that was out of the question. I manage to keep myself busy with the store and all."

Beth said, "I better get going. I'm going to Womble's to pick up ground beef. I'll talk to you later."

Ms. Maggie said, "Keep me posted."

Beth said, "No worry. I always do." She left the drugstore.

* * *

Around lunchtime, Jennifer enters the drugstore and takes her items to the counter.

Ms. Maggie starts to ring them up in the old register and says, "Hello, Jennifer. Nice to see you again." She tears off the receipt and tells Jennifer the total. "I heard about your father. I hope he's OK."

Jennifer pays and takes her change. "He's fine. It was a scary thing. Poor Kenny was scared out of his mind. It's not good for a boy to have to experience things like that."

Ms. Maggie thought, *What a two-faced liar*. "Is he doing OK now?"

Jennifer said, "Yes, he's fine. He loves his papa."

Ms. Maggie said, "That's good." Jennifer took her bag and left the store.

* * *

After Thorne left for the office, Carly called her gynecologist, Dr. Ellen Whitmore's office. Surprisingly, she was able to get an appointment that afternoon.

She called Thorne. He answered, "Davenport Investigations."

Carly said, "I called Dr. Whitmore's office. They gave me an appointment this afternoon at 1:30."

Thorne quickly said, "I'll come home and take you."

"No, Thorne, I'm fine to drive. Really."

He said, "Call me as soon as you get home and let me know what she says. Drive carefully."

Carly replied, "I will. I'm sure I probably just need a vitamin or something." They hung up.

Thorne sat back in his desk chair and thought back to the time his first wife, his new bride, had driven herself to the doctor to check on her pregnancy. He felt the feeling of great loss come over him. He was so afraid that on this day he could be reliving that same nightmare. He got up from his desk. He had to get a little fresh air, a change of scene, to wipe away his anxiety. He walked down to the nearby donut shop.

Even though it was chilly outside, he had his donut and coffee at an outside table. He went across the street to the Quick-Mart and bought a newspaper. Nothing helped. He looked at his watch. Back at his office, his phone rang. He answered, "Davenport Investigations." Wrong number, he hung up the phone. He looked at his watch again, at 12:30. He put on his jacket, left the office, and drove home.

Carly was surprised when he came in the door just as she was getting ready to leave. "Hey, Thorne. Anything wrong?"

He looked at her. "I see I'm just in time. You ready?"

Carly said, "Thorne, I told you that I am fine to drive."

"I know what you said, but you're my wife and I want to take care of you. You don't feel well, and I'm driving. End of story." He hugged her. "Come on, let's go."

Carly realized that he was remembering what happened to his first wife on her way to the obstetrician's office. She understood.

They only waited minutes in the doctor's waiting room before Carly was called back to the exam room. She explained her feelings to Dr. Whitmore. "A couple of mornings last week, I felt a little nauseated, but not since. The only thing is that I feel more tired than usual in the last few days. Otherwise, I'm fine."

Dr. Whitmore did an initial exam and took a blood sample. "I'll be back in a few minutes. You can put your blouse back on and wait in the chair."

In about fifteen minutes, Dr. Whitmore returned, holding Carly's chart. She sat in her chair, looked at Carly, and said, "My dear Carly, you are going to be a mother."

Carly was shocked and felt dizzy. "Really? Oh my, I had no idea. I know we've wanted this. It's not a surprise but it is."

Dr. Whitmore understood. She had seen this reaction many times. "Carly, I just need to ask you a couple of questions."

Carly said, "Sure, OK."

Dr. Whitmore asked, "What was the date of your last menstrual cycle?"

Carly tried to bring thoughts to her mind. Her brain felt like it was in a fog. She remembered Thorne was in the waiting room. "Oh, I've got to go tell my husband!"

Dr. Whitmore quickly said, "Just another minute, Carly. Do you know the date of your last period?"

"Ah, let me think. It was the first week in October, I'm fairly sure. We had not been home too long from our honeymoon."

Dr. Whitmore noted that in the chart. She said, "I want you to come back in three weeks for a full examination. Congratulations. Now, go tell your husband. We'll send you a notice of the appointment date and time. Again, congratulations to you and your husband."

Carly almost fumbled over her own feet when she walked out the door. Thorne saw her coming down the hall and stood up to meet her. When he saw her face, fear went through him. She looked as pale as a ghost. Oh no, he thought. Not something terrible. Carly focused on Thorne, then a huge smile came on her face, and her eyes sparkled with tears. Louder than she intended, she said, "We're going to have a baby!"

Thorne wrapped his arms around her and squeezed. "Oh, sorry, I didn't mean to squeeze you so hard."

Carly laughed, "I'm not breakable, dear daddy." Thorne gave her a quick kiss on the forehead. "Never mind that. I'm going to pamper you like you've never known." They walked to Thorne's car.

On the way home, Carly said, "I want to stop and tell Nellie the news. The diner shouldn't be busy as it's after lunch. In fact, she's probably getting ready to close for the day."

Thorne pulled into the parking lot at the diner. Carly got out and reached the door before Thorne did. She walked into the diner. Nellie took one look at her and said, "You're not!"

Carly, confused, asked, "Not? Not what?"

Nellie answered, "Pregnant!"

Thorne heard the conversation and said to Carly, "I told you, that woman has a seventh sense. She knows things." They all laughed. Nellie hugged Carly, then Thorne.

Nellie said, "What can we do to celebrate? I don't have any celebrating type of food here, or drink, for that matter. Not that you need any of that stuff." She laughed.

Carly said, "No worry, Nellie. We just got out of the doctor's office and HAD to come give you the news first before anyone else." Carly thought about saying something about Nellie being the baby's godmother but decided to wait until she discussed it with Thorne. She said, "We need to get home, Nellie. I'll see you later this week."

Nellie, as always, said, "You take care, and you know I'm here if you need me."

When they got home, Dinkle greeted them, tail wagging, barking hello. Thorne gave Dinkle a rub on the head. He said, "Dinkle, you have a new job. You must look after your momma and don't be asking her to wait on you all the time. You are going to be getting a little sister or brother to love and take care of." Dinkle wagged her tail.

Thorne looked at Carly for interpretation. She said, "Dinkle is happy about it."

Thorne said, "You lie on the sofa. Can I fix you anything?"

Carly stopped him as he started to the kitchen. "Listen Thorne. I am not an invalid. I am not helpless. You are too sweet to offer to do everything but I'm able to be a normal person. If I have a bad day or something, then I'll let you wait on me. OK?"

Thorne hugged her and agreed. "Sorry, I guess I got carried away. I'll try to do better." They fixed supper and went to bed early. Surprisingly, both slept well that night.

The next morning, Carly remembered the prescription for the prenatal vitamins given to her by Dr. Whitmore. She got it from her purse and said to Thorne, "I forgot that yesterday, Dr. Whitmore gave me a prescription for prenatal vitamins. I was too shocked, surprised, stunned, elated. Do you think you could pick them up at the drugstore sometime today? You could drop it off and pick it up later when you're on the way home. Whatever works. If it's inconvenient, I can go into town and get them sometime today."

He took the prescription. "No problem. I'll see you this afternoon. You take it easy and be sure to call me if you need me." They kissed and he left to go back to work.

Chapter Thirty-Seven

Jennifer got Kenny off to school. She called her boss to explain the situation to her father and asked for the day off. When she arrived at the hospital, she went to her dad's room.

"Good morning," Mr. Ward said as she walked in.

"Hey, Dad, you're looking a lot better. How do you feel?"

He replied, "I'm ready to get back home. Hopefully, the doctor will release me this morning." He sat up straighter in his bed. Jennifer walked to him and kissed him on the cheek. "Aren't you supposed to be at work?"

"No worry. I called and told my boss that I needed today off. He understood."

Mr. Ward said, "The doctor should be at any time to tell me that I can go home." He sat up and hung his legs on the side of his bed. "How's Kenny?"

"Besides the fact that you scared us half to death, he's OK. In fact, I see somewhat of a change in his behavior. He seems a little more open and not so sulky."

"That's good," Mr. Ward said. "I really hate that our weekend got messed up. I'm sorry that I upset you and Kenny so much. I guess he went to school today?"

"Yes. He didn't want to, but he did. I'll pick him up this afternoon and we'll come over to fix your supper."

Mr. Ward said, "Now you listen. I don't want you to interrupt your life, your job, or Kenny's. I'm fine. Besides, Edna will more than likely be coming over often."

Jennifer said, "Yes, we met Ms. Cooper in the waiting room right after you were brought in. She seems like a nice person."

"Oh, she is. I've known her for many years. Her husband ran out on her not too long after they married. She's alone and doesn't have any children."

Jennifer added, "It is really nice of her to do this."

The doctor came into the room and said, "Mr. Ward, I'm going to discharge you today. All your tests were negative. It seems you were dehydrated. You should try to drink more water and take it easy for a while. So, you're good to go." He looked at Jennifer. "I guess you will be taking him home?"

"Yes. Thank you very much for your care of my dad."

Ms. Cooper came over as soon as they pulled into the driveway. She said, "I'm sure glad you are OK and back home, Vernon." Inside the house, Ms. Cooper reassured Jennifer, "Don't you worry about anything. I'll keep a close eye on your dad."

That afternoon, Jennifer picked up Kenny from school and they drove to Papa's house. Kenny sat in the living room and talked with him while Jennifer helped Ms. Cooper with supper. After they finished eating, Jennifer said goodbye to Ms. Cooper, "Be sure to call me if anything changes or you need me for anything. I appreciate your doing this."

Ms. Cooper assured her that she would. Kenny gave Papa a hug and said, "Get better fast. I think we need to catch more catfish."

Papa replied, "You bet. Soon, we'll do just that. You do good in school, OK?" Kenny shook his head.

Jennifer hugged her dad and said, "I think you're in good hands, Dad. Take care."

As they rode home, Jennifer asked Kenny, "How was your day at school?"

"It was OK. I'm just glad Papa's OK." They were quiet the rest of the way home.

Chapter Thirty-Eight

Shortly after Thorne got to work Tuesday morning, his phone rang. "Davenport Investigations," he answered.

"Thorne, Chief Logan here. Just checking to see how your investigation is going on Eli Gruber's case."

"Hello, Chief. Pretty well. I have found out some good information. I met with a neighbor who knew the family back years ago. She knew quite a bit about the past but nothing current. I found out that Eli had a brother. There wasn't any property listed in his name. I've contacted the Department of Motor Vehicles to get an address. I thought he must at least drive a car. I haven't heard back yet and with Thanksgiving this week, it will more than likely to be next week before I get that information."

"Sounds good, sounds good. Keep up the good work. Oh, and have a nice Thanksgiving."

Thorne said, "Thanks, Chief, you have a nice one also."

Thorne left work by midafternoon. He decided to get Carly's prescription filled at the pharmacy in Dunn instead of in Lillington. He knew how Ms. Maggie talked and with the prescription being for prenatal vitamins, the whole town would know about their having a baby before they were ready to announce it.

When he arrived home, Dinkle met him at the door. Carly was sitting on the sofa drinking ginger tea and eating saltines. Thorne walked to her and sat down, placing the prescription bag on the coffee table. Dinkle jumped on the sofa beside Carly. He said to Dinkle, "I see you are taking good care of your momma," and gave Dinkle a rub. To Carly, he said, "I got this prescription filled in Dunn. I assumed that Ms. Maggie would tell the town and we might want to do that ourselves."

Carly said, "Good thinking. I'm glad I don't have to worry about that with Nellie. That's one thing about her, you can trust her to keep things confidential."

Thorne asked, "Have you eaten anything besides crackers all day?"

"I had a piece of buttered toast around midday. When I told Dr. Whitmore about my queasiness, she said that it is common in the first trimester of pregnancy and recommended eating a few saltine crackers." She took a sip of her ginger tea. "There is some leftover soup in the refrigerator for you to have tonight if that's OK."

"Fine. I'll take care of it."

Carly asked, "How was your day?"

"Not very exciting. Chief Logan called to get an update on Eli Gruber's case. I told him that I was waiting for the DMV to get me an address for Eli's brother. I told him that with the holiday, it will be next week. I made an executive decision to leave work early and, in fact, take the rest of the week off."

Carly leaned against him. "Sounds good to me. I hope I can be a better company. I would hate to spend the whole week eating crackers, especially with Thanksgiving coming up."

"I definitely want you to feel better, but I'm here even if you turn into a grouchy lady."

Chapter Thirty-Nine

With the next day being Thanksgiving, Nellie was busy preparing her usual feast for all the folks in the area that didn't have family or friends with whom to celebrate. All the other restaurants in town would be closed. The customers were always scarce in the diner on the day before Thanksgiving, as most of them were home preparing for their own dinners.

She knew Doc Skinner, Ms. Maggie, Chief Logan and Beth, and Mr. Matthews would be among the customers. She didn't charge, but everyone left varying amounts of tips for her. She had the turkey in the oven, so it would be cool the next morning because Doc Skinner always carved it for her. She was preparing the desserts, apple pie, pecan pie, cherry pie, and fudge cake with chocolate icing. The diner's phone rang and Nellie wiped her hands on her apron. "Green Hornet," she answered.

"Hey, Nellie, it's Carly. I know you are busy preparing for tomorrow. I just couldn't remember if I told you that we are going to Bonnie's house for Thanksgiving."

Nellie said, "I'm not surprised now that you have family. I've just about finished with the desserts. I sure hope a lot of folks show up. I'm going to have enough food for five counties."

Carly said, "Thorne took this week off work, and we've just enjoyed being around the house, being lazy. I hope you have a wonderful time with all your friends. I'm sure they will love the feast you are preparing. I'll let you get back to it and we'll see you when we get back."

"I hope you have a safe trip and enjoy your visit. Tell that handsome detective husband of yours that I said hello and happy Thanksgiving." They hung up.

As soon as she hung up with Nellie, her phone rang. Carly answered, "Hello."

"Hello, daughter," Joey cheerfully said.

Carly couldn't yet call him Dad, so she answered, "Hello to you. You sound cheery."

Joey continued, "I'm calling to say I hope you and Thorne have a nice Thanksgiving. Do you have any plans?"

Carly said, "Yes, we are going to Bonnie and Josh's house tomorrow. What about ya'll?"

"We'll stay around here. The boys can't make it this year. So, we'll just have a quiet time at home."

Carly thought and said, "I've got some good news. You're going to be a Granddaddy." She waited for his response.

She heard him call loudly to Janice, who was in the kitchen. "Janice, come here. Guess what?" Carly couldn't hear anything until Joey said, "Carly and Thorne are going to have a baby!"

Janice said, "Give me that phone." She took the phone and said, "Carly! Oh, my goodness, what great news! That's wonderful. Something to really celebrate for Thanksgiving."

Carly said, "I agree. We were surprised and we were very happy. We're going to Bonnie and Josh's tomorrow for Thanksgiving dinner. I can't wait to tell Bonnie that she's going to be a great aunt."

Janice said, "Ya'll have a safe trip and I'm so happy for both of you. Take care and I hope to see you soon. Here's Joey." She handed the phone to Joey.

Joey said, "That's great news, Carly. I'm sure Thorne will take good care of you and the little one. Tell him I said congratulations."

"I will. Ya'll have a nice day and tell your boys we said hello." They hung up.

Carly went back into the living room. Lately, Dinkle had taken up sitting with Thorne on the sofa. Carly said, "Nellie is busy as usual. I don't see how in the world she does all that she does." She stood in front of the sofa and looked at Dinkle and said, "I guess you've fallen in love with him too. I think I'm jealous. You might end up loving him more than you do me." Carly said to Thorne, "I embarrassed her. She knows I have her number." They laughed.

* * *

Bonnie busied herself preparing food for their holiday. She always had baked ham, potato salad, green beans, fruit salad, sweet potatoes, homemade biscuits, cornbread, and a couple of pies, pecan, and chocolate. Josh was helping by cutting up the vegetables and washing the dishes as they went along.

Bonnie said, "You know, I can't believe all that has happened this year. Finding out that my sister gave a baby up for adoption is still unbelievable to me. And Carly is so sweet. Her husband seems like a fine man. I'm happy for her that her life wasn't ruined by what Kate did. A mother who turns away her child, really, it's unbelievable. I just don't understand it." She put the pecan pies in the oven and turned to Josh. "Don't you agree?"

"Yep, but I'm not all that surprised. It was a shock, yes, but not surprising. I never thought Kate was as perfect as she comes across. One thing, for sure, Carly is fortunate to have you as an aunt."

"Thanks, sweetie." They continued preparing the food.

* * *

Jennifer Owens worked a half day on Wednesday. Kenny was out of school and spent the day at Papa's. When Jennifer left work, she drove to her dad's house. Edna Cooper was already in the kitchen making banana pudding for tomorrow. Kenny opened the door when his mom arrived.

He greeted her, "Hey, Mom. Papa's in the kitchen watching Ms. Cooper work." He laughed.

Jennifer went into the kitchen. She kissed her dad on the cheek. "Hey, Dad. Happy Thanksgiving. I'm sure thankful you are here." She looked at Ms. Cooper. "You look like you are hard at work, Ms. Cooper. What can I do to help?"

Ms. Cooper said, "First of all, you can call me Edna." She rinsed the pot she had washed. "You just spend time with your dad. I'm nearly done."

Jennifer asked, "Edna, what time do you want us to come tomorrow?"

"As early as you like. I figure we can eat around 1 o'clock. I'm going to bring over some country ham and biscuits for our breakfast, so come early. We'll make a day of it."

Jennifer and Kenny stayed a while longer, then went back home.

* * *

The realty office opened a half day on Wednesday. Mr. Templeton said to Stacy that morning, "I realize that you and I don't have relatives in town, and I don't care to go to Nellie's for the day. I had an idea. I have steaks in the freezer. Why don't you come over and we can spend the day together, just the two of us?"

Stacy looked up at him and said, "I would like that. What time?"

"Anytime you like. I'll be there. I planned to grill the steaks, but since it's too chilly outside, I'll just broil them in the oven."

Stacy asked, "What can I bring?"

He answered, "Your beautiful self."

They put the closed sign on the door and left.

Chapter Forty

Thanksgiving morning, Thorne was in the kitchen making the coffee. Carly walked in and said, "I hate to leave the doggie door open all day for Dinkle. I'm so scared she will get hurt again. I won't be able to relax worrying about her."

Thorne asked, "Don't you still have some of those training pads you used when you first got her?"

Carly thought. "Yes, I believe so. That's a great idea. I'll just put them in front of her doggie door. She's a smart girl. She'll understand."

They showered and dressed after having coffee at the kitchen table, talking about their trip. Thorne said, "It's about two and a half hour's drive, so I guess we better get going."

Carly put the training pad on the floor at the doggie door at the kitchen door. She looked at Dinkle, "Here, sweetie. This is for you today. You understand?" Dinkle barked. Carly looked at Thorne. "See, I told you she's a smart girl." Carly picked up Dinkle and gave her a little hug, Thorne rustled her fur. "We'll be back later. You be a good girl."

They drove straight through to Bonnie and Josh's house. When they drove up the driveway, the Australian Shepherd and Dachshund were gaited on the patio part of the porch. They barked in greeting. Josh came out of the house to greet them. "Welcome! Come on in." They went inside and took off their coats. Thorne said, "Something smells mighty good." He shook Josh's hand. "It's very nice of you to have us for Thanksgiving, Josh."

Josh said, "It's too bad we don't live closer so we could visit more often."

Carly hugged Josh. Renee was sitting in her chair making potholders on her loom. She got up and walked over and hugged Carly. She went to Thorne, and he reached out and hugged her too. Carly said, "That was such a good hug, Renee. Show me what you are making." Renee went back to her chair, picked up her loom, and handed it to Carly. "Wow, you do a good job. This is beautiful. Do you make a lot of these?" Renee shook her head yes. "Do you think I could have one sometimes?" Renee reached beside her chair and took one out of a box and handed it to Carly. "For me?" Carly asked.

Renee said, "Yes."

Carly called to Thorne, "Look, Thorne, Renee gave us one of her woven potholders for a present!"

Thorne came to her, took the potholder, turning it over in his hands. He said to Renee. "This is beautiful. Looks like you work a lot. Thank you so much, Renee."

Renee pointed to the television. Carly asked, "TV?"

Josh said, "Yes, Renee watches her shows every day."

Carly said, "I certainly don't mind if she watches her television." Renee smiled and looked at Josh as if to say, OK? Josh gave the remotes to Renee. You could tell that she was happy to have her regular routine.

Josh said, "Bonnie's in the kitchen. Go on in Carly. Don't be offended if she doesn't allow you to help. She kind of likes to do things her way," and smiled. Josh said to Thorne, "We can leave them to it, Thorne. Would you like to see where I do my work?"

"Yes, I sure would." The two men grabbed their jackets and went back outside, walked down the dirt driveway to the trailer that Josh used for his studio. It was a little chilly inside, so they kept their jackets on. Josh switched on the lights.

Thorne looked around, the tables and walls were covered with paintings, sculptures of many types of birds, and many faces. He was amazed. "This is unbelievable," he said. "You really are talented, man."

Josh pointed down the small hallway. "There's more down there, in the bathroom. Let me know if you see something you like."

Thorne smiled and said, "Something I like? How about everything?" It was unbelievable at the creative ability that Josh had. His birds looked right at you. They looked alive. The faces, so many faces, all different, also alive with personalities. As he walked through, he said, "Man, you ought to be a millionaire."

Josh laughed, "Yeah, I always thought so too."

They stayed about an hour, Thorne admiring so many pieces of art, asking various questions. He said, "These faces, are they made out of clay?" He pointed to a Native American face sculpture and asked, "How did you get this one to have this surface color?"

Josh answered, "Before it was fired, I added oxides to it. With firing, it turned out like that. Before we moved here, we did many clay art pieces. It was so much fun, a lot of work and time, though. I would form the face, let it cure, keep it turned, and when it was thoroughly dry, Bonnie would load the kiln. She's better at that kind of thing than I am. Then the kiln would fire for most of the day. Afterward, the kiln had to cool before you opened it. Most of the time, everything turned out, occasionally a piece would crack."

Thorne asked, "Did Bonnie make clay too?"

"Yes, she would make handmade pots, as well as throw pots on the pottery wheel."

Thorne pointed again to the Native American face sculpture. "That is superb."

Josh said, "Thanks."

Thorne asked, "How long did you do clay pieces?"

"We started out making our own clay. Bonnie researched recipes for how to do it. We had five-gallon buckets with different chemicals that we used in the mud we dug from the ground. In the very beginning, we tried firing the clay in a sawdust kiln. Then we invested in an electric kiln. That was much more successful."

They walked back to the front room. Josh asked, "What about you? Your job sounds interesting."

Thorne laughed and said, "Sometimes yes and sometimes no. It can get frustrating when you can't find helpful information or leads. I'm working on a case now that seems to be one of those times."

Josh cleaned a couple of items off the recliner and said to Thorne, "Have a seat. It will be a while before Bonnie has dinner ready." Thorne sat and Josh walked over to the chair behind his worktable. He asked, "What kind of cases do you get mostly?"

Thorne said, "It varies. The most intense are the ones for missing people, especially children. It gets difficult to sleep at night. When the outcome is good, of course, it makes it all worth it."

Josh said, "I would offer you something, but my studio isn't set up for entertaining." He smiled.

Thorne said, "No problem. I'm fine. I'm just looking forward to the dinner."

Josh said, "The case now you say is not going good?"

Thorne thought about where to start. "This guy died, and the cause was undetermined. In his house, they found an expensive wooden box that was locked, and no key was found. Nobody wanted to destroy the box, so the chief of police called me to check it out, the box and the death, as well as to find any relatives of the man. So far, nothing but suspicious findings, nothing helpful. I did find that he has a brother, but no address. Next week, I hope to get a location for him from the DMV."

Josh said, "Sounds interesting." He looked up at the clock on the wall and said, "You want to go see if it's about time to eat?"

"Sure." Thorne answered and got up from the chair.

While the guys were at the studio, Carly sat in the kitchen watching Bonnie busy herself with the last-minute details. Carly said, "Let me at least set the table."

Bonnie said, "Yeah, that would be good. I don't mean to be this way. It's just that I'm used to doing the cooking and when someone helps, I get distracted and mess up something."

Carly said, "No problem. I understand." She wanted to tell Bonnie about her pregnancy but decided to wait until they were all together. Carly said, "Your story is coming along pretty good."

Bonnie asked, "Can you tell me a little about it?"

Carly began. "Like I said, it's all fiction, although it is based on all the things you told me about your life. Anyway, a little summary so far. A young woman moves to town and finds a box in the attic. After reading the journals and notes, she hires a private investigator to try to find out who lived in the house previously. On and on, and you know how the rest goes. I, of course, changed the locations, the names, most everything. I'll let you read it when I get it all finished, and the final edits done. I'd like to know what you think."

Bonnie said, "I would like that. At least I think I would. To tell you the truth, I'd just as soon forget about all of it."

"I can understand." Carly said. "One thing I realized is that you didn't mention your parents in recent years. Are they still living?"

Bonnie took the ham out of the oven to cool before Josh sliced it. She turned to Carly and said, "My mother died a few years ago, four or five years, I'm not sure. It's weird, my feelings. I was numb, really. I felt guilty in one sense for not being sad, and even having no feelings. On the other hand, I understood and allowed myself to feel, however, felt natural." Bonnie pointed to the drawer beside the sink. "The silverware is in that drawer. It's all jumbled up, not organized in a nice divider tray like most folks. It suits me that way."

Carly asked, "And your dad?"

Bonnie said, "That's another thing. You understand, these are just my thoughts and feelings. Like I said, I'm not like the rest of my siblings, or anybody, that I've ever met, for that matter. First, you know Josh is my first cousin. His dad was my dad's older brother. It seems to me that I am more like Josh than I am my own siblings. I wondered for a long time if his dad was my dad too. Josh and I like the same things, we understand each other."

"Of course, we've been together about 35 years, so I guess that's expected. Anyway, back to my dad. I would describe him as a good man, calm, never angry, always joking, hardworking, tolerant. The one thing is that I have no idea what he really thinks or feels about things. I do believe he has pride in things, and he is very thrifty."

"I assume that is because he grew up around the Great Depression. He will spend hours repairing something that would only cost a few dollars new. My kids love him. Melanie, especially. What's sad is now he is getting dementia or Alzheimer's, not sure which. He has been aware that his memory and other things have been changing, but now I'm not sure he realizes it so much. Again, I have mixed feelings. I guess he loves me, but he only told me once. Maybe I'm getting indifferent because I don't want to face the reality of the situation."

Bonnie heard the front door open. Josh and Thorne appeared in the doorway of the kitchen. Josh said, "I'm almost starving to death!" Thorne laughed.

Bonnie said, "It's almost ready, I'm just waiting for the biscuits to get done. Josh, the ham is ready for you to slice. Then we'll be all set." She looked through the oven glass to check the biscuits and said to Thorne, "Did you enjoy the tour of the Louvre?"

Thorne smiled. "Unbelievable. Amazing." He looked at Carly. "You've got to see it. You won't believe it."

Bonnie took the biscuits out of the oven, putting them in a woven cloth-lined basket. She said, "This cloth was woven by Sara. She gave it to me for Christmas a couple of years ago. She also has started quilting. We have a lot of fun talking about different patterns we are working on." Bonnie took the biscuits to the table. Renee came into the room. Bonnie said, "Alright, let's all have a seat. Renee, you sit here, sweetie. We always have ham instead of turkey. I'm not that fond of turkey."

They all took their seats and Bonnie said to everyone. "I don't particularly care for praying out loud, so if everyone could give thanks quietly, in their own way, we can eat." They all bowed their heads for a few moments.

They passed the food around, each taking their serving. Bonnie fixed a plate for Renee. All was quiet for a long while, except for a lot of "ums, yummy, delicious," words spoken as they ate.

After they finished, Carly said, "Thorne and I will do the dishes, Bonnie."

Bonnie quickly said, "No way. These can wait until tomorrow. I'll just put a few things in the refrigerator. We're not about to spend time doing dishes." They went into the living room. Carly looked at Thorne with a questioning look. He gave her an approving nod. Carly cleared her throat rather loudly and said, "Ding, ding, ding. We have an announcement to make." They all looked at her, waiting. She said, "Thorne and I are going to have a baby!"

Bonnie said, "That's wonderful. I'm going to be a great aunt. Do you know when the baby is due? I can make her or him a baby quilt. In fact, I can keep them in quilts as they grow up!"

Carly answered, "I will treasure them, Bonnie, and keep them to give to him or her when they grow up. I should find out my due date on my next visit to the doctor when she does a thorough exam. At my last visit, she did blood work which let me know. I had been a little queasy feeling and more tired than usual. That's why I went to see her. Surprise, surprise!"

Josh walked over to Thorne, shook his hand, "Congratulations, Thorne."

Thorne said, "Thanks. It was what I wished for when I blew out the candles on my birthday cake. So, there is magic in that tradition." They all laughed.

Bonnie said to Carly, "Would you like to see my little house? That's what I call it. It's where I keep all my quilt making fabric and things."

Carly said, "I would love to."

They put on their coats and walked around the house to the cutest little cottage-type building. The sign on the covered porch read, "Bonnie's Lil House." Carly said, "This is darling. It looks like a playhouse." A cedar bench and glider were on the porch. The sign was mounted on a piece of plywood attached to the side of the porch to make the porch more private.

Bonnie said, "It is my playhouse. I love it out here." They went inside. There was hardly enough room for two people. Bonnie told Carly to sit in the chair while she took a seat in the chair at her sewing machine.

Carly asked, "Did Josh build this for you?"

Bonnie smiled and said, "A couple of years ago, I was on the computer and found a picture of a place a lot like this one. I posted it on Facebook and said something about when I win the lottery, I'll have one of these built. My oldest daughter, Melanie, posted a reply that said, 'I know people that can make it happen.' She's the most resourceful person I've ever known."

"Anyway, she and her boyfriend at that time made the plan. They worked many weekends. They also built the covered patio, where the dogs are. I sit out there a lot, especially now that I don't smoke in the house anymore. They would order the supplies to be delivered. They worked on it on weekends for over three months. The building used to have shop lights and they replaced them with these which are perfect and look much prettier too. They put in the windows, my beautiful new door, and even the porch with a tin room, and a little patio."

Pointing to the ceiling, she said, "Melanie had the idea of hanging that dragonfly tapestry-like quilt on the ceiling. I would have never thought of that. It is my heaven, for sure. As you can see, its full of my little special things."

Bonnie pointed to the needle-felted doll collection across the top shelf, the pysanky eggs hanging from one shelf over the window, her children's photos on top of the shelf, and explained about each. Then she pointed to the magnets on the side of one metal shelving unit and said, "These are pictures of artwork that three of my great-grandchildren make in school. They sell them on an online art site. You can get coffee cups and other things with the art on them. Last year, I ordered quilt squares of all they had done and made each of them a quilt with their artwork squares for the top."

Carly said, "I'm sure they will treasure them forever. Bonnie, I'm so glad everything has turned out for you and your children. You deserve all the good things possible."

Bonnie said, "I thank God all the time for my life and everything I have and don't have. Speaking of thankful, your baby is going to have a special quilt. And when they wear it out, I'll make them another one."

Carly said, "That will be a treasure. I'll keep them so they can hand them down to their children. How's Melanie doing these days, and the rest of your children?"

Bonnie began. "Melanie still works for an optometrist. Her kids are doing good, and she has five grandchildren. It's hard to believe. She is seeing a new guy. I've only met him twice, but he is something special, different from guys she has been with in the past. Who knows, we'll see how things turn out."

"He's a family guy. He is also a fixer-upper. The electric line to the well house used to hang low over the driveway, which made it impossible to get deliveries and things. He came one Saturday and dug a trench, buried it, and hooked up a more attractive box for the connection stuff. Super job. Then he trimmed the whole driveway and turned around the area with a weed eater. Josh and I very much enjoyed talking to him."

"Sara is still happily married to her wonderful husband. The three kids are doing good too. Her husband put the roof on our house when we moved in. It's a much better job than any roofing company would have done. If they lived closer, I could worry him to death by asking for favors all the time, but they live about an hour away, so I try to hold off for emergency help. We haven't been able to find anyone around here that is dependable to do anything."

"Sara used to spend time with me. She would spend the night and we would work in here, each on our own quilts. Sara is now a traveling registered nurse. She is the best nurse you have ever seen. She genuinely cares about people and her personality is perfect for the profession. Like I told you, I couldn't be prouder of my children. Despite their start in life, they are beautiful, wonderful human beings."

"Jeremy and his wife and their four children live in Colorado. He has a very good job, lots of security involved, so he doesn't tell me much about it. Their kids are home-schooled and are growing up so fast. He talks to me on that app, Marco Polo, quite often and I get to see them that way. They visited us once since we lived here, but since then, not the whole family. Jeremy has been twice."

"I'm not sure why they don't come more often, but I believe it's because I smoke, and my house is not as clean and organized as it should be. I used to worry about it, but I'm me, and they are them. Everybody must live with their decisions. You can't really change anyone. I just accept that. But like I said when telling you my story, my candle is always lighted full of love for all of them. I just want them healthy and contented."

Carly looked at her watch. "Oh my, it's later than I thought. We need to be getting home." They walked back to the house. In the living room, Carly said to Thorne, "Are you ready to head for home?"

Thorne said, "If you are," and looked at his watch. "Where has this day gone? Time has flown by." He turned to Josh. "Listen, man, thanks for the art tour, and good luck on your sales."

Bonnie broke in and said, "I fixed ya'll a plate to take home. Let me get it. We'll never eat all this food."

Josh said, "On your way out, stop by the studio for a minute. I've got something to show you."

Thorne said, "Just for a minute. We really need to be getting home."

Bonnie hugged Carly and Thorne. She said, "Call me and let me know you got home, OK?"

Carly thanked her for the food.

Josh walked to his studio. When Thorne pulled into the little driveway, Josh came out with a plastic bag, padded and heavy. He said to Thorne, "A little something I want you to have."

Thorne said, "I can't take your art."

Josh said, "You're not taking it, I'm giving it to you. Bonnie gave you a quilt for your wedding. Call this my wedding gift."

He looked at Carly and said, "Maybe next time, you can look at my art. I know ya'll need to get going. We enjoyed having you. Have a safe trip."

Thorne and Carly said at the same time, "Thank you very much, Josh."

* * *

On the way home, Carly and Thorne talked about their day. "Renee is a special girl. She gives sweet, sincere hugs."

Thorne says, "Yes, she is pretty special. Seems she is dedicated to making her potholders."

Carly said, "Yes, and they are beautiful. She is dedicated to watching her television shows too. She looked a lot happier when Josh gave her the remote controls." After a few minutes, Carly said, "you know when I was talking to

Bonnie today, she told me about her parents, and I got to thinking. I don't think you have ever told me about your parents, or if you had any brothers or sisters."

Thorne said, "Not much to tell, really. I think I remember that my mom had miscarried once. I'm not sure if that was before me or after me. They were good parents. My dad was a life insurance salesman and my mom stayed at home. We weren't rich, just average, I would say. I believe they were older when they had me. Both died several years ago, about six months apart. My mom first, then my dad, both from natural causes."

Carly asked, "Did you feel loved by them?"

Thorne thought. "I never really thought of it that way. I believe they cared about me, my safety, and well-being. I do remember my mom giving me hugs sometimes."

Carly asked, "Did they ever argue?"

"Not that I can recall," Thorne answered. "Why do you ask? You're not planning to write a book about me, I hope."

"You never know. But, no reason, I was simply curious." They were quiet most of the rest of the way home.

When they entered the front door, Dinkle met them, barked, and ran to the kitchen. Carly hurriedly followed and saw that she was standing beside the doggie door. "Poor baby," she said. "You've held yourself all day. Here you go." She opened the door and Dinkle ran outside. Carly went back to the living room. They removed their jackets. Carly said, "Poor baby, she held herself all day. I'm glad we weren't any later."

Thorne took the bag with Josh's gift into the living room and opened it. "Ah, that man, he must have seen that this is my favorite." He looked at Carly and held up the Native American clay face sculpture. "Can you believe that guy?"

Carly walked over, took the face sculpture, and said, "That is absolutely perfect. Where should we hang it?" They both looked around and thought. Carly said, "How about over the lamp at the end of the sofa? We can see it every time the light is on."

Thorne said, "I agree. Let me get the hammer and a nail." He returned and hung the face on the wall, stood back, and admired it. In a few minutes, Dinkle came back through the doggie door and into the living room. She looked at what they were staring at and barked twice. Thorne said, "Dinkle likes it too."

They smiled, Carly put Dinkle in her kennel, and they retired earlier than usual because they were both tired from their long day.

Carly said, "I'm so glad that I wasn't nauseated today. Goodnight."

Native American Clay Sculpture by Don Reardon

Chapter Forty-One

After Thanksgiving, the diner was closed until Monday, Nellie spent the day cleaning, dusting vacuuming, checking the food in the refrigerator and freezer. She felt happy that so many people had come for her Thanksgiving dinner. She thought back over the day with fond memories. She had been surprised to learn that Doc Skinner was going to retire and had hired a new vet to take his place. She thought about her own age and how much she enjoyed her job. She hoped she could keep working and not retire. *What would I do with myself,* she thought?

She was about ready to close the diner when the phone rang. "Green Hornet," she answered.

"Hey, Nellie."

Nellie sat on a stool. "Hey, Carly. How was your Thanksgiving?"

"It was very enjoyable. Big thing is, I wasn't nauseated, thank goodness."

Nellie said, "I'm glad it went well."

Carly asked, "How about yours?"

Nellie said, "It was special. So many people came, even a few new people I hadn't seen before. I guess word gets around. I still have plenty of leftovers if you want some."

Carly said, "Bonnie gave us two huge plates of leftovers which will last us all weekend."

Nellie said, "I've been cleaning all day and feel beat, so I'm going to rest until Monday since we're always closed for the holiday weekend." She paused and said, "Oh yes, I almost forgot. Yesterday, I found out that Doc Skinner is retiring and has already hired his replacement."

Carly said, "What? I just took for granted that he would always be our vet. Oh my, we need to plan a retirement party for him. What do you think?"

Nellie said, "Why, I never even thought about it, but I agree. We can have it here at the diner. I understand next week is his last week. So next weekend? I can put up a sign about it so the people who come here will know."

Carly said, "Good idea. I'll ask Mr. Bennett about putting an announcement in the paper next week. Doc Skinner has been here forever and I'm sure even the people without pets would want to know about it."

Nellie said, "We'll talk about it more, work out the details. I'm gonna call it a day. Ya'll have a nice weekend." They hung up.

Chapter Forty-Two

On Sunday afternoon, Carly and Thorne were relaxing in the living room, Dinkle on the sofa with Carly. Carly broke the silence. "I've been thinking, Thorne. I really would like to finish Bonnie's story before the baby comes. I was thinking about quitting the newspaper. Besides, when the baby comes, I want to be able to give our baby my full attention. What do you think?"

Thorne looked up from the book he was reading. "I think that is a great idea, as long as you will be happy. That's all I care about. I do agree that the baby should come first." He smiled and added, "after me, of course." Dinkle barked. Thorne said, "Oh yes, and don't forget Dinkle."

Carly changed the subject. "I'm going to meet with Nellie on Monday. We're going to plan a retirement party for Doc Skinner. She found out on Thanksgiving that this coming week is his last week before the new vet starts."

Thorne said, "He's been the vet around here for a very long time, I understand."

"Yes, for as long as I can remember. The last time I took Dinkle to him, I noticed that he looked tired and a little older than usual. I asked Ms. Maggie had she heard anything about him being sick or anything. She said she had not. So, I think it's a good thing. Nellie told me that a new vet was moving here this week and start working next week. I guess Doc Skinner will spend a few days with him until he's comfortable with everything." She got up and walked toward the kitchen. "I'm going to make some tea. Would you like some?"

Thorne answered, "No, I'm fine." He went back to reading his book.

Chapter Forty-Three

Monday, after Thorne left for his office and Carly had let Dinkle outside and back in, she dressed and went to see Nellie. Nellie was glad to see her, as always.

Nellie asked, "You want some coffee?"

Carly said, "No thanks. I thought, if you're not busy, we could talk about Doc Skinner's retirement party."

Nellie walked over to join Carly at the table. "I've been thinking about the menu. I know Doc Skinner loves the chicken salad and chocolate pie. So, I thought I could make that for sure. Maybe some French fries. Do you have any ideas?"

Carly thought. "Maybe some fruit and a mixed green salad?"

They discussed it a little more. Carly said, "I'm headed to the newspaper to talk to Mr. Bennett about putting an announcement in the paper. What time do you think is good to start?"

"I'd say around 12:30 or so."

Carly got up to leave. "OK. I'll tell Mr. Bennett. I'm sure he will do it for Doc Skinner."

She left the diner and went to the newspaper office. On the way, she contemplated whether to tell Mr. Bennett about not working there anymore. It made her nervous but knew it was something she really wanted to do. The baby comes first. And Thorne and Dinkle, she added to herself and smiled.

Mr. Bennett was in the front office when Carly arrived. "Hello, Carly. Come right in." She followed him to his office. She sat in the chair across from his desk. He began, "I'm glad you stopped by. I needed to tell you that Harry is planning to come back to work next week. His parents are in a senior care facility and his older brother is taking care of the particulars, so he's free to come back."

Carly felt a sense of relief and said, "That's good. In fact, I wanted to talk to you about my job. That's why I came. I'm currently working on a novel which I would very much like to spend more time on it so I can finish sooner than later. We haven't spread the word yet, but Thorne and I are going to have a baby. I want to be able to give my baby my full attention. I hope you understand."

Mr. Bennett said, "Of course, what wonderful news. Congratulations to both of you. Since Harry is coming back, I don't see a problem. You do know that you will be missed around here, and I know the town's people will miss your articles. I've had several good comments from folks about how much they enjoy them."

"That's nice to know. I appreciate your understanding. The other reason I stopped by is because Nellie at the Green Hornet found out during her Thanksgiving dinner that Doc Skinner is going to retire and that a new vet will be starting next week, I believe. We want to have him a retirement dinner at the Green Hornet, and I was wondering if you would put an announcement in the newspaper this week."

Mr. Bennett said, "Ole Doc Skinner. My how time flies. Of course, I'll be glad to. What time will the get-together take place?"

Carly said, "12:30 on Saturday. Everyone is invited. I really appreciate it."

"You're welcome, Carly. Again, congratulations to you and Thorne. I guess this will be your last week writing an article for us. So, I don't want you to be a stranger. You drop by anytime, just to say hello, OK?"

"I certainly will, Mr. Bennett. I thank you for all the experience you have given me. I'll talk to you soon." She left the office. She felt tired and decided to go back home and take a nap. *Dinkle will like that*, she thought. When she drove past the diner, she saw that Nellie had already put a sign in the window about Doc Skinner's party. She thought, *Ain't nothing slow about that woman.*

* * *

Carly was still resting on the sofa when Thorne came home from work early. He put his jacket and shoulder holster in the closet and called, "Hello, my everything." Dinkle ran to greet him. Carly sat up on the sofa. Thorne joined her.

She said, "Hey, Thorne, you're home early. Is there a problem?"

"No, just a slow day. I didn't get the information from the DMV I wanted. Hopefully tomorrow."

Carly said, "I went by the diner. Nellie and I made the plans for Doc Skinner's party. It's going to be Saturday at 12:30. I went to see Mr. Bennett about putting an announcement in the paper and he agreed to do that, of course. The good news is, he told me that Harry is returning next week. His parents are in a senior care facility and his older brother is taking care of the paperwork and other things. Anyway, I felt relieved. The timing is perfect. So, I told him about the baby. He said to tell you congratulations. He understood about my wanting to finish the book and spend full time with the baby. It worked out perfectly."

Thorne said, "I'm glad. Sounds like perfect timing all the way around."

Carly said, "I haven't thought about anything for supper. We still have a few leftovers from Bonnie's or I can fix something."

Thorne said, "I had a late lunch. I'm fine for now. On the way home, I saw a U-Haul at Donna's house. So, I guess we have new neighbors."

Carly said, "I'll give them a little time to settle in and go welcome them to our huge neighborhood."

Thorne smiled and put his arm around Carly. Dinkle loved it when they sat quietly on the sofa. *A real happy family, I'm sure*, Dinkle thought.

Chapter Forty-Four

When Jennifer awoke Monday morning, she knew it was too early to call her dad. She slowly got out of bed, dreading the ordeal with Kenny about going to school. She put on her housecoat, walked down the hall to his room. To her surprise, he was already awake and dressed. She said, "Good morning!"

"Hey, Mom," Kenny said.

Jennifer yawned. She said, "What a nice surprise. I think we're going to have a good day. What do you want for breakfast?"

Kenny said, "I'll just have some cereal." He finished his cereal, picked up his backpack, and headed out the door. "Bye Mom."

Jennifer sat at the table, drinking her coffee. She thought, *My dad must have worked a miracle. Hope it doesn't change.*

When Kenny got off the bus and walked to the school entrance, he saw Bucky Winthrop. He felt a tinge of dread. Bucky walked up to him and said, "Kenny, look, I'm sorry for what I said to you last week. I didn't really mean it."

Kenny, at first, didn't know how to respond. Then he said, "No problem. I'm sorry I got so mad. I don't know what got into me."

Bucky said, "I heard your grandfather went to the hospital. Is he OK?"

Kenny said, "Yeah, for now. It was very scary. We had gone fishing, cooked the fish outside on a fire. He was sitting at the table while I was washing dishes and when I turned around, he was slumped in his chair."

"Oh man, how awful!" replied Bucky.

"Anyway, he's home and doing better."

They walked into school. The assistant principal, Ms. Kennedy, was standing near the entrance with her hands on her hips like a drill sergeant.

* * *

After work, Jennifer drove to pick up Kenny from school. When Kenny saw her, he jogged over and got in the car. "Hey, Mom, you'll never guess. You know the guy I hit because of what he said? This morning before school, he came up to me and apologized. He seemed to mean it too."

Jennifer asked, "Is that who you were talking to?"

"Yep. I think we might end up being buddies. We'll see."

* * *

They arrived at Papa's house. Edna Cooper opened the door. "Come in. All is good here. Did ya'll have a good day?" She looked at Kenny and said, "Kenny, you can put your bookbag over there," and pointed to the floor next to the sofa.

Kenny heard a noise in the kitchen and went to see Papa. Jennifer asked Edna, "How is he?"

Edna answered, "He's doing fine. Eating better than ever. His spirits are good. Come on in the kitchen. I have supper ready."

"You didn't have to do that, Edna."

Edna said, "No problem."

Kenny was already sitting at the table with her dad. "Hey, Dad. You're looking much better." She leaned to kiss his cheek.

Her dad answered, "I'm fit as a fiddle, thanks to Kenny's fast response in getting help."

Kenny said, "You sure scared us, Papa. Everything's going to be fine now, I just know it."

After supper, Edna and Jennifer cleaned the kitchen while Papa and Kenny played a game of checkers at the kitchen table. Papa won, as always.

They all said their goodbyes and Jennifer drove home. She felt more optimistic than ever about the future.

Chapter Forty-Five

When Thorne got home from work on Tuesday, Carly and Dinkle greeted him. After hanging his jacket and shoulder holster in the closet, he leaned his head back to look at Carly and said, "You are getting more beautiful every day, Mrs. Davenport."

Carly said, "Thanks. I'll make you an appointment to have your vision checked." They smiled.

Carly said, as they walked to the living room, "I'm having tea. Would you like a cup?"

"No thanks, I'm fine."

Dinkle sat on the sofa, closer to Carly than usual. Carly said, "You know, I believe Dinkle somehow knows I'm having a baby, his new baby boss. He has sat closer to me all day."

Thorne said, "Dogs are smart like that, especially the vicious guard dog." He looked at Dinkle. "Isn't that right, girl? You are smarter than the average bear." They smiled. Thorne said, "Today, I finally got the report from the DMV about Joshua Gruber. Seems he owns an older model Ford pickup and I have his address in Charlotte. I plan to drive there on Thursday and hopefully get enough information to figure out this case or at least make some headway."

"I hope you do," said Carly and she took a sip of tea. "Nellie called me today. She said that many of her customers plan to come to Doc Skinner's retirement party. I'm glad and not surprised. Everybody in town loves Doc Skinner."

"Is it going to be a surprise, or does he know about it?"

"Considering everyone who knows by now, I'm quite sure he knows too. No matter, I think he will still feel special."

Thorne said, "I didn't see the U-Haul, so I guess our neighbors have moved in. Do you want to go welcome them tomorrow?"

"That will be good. Maybe in the afternoon when it's a little warmer."

Thorne said, "Sounds like a plan."

Chapter Forty-Six

Mike and Shelly Lawson, and their daughter, Jill, were getting things sorted in the house. Shelly said, "I'm glad this house was furnished. It made moving so much easier."

Mike said, "I thought it would. It would have taken a lot longer if we had to buy all the furnishings." He put Jill in her playpen and turned to Shelly. "I was thinking maybe we could go into town and let you meet the realtor, Mr. Templeton. Also, the little diner I was telling you about is on the way, so maybe we could stop there for lunch. Seems it's the place to go around here. I understand the lady who owns it is nice. She was busy the day Mr. Templeton and I stopped it. Maybe today, we can get a chance to talk to her."

"I would like that," Shelly said.

They drove to the real estate office, met Stacy and Mr. Templeton. Mike said, "We're going to drop by the diner, the Green Hornet Grill, for lunch. Maybe we'll get a chance to meet Nellie."

Mr. Templeton said, "I'm sure she would love meeting you and I know she'll talk to you unless she is swamped with customers." He looked at Jill in the stroller and said, "You are a pretty little girl. I like your teddy bear." He turned back to the Lawsons. "I'm glad you stopped in. I hope your new house will be a home for you."

They said their goodbyes.

* * *

Mr. Templeton came out of his office and Stacy said, "Another boring day."

He smiled. "I know what we could do to make it a lot less boring."

Stacy smiled, then asked, "Are you going to Doc Skinner's retirement party at the diner on Saturday?"

"Oh yes. I really don't want to, but one has to keep up appearances. What about you?"

"No, I try to just keep to myself, mainly. This town is full of nosy gossips. Speaking of gossips, I need to go by the drugstore later."

* * *

Mike drove to the diner and carried Jill inside, Shelly followed. Mike said, "I assume they have a highchair for Jill."

When they entered the diner, Nellie greeted them immediately. "Hello, and welcome to the Green Hornet." She showed them to a table at the window. "Let me get a highchair for the little one." When she returned and Shelly placed Jill in her highchair, Nellie looked at Mike and said, "I believe you were in here a couple of weeks ago with Mr. Templeton. Am I right?"

Mike spoke up, motioning toward Shelly and Jill, "Yes, you're correct. This is my wife Shelly, and our daughter, Jill."

Nellie said, "I'm so glad to meet you and I appreciate your coming in for lunch." She handed them a menu and asked, "Do you live in town?"

Shelly said, "In Flat Branch. Mike is starting next week as the new veterinarian."

Nellie said, "I heard about that. You'll find that word spreads fast around here." She looked at Mike, "So you're our new vet? Doc Skinner has been the vet around here for many years. We're going to have a retirement party here at the diner for him this Saturday at 12:30. I hope ya'll can come so everybody can meet you."

Mike said, "That sounds nice. Yes, we'll be here. Wouldn't miss it. I need to meet Doc's patients or rather owners of his patients."

Nellie said, "I'll be right back to take your order."

After finishing their lunch, they wave bye to Nellie who was busy with other customers.

* * *

When Mike drove to their house, they saw their neighbors walking down the road. Mike pulled in the driveway. He got Jill out of her car seat. They walked to greet Thorne and Carly.

135

Mike said, "Hello, you must be Carly and Thorne. We're the Lawsons; I'm Mike. This is my wife, Shelly, and our daughter, Jill."

Thorne reached out to shake Mike's hand. "We just wanted to stop by and welcome you to the metropolitan city of Flat Branch." They laughed.

Mike smiled and said, "That's exactly why we moved here, all the activity."

Shelly said, "Mike is going to be the new vet doctor in Lillington. He starts next Monday."

Carly said, "Doc Skinner has looked after Dinkle, my Yorkie Mix."

Thorne interrupted, "Spoiled rotten, vicious guard dog, is what she is." He smiled.

Carly said, "She's not. She's just a little jealous. Do you know about Doc Skinner's retirement party this Saturday? It's going to be at the Green Hornet Grill at 12:30."

Shelly said, "Yes. We stopped there for lunch and Nellie told us. We will definitely be there."

"How old is your daughter?"

Shelly said, "She's two and a half. I recently found out that I'm pregnant again."

Carly said, "That's wonderful. I just found out a couple of weeks ago that I'm pregnant, my first. Thorne and I just got married in September."

Mike said, "Congratulations on both! Listen, we don't have to stand out here and talk, it's chilly. You want to come inside?"

Thorne said, "No, we don't want to bother you, just wanted to say hey and that we are your one and only neighbor. Also, to say that in case you need us, please feel free to call or come by."

They said their goodbyes and walked to their perspective homes.

* * *

When they went inside, Shelly said, "We forgot to ask them where they work."

Mike said, "Thorne's a private investigator, and Carly's works at the newspaper."

Shelly responded, "His job sounds interesting." She put Jill in her playpen and said, "I liked them, didn't you?"

Mike said, "I think they'll be good neighbors. Since we plan to live here a long time, let's hope we become friends."

Shelly said, "Carly and I will have babies around the same time, so that should give us something in common." She walked over and kissed Mike on the cheek, "You did good my sweet husband."

* * *

When they got home, Carly asked Thorne, "Well, what did you think?"

Thorne asked, "What do you mean, what do I think? We just met and talked for five minutes. I can't form an opinion on that."

Carly laughed, "Some detective you are. I like them. It's neat that Shelly is pregnant too. Jill is so cute, her curly brown hair and brown eyes. She's a little dream doll."

Thorne said, "We'll see how it goes. They seem like regular folks to me."

They had a nice uneventful evening. Carly fed Filet Mignon to Dinkle. She and Thorne had soup and a grilled cheese sandwich. Thorne read his book for a while. Carly rested on the sofa. Later, she put Dinkle in her kennel.

* * *

When Kenny got home from school, without being asked, he began telling his mom about his day. He said, "Me and Bucky—"

His mom interrupted, "Bucky and I."

He continued, "Bucky and I ate lunch together in the cafeteria. I found out that he lives only two blocks from us." She could hear the excitement in his voice. "Do you think he could come over sometime?"

"Of course, as long as I'm here. That would be nice."

Kenny said, "I was thinking maybe we could plan some things together. Maybe camp out in the backyard or visit Papa and even go fishing."

"I'm happy for you that you have found a friend. Those ideas sound like fun. Just talk to me about any plans before doing them, OK? You know Papa still needs to get better, so you might not mention fishing this soon."

"OK, Mom." Kenny went to the phone and called Bucky.

Jennifer sat in the living room, reading her novel, and was quite happy with the new attitude in Kenny. She owed it all to her dad.

Chapter Forty-Seven

Thursday morning, Thorne left after breakfast to interview Joshua Gruber. He was going over the facts that he knew in preparation. Late morning, he found the street and then the house. It was a normal-looking neighborhood, well-kept brick homes, neat lawns, few cars, as he assumed people were at work. He saw Joshua's address, the same type of brick home, a weedy front lawn, and a beat-up old Ford pickup in the driveway. *Good*, he thought, *looks like he's home.* He parked, got out and walk to the porch, and knocked on the door.

He paused when the man opened the door. He wore a dingy-white t-shirt with the sleeves cut out, tattoos on his arms, blue-jeans, barefoot, and greasy shoulder-length dark hair. He held a beer can in one hand. He said, "Yeah?"

Thorne replied, "Are you Joshua Gruber?"

"Whose asking?"

"Mr. Gruber?" Thorne asked.

Joshua interrupted, "That was my old man. Call me Joshua."

Thorne said, "Joshua, I'm Thorne Davenport. I'm here to talk to you about your brother, Eli."

Joshua laughed, took a swig of beer, and said, "That scoundrel? What has Mr. Goody-two-shoes done?" He took a long drink of his beer and crushed the can with his hand.

Thorne asked, "May I come in?"

"Sure man, come on in." Thorne followed him inside. The walls needed painting. The living room was furnished with a cheap-looking sofa and two chairs, a coffee table, and two end tables with big based blue lamps on them, ashtrays on every table full of cigarette butts. There was a well-worn piece of carpet on the floor.

Joshua said, "Sit."

Thorne began to doubt that this interview would produce helpful information. A female appeared in the doorway. She had short chopped-off blond hair that stuck out like a porcupine, a too-low-cut extremely tight sleeveless top, and jeans that appeared glued onto her legs and hips. Joshua looked up and said, "Don't just stand there gawking, get the man a beer and me too."

Thorne said, "No, I'm fine."

Joshua looked at Thorne. "Now, what's this you wanna know about my illustrious brother?"

Thorne got out his notepad. "Sounds like you two didn't like each other very much."

Joshua took the beer from the woman, popped the top, and took a swig. No, thank you, no introduction, just a quick slap on the buttocks as she walked away. Joshua began, "Well, let's see. First, he never amounted too much. He did good in school, never got in trouble. Me, I skipped as much as I could. Won't nothing I wanted to learn. I wanted to live, just live, you know, experience life."

Thorne said, "What about your parents?"

Joshua took a swig of beer and propped the can on his knee. "My old man. I don't know what to say exactly. He was a big man, not mean, but a little scary sometimes, especially after Momma left. Everything was going fine until she ran off with some dude she met at the dancehall. That upset my old man a lot. Something about him changed. I can't explain it, but all I know is, he changed. He lost his job at the factory, started drinking more. Sometimes he would stay gone a day or so and leave me and Eli to do everything on our own."

"Of course, perfect Eli was fine with that. Him being two years older than me, he acted like my boss. I wasn't going to stand for that, you see. I know I frustrated him, but we made out, I guess you could say. Ate a lot of pizzas. The old man would leave cash on the table when he left, so we bought pizza. That's how we knew he would be gone a while."

Thorne asked, "Did your dad have many friends?"

Joshua took another swig of beer and laughed. "Friends? Heck no. He had 'business acquaintances' or that's what he called 'em."

The female appeared at the doorway again and looked at Thorne. She said, "I'm Natalie, you can call me Nat."

Thorne acknowledged her and said, "Nice to meet you, Nat. I'm Thorne Davenport."

Joshua said to her, "Would you mind? We're having a serious conversation here." She winked at Thorne, turned, and left the room.

Thorne asked, "Is that your wife?"

"Heck no, ain't about to get married again."

"So, you were married before?"

Joshua explained, "Yeah, for what it was worth. I fell in love, or just horny; anyway, she had inherited her parents' house. They were killed by a burglar, the story was. I moved in with her until I couldn't stand her nagging anymore. Then I met Nat. She don't nag, no sir, no nagging. She loves me, let me move in here with her." Thorne thought, *That's why no property in his name.*

Thorne said, "Back to your dad. You say he had some business associates?"

"Yeah. Two mean-ass guys, big, not real talkative. The old man would shew us out of the room when they were around."

Thorne asked, "Did you ever hear anything they were talking about?"

Another swig, canned crushed, Joshua hollered, "Hey hon, bring me another beer!" He took it when she brought it to him, popped the top, took a swig, and continued. "I heard a couple of things. They got a little loud, so it wasn't hard to hear what they were saying. Something about the jewels, the money for the jewels. I didn't really know what that was about until much later."

Thorne thought about the jewelry store robbery mentioned in the newspaper article that he had found in the expensive locked box. He asked, "Do you think they had robbed a jewelry store?"

Nat brought him another beer. Joshua popped the top. "They looked like the type, but no, I found out later more about it. I was married and lived with my wife. One night I go over to see the old man and when I got inside, he was sprawled out on the kitchen floor. I called 911 and at the hospital, I found out that he had been shot."

Thorne asked, "Do you think it was one of his business associates who shot him?"

"Yeah, man, of course. Who else?"

"Do you remember anything about these men, anything at all?"

"All I know is they was mean, big, and scary-looking. One of 'em had a gruff voice. They drove a black town car if I remember right."

Thorne jotted in his notepad. Joshua chugged the rest of his beer and said, "That's when I found out that I was my old man's favorite, not Eli. I felt real proud. I went to see him in the hospital because they told he was dying. He told me things. Mainly about the jewels. Seems he had sold them and had the money, at least what was left after his gambling. He had hidden it and wanted me to have it so, he told me where to find it. I got pure excited. He died a little bit later."

Thorne felt like he was pulling eye teeth to get this guy to continue. He asked, "Did you find the money?"

"Heck yeah, I found it, it was a lot, didn't really count it exactly, just knew it was many thousands of dollars."

Thorne asked, "Do you still have the money?"

Joshua almost choked on his beer. "What do you think? After all this time. I mean, really, those casinos are rip-offs, you know. They are rigged. They let you win a while, then they snatch it all from you. Thieves, that's what they are. Legalized thieves."

Thorne asked, "Where was Eli during this time?"

"I didn't keep up with him. I just lived my life, you see. When I found the money, like a bad penny, Eli shows up one day. I sure didn't tell him nothing. Come to find out, he got the old man's house. When my mamma was there, she had made the old man sign a will, you know that leaves their stuff to somebody. They had left the house to Eli, not me. I guess they figured I wouldn't want it. Eli came to see me, and I told him that the old man had been shot and that he might not wanna live in that house."

"He got upset because he was nowhere to be found when all this with the old man came down. It's all a mess to tell you the truth. Eli said that he was going to move away, far away, he said. I got some of the old man's money and went and bought Eli a brand-new Lincoln Continental. I mean, why not, it would help him get out of town. I told the man to deliver it to Eli at the old man's house. You know, I never heard from him again, the scoundrel, just take and take and take. No appreciation, no thanks. So be it."

He gulped the rest of his beer, crushed the can, and put it on the coffee table. He yelled to Nat to bring him another one. He looked at Thorne and said, "You sure I can't get you a beer, man?" Nat returned with the beer and left the room.

Thorne declined and continued. "Let me see if I understand all of this. Your parents were OK until your mom left with another man. Then, your dad changed, started drinking more, staying gone for days, you got married and moved into your wife's house that she inherited, lost touch with Eli, your dad was shot, told you about his money before he died, you left your wife and moved in here with Nat, Eli inherited your dad's house, you bought Eli a car, and he left town. Is that right?"

"Man, you summed it up and I mean quick too. Yep, that all sounds like what I told you."

Thorne asked, "Did they ever find out who shot your dad?"

"Nah, nobody cared really, don't seem like it to me know how. I never heard any more about it. Never heard from Eli either. Just a messed-up family, I reckon."

Nat appeared in the doorway and whined, "Josh, honey, I'm hungry. You hungry?"

Joshua said, "How many times have you told you not to call me that. My damn name is Joshua. And, no, I'm not hungry. Find something yourself and bring me another beer while you're at it." He looked back at Thorne and said, "Women!"

Thorne didn't acknowledge the comment or the conversation. He said, "I have to tell you, Joshua, that your brother Eli died a few weeks ago. I apologize for the delay in letting you know but there was no next of kin found."

Joshua jumped off the sofa. "What? You telling me that Eli's dead? How? What happened?" He sat back down. "Damn."

Thorne waited a moment and added, "There is a question about the cause of death. There were no signs of a struggle or injury, but there was a question of suffocation. They just can't be sure."

"Not surprised. Nobody gives a damn. We ain't high society or important to nobody." He was quiet, leaned back on the sofa and said more to himself, "I never thought nothing like this would happen to Eli. Me, maybe, but not him. Damn."

Thorne decided the interview was about finished. He stood and said, "Joshua, I'm sorry about your brother. I'm also sorry that I couldn't find you sooner. I appreciate your help. I'll do all I can to figure out who did this, but I have to say, right now, it's not looking promising."

Joshua got up. "Hey, man, at least you're doing something. Find out or don't, it won't change nothing." Thorne left the house and got in his car.

He looked at his watch. It would be after supper by the time he arrived home. He called Carly. "Hey, my wife."

"Hey, my husband. Where are you?"

"I just left Joshua Gruber's house. What a story. I'll tell you about it when I get home. I'll just grab something at a drive-thru and see you around 6:30."

"Be safe. I'll see you then." They hung up.

Chapter Forty-Eight

When Thorne got home, Carly and Dinkle were on the sofa. She had fallen asleep. He took off his coat and shoulder holster and hung them in the hall closet. Dinkle looked up and thought, *Oh, it's you, we're sleeping, don't disturb us.*

So Thorne went to the kitchen for a glass of water. Carly woke up when she heard the water running. Dinkel jumped off the sofa, ran to the kitchen door, and said, we're up, you can come in now. Thorne thought, *I must be losing it, I'm hearing the dog's words.* He called out, "It's me," and walked into the living room. "Sorry, I didn't want to wake you. Dinkle told me to get out and not disturb you." He smiled.

It took Carly a few seconds to understand what he was talking about. She pushed her hair back and sat up. "I don't know what I'm going to do with you two." She stood and walked over the Thorne. "I'm glad you're home. I didn't mean to fall asleep. It happens easily these days."

Thorne said, "Your body is using all its energy to make a little one." They kissed.

Thorne said, "I'm beat. I'm going to take a shower. Maybe a glass of wine afterward and I can give you the highlights of my meeting with Joshua Gruber."

Carly kissed him again. "I'll get your wine. Hurry, I can't wait to hear about it." She went to the bedroom and put on her gown and housecoat and bedroom slippers. While waiting for Thorne, she fixed herself a cup of tea, poured his glass of wine.

He came back in, sat on the sofa, and took his glass of wine. "Thanks," and took a sip. "Where do I begin? A real pair, I have to say. I think a good word might be low life. He looks like a greasy, unclean guy who treats his girlfriend, Natalie, Nat for short, like a slave or something. She could pass for a street hooker. She stayed gone, except to bring him umpteen beers. He drinks like a fish. He never appeared intoxicated, however."

"I found out enough to know that I believe his old man, as he called him, was the one who robbed the jewelry store. It sounds like a couple of rough guys, serious business acquaintances, as Joshua called them, may have been the ones who shot and killed him. Before the old man died, he told Joshua where the money was. So many details, really. Bottom line, Joshua squandered away the cash, gambling, and who knows what else. Joshua had married and he didn't keep up with his brother, Eli."

"After the dad died, Eli came to see Joshua and Joshua told him about the old man getting killed. Eli had inherited the old man's house. Joshua didn't tell him about the money but advised him to move out of the house because of the killing. Eli agreed to do that, so Joshua bought him a new Lincoln Continental, paid cash. He had the dealer deliver the car to Eli. Go figure. Eli left town and he hadn't heard from him since."

Carly exclaimed, "Wow, that is quite some story! Remind me to make notes to include in one of my future novels." She finished her tea. "Have you reached any conclusion?"

Thorne said, "I thought about it all the way home. I believe that with Eli getting the new car delivered to him, there is no sign of Joshua being involved. The bad guys saw this and assumed that Eli was the one with the lute from the robbery. They traced him to Lillington and when he didn't know what they were talking about when they wanted to know where the money was, they killed him, quietly, by smothering him."

Carly said, "Oh my, mistaken identity. How awful. So, I guess Eli wasn't married."

"Not much is known about him. I'm going to fill the chief in what I've learned and see if he agrees with my conclusion. I think the case is unsolvable. I don't believe those guys will ever be found. No evidence, no clues, no witnesses, nothing. I don't see anything further I can do."

Carly said, "I agree. It sounds that way to me too." She got up to put Dinkle in her kennel. To Thorne, she said, "Are you coming? I'm ready to call it a night."

Thorne said, "Me too. This has been a rough day." They both slept soundly all night.

Chapter Forty-Nine

Thorne left home Friday morning to return the expensive box and its contents to Chief Logan and to give him his conclusion of Eli Gruber's case. When he walked into the office, Deputy Goss wasn't at his desk, so he waited a minute. The chief came down the hall and saw Thorne. "Hello, Thorne. Deputy Goss will be in later. He had family business to take care of first thing. How's it going?"

"Hey, Chief. I hope it wasn't anything really serious."

The chief said, "No, no, just a minor thing."

Thorne held out the box. "I'm returning the box and, if you have time, I can give you the details of my investigation."

The chief said, "I ain't got nothing but time. Come on in my office." Thorne followed him and sat in the wooden straight-back chair across from his desk. The chief said, "Tell me all about it." He took the box from Thorne and placed it on his desk.

Thorne began. "I had a locksmith open the box. The contents are still inside." The chief opened the box and took out the few items. Thorne continued, "I began with the newspaper article about the jewelry store robbery in Charlotte. I looked through the microfiche at the Charlotte library, found it, but no follow-up. I searched for the name Eli Gruber, and the only thing that came up was an obituary for his father. That's when I found out that he has a brother. There was no property listing in the brother's name, Joshua Gruber. I contacted DMV and after getting the report, drove to the address in Charlotte to find out what I could from him."

Chief cleared his throat. "Good work, good work. Was he helpful?"

Thorne continued. "Joshua recounted a lot of the family history and different situations. To summarize, his dad, Frank Gruber, committed the robbery, sold the jewels. Sometime later, he was shot and died. But before dying, he told Joshua where the money was hidden. Eli was not around during all this. When Eli did show up and Joshua informed him about the robbery and his father's being shot, Eli wanted to get out of town."

"Since Joshua had more money that he knew what to do with, he paid cash for a Lincoln Continental to help Eli's departure. My guess is that the same thugs that killed the father, being aware of the new expensive car, assumed that Eli now had the money. They tracked him down and he denied having the money, of course, and they killed him. In summary, Chief, I believe this case is not solvable. There is no evidence. Oh, and the police report about the father's shooting was less than informative."

Chief rubbed his chin. "Sounds about right. Seems to be open and shut, no witnesses, no evidence, nothing."

Thorne handed him a folder. "Here's a copy of my reports for your files. Also, my invoice that you asked for."

The chief opened the folder and took out the invoice. When he looked at it, his eyes became a little larger and he said, "Man, I'm in the wrong profession," and laughed. "You're good at your job, Thorne. With the crime increasing around here, I'm sure I will have to call on you again."

"I'll be glad to be of service, Chief. I appreciate your confidence."

They shook hands. The chief said, "I'll get this to the City Council at the end of the month and you should get your money shortly after."

"Sounds good." Thorne left the office.

Chapter Fifty

That night, Thorne was on his way home. He didn't like it in the winter when the days were so short that he had to drive home in the dark. A short distance from his house, he saw something on the side of the road. Two glowing eyes. A deer, he wondered. He slowed as he got closer, he saw that it was a dog, laying on its side, but holding its head up, panting.

He pulled off the road, left his headlights on high beam, and got out. Very, very slowly, he began to approach the animal, speaking softly and calmly. "It's OK, boy, it's OK, I'm not going to hurt you, just relax, take it easy, you're a good dog, yes, just relax, let me take a look." The dog tried to raise up but just whined. As Thorne got close enough, he didn't see any blood. "What happened, boy? Is your leg hurt?"

He let the dog sniff the top of his hand. It was a big dog, like a German Shepherd or some of the hunting dogs he had seen, brown, black, and white, short hair. He was wearing a collar but there was no tag on it. When he felt that it was safe, he went back to his car, opened the back door, and took the blanket from the floorboard to wrap around the dog. He returned.

"I'm going to get you warm, boy." He gently and carefully let the dog smell of the blanket and wrapped it over him, lifted him from the ground, and took him to his car. When he got back in the car, he knew the new vet's house was just a short distance away and decided to stop there.

He drove up in the driveway. Mike had seen his car pull in and walked out the door to meet him. "What's up, Thorne?"

"Hey, Mike. I've got an injured dog in my backseat. I picked him up not far down the road and, you know, since you're the vet, I figured you might be the person he needs to see."

Mike hurried to the car. "Here, let me take him." He reached in and talked softly, gently, yet firmly to the dog. "It's OK, boy, you're going to be fine. I'll take good care of you. Let's get you inside. I bet you're thirsty." He walked past Thorne and said, "Come on in, and we'll see what the problem is."

Thorne followed him inside to the little room off the back of the kitchen, a makeshift animal care room. Thorne commented, "This is perfect for a vet. In fact, I know where to come if I cut myself." He smiled.

The vet lay the dog on the counter, examined his eyes, ears, gently rubbed his body, then legs. The dog let out a whiny yelp when the vet examined his back left leg. "I think I know what the problem is. Now we can fix you up." He looked at Thorne and said, "His left back leg is broken, I'm afraid. He must have been struck by a car. Lucky he wasn't hurt worse. I'll get this bandaged up and give him food and water, and something to help him sleep through the night. He should be up and around tomorrow."

Thorne asked, "Do you think he could stay here tonight? I need to try to find his owner, I guess. Dinkle might not take too kindly to an intruder on her turf."

Mike smiled, "You're probably right. No problem, I have a kennel just right for him. We'll fix him up. Don't worry. I'll just plan on keeping him until we find the owners."

Thorne turned to leave. "I really appreciate it, Mike. Tell Shelly I said hello and give Jill a kiss."

* * *

Thorne parked in his driveway. Even though it was late, Carly met him at the door. "Thank goodness. I was beginning to worry."

He said, "I should have called." He took off his jacket and shoulder holster and hung them it in the closet. "Not far from here, I found this dog on the side of the road, hurt, and decided to take him to Mike's house."

"Oh no, what happened? Is he OK?"

"Yes, Mike examined him. He has a broken back leg. Mike has a small room set up like a room at his clinic. He took care of it and even agreed to keep him since he has the kennel and necessary things the dog will need until we can find the owners. Mike figures he must have got hit by a car."

"Poor thing. What kind of dog was it?"

"I have no idea. Looked a little like a hunting dog. He was heavy, seventy-five pounds or more. He liked me; I think." He smiled and looked at Dinkle, who was staring at him in disbelief. Thorne said to Dinkle, "I know, you don't have to worry. You cannot be replaced. You are our special one." Dinkle

149

wagged her tail. Carly picked up Dinkle, waved her paw goodnight to Thorne, and took her to her kennel.

They both had already had supper, so they went to bed early. Carly said, "What if you can't find the owners, Thorne?"

Thorne said, "Let's cross that bridge when we get to it." He kissed her shoulder, wrapped his arm around her. They slept.

Chapter Fifty-One

Saturday morning, Nellie had all the preparations done for Doc Skinner's retirement party. Carly and Thorne had arrived early to help. Around 12:15, the people in the community began arriving. Chief Logan and Beth, Deputy Goss, Mr. Templeton, Mr. Matthews from the meat market, Ms. Maggie, and, of course, Mike and Shelly Lawson with their daughter, Jill. Nellie had prepared a table just for Doc Skinner and his replacement, Mike Lawson, and his family. Everyone liked the food. Coffee and tea were served. Nellie asked Doc Skinner to say a few words. He declined. Many of the people who had him as their vet, got up and told how much they appreciated Doc Skinner.

When everyone left, Doc Skinner, being the last, Carly and Thorne, helped Nellie clean the tables, while Nellie put away the few leftovers.

Nellie said, "You know Christmas is just around the corner. Time flies, it seems."

Carly said, "I know. It's hard to believe that the year is almost over. Do you know when Mr. Greenfield is going to set up his Christmas tree sale lot?"

Nellie replied, "I believe Archie usually opens the first or second week of December. I'm going to put up my small artificial tree like I do every year. Those needles from the real trees just make more work for me."

Carly said, "I want us to have a real tree this year." She looked at Thorne, who nodded in agreement. She said, "Nellie, we're going to head home. Is there anything else you need before we go?"

Nellie said, "No, ya'll have a good rest of the weekend and I really appreciate your help." They said their goodbyes.

On the drive home, Carly said, "I'm so glad I'm not nauseated anymore. I remember when I was young, I would get a queasy feeling when I had a test or something in school. My mom would give me Pepto-Bismol which would make it better. That was nothing compared to pregnancy nausea."

Dinkle was waiting at the door for their arrival, as always.

After the party, Chief Logan returned to the police department. Beth drove to the drugstore. She could hardly wait to talk with Ms. Maggie about the Eli case and the money. She parked and entered the store. Before Ms. Maggie could greet her, Beth began. "Let me tell you the latest. You won't believe it."

Ms. Maggie had left the party early so she could be at the drugstore. She said, "Give me a minute, I haven't even opened the register."

Beth said, "I'll talk while you do whatever you have to do."

Ms. Maggie fiddled with the register and said, "Now, go ahead. What's this about?"

Beth began, "They have concluded that Eli Gruber's death is unsolvable! The detective, Davenport, checked it out, did interviews with people. He did find out that Eli had a brother who is still alive and a real loser, according to Logan. The father had been shot and killed not long after he robbed a jewelry store and it was said that the brother, Joshua is his name, was told by his father where the money was hidden."

"After the father died, Joshua found the money and bought Eli an expensive new car so he could leave town. The bad guys thought Eli was the one who got the money, with the new car and all. So, they must have killed him. Davenport told Logan that the brother, Joshua, said that he gambled and lost it all." Beth took a tissue from her pants pocket and wiped her lips. "I don't believe it for a minute. What do you think?"

Ms. Maggie put her bony finger on her lips and thought. "I bet you anything, none of is true. We'll have to cipher on this one. Sounds a bit complicated. You say the father stole the jewelry, sold it, and hid the money, then got shot and told the brother, Joshua, where it was. Joshua got the money and squandered it away. The bad guys mistakenly thought Eli was the one who had the money and killed him." She thought some more. "I bet he told them where the money is hidden and then they killed him."

Beth said, "You know, I bet you're right. Wonder where the money is? Maybe he lied and it's buried on the property at his house!"

Ms. Maggie said, "Are you going to tell all this to the chief? He might want to dig around or something and try to find it."

Beth said, "Nah, no sense in getting him all riled up. He doesn't put stock in anything I say, anyway."

A customer came in and cut short their conversation. Beth said, "That was a nice party for Doc Skinner, don't you think?"

Ms. Maggie agreed and quietly said, "I wonder if this new guy who's taking his place is going to be any good."

Beth said, "We'll see. Listen, gotta run. I'll talk to you later." She left the store.

Chapter Fifty-Two

On Sunday, Jennifer and Kenny spent the day with Papa. Edna came over around lunchtime. After lunch, Papa and Kenny played several games of checkers. She and Edna had friendly conversation, Edna sharing her favorite recipes. Jennifer heard Kenny say from the living room, "Can't you let me win just once, Papa." She smiled and felt happy about their relationship. She reassured herself that moving here near Papa had been a great idea.

* * *

Thorne read most of the day. He enjoyed mysteries. Every now and then Carly would hear him say aloud, "No, don't do that!" He really got into the stories sometimes. She took a break from working on her novel about Bonnie's life, went to the living room, walked over, and kissed Thorne on the cheek. She said, "You tell 'em, detective." They laughed.

Thorne said, "I guess I get carried away." They had lunch and spent the rest of the day being lazy and trying to figure out what to give everyone for Christmas.

* * *

Mike and Shelly Lawson talked about Doc Skinner's party and the people who admired him. Shelly spent most of her day rearranging the kitchen cabinets. Mike straightened the carport area. He was surprised that there was a lawnmower and other tools still there.

For supper, Shelly had fixed homemade spaghetti and garlic bread with sweet tea. Shelly said, "Yesterday, Carly told me about a man who has a live Christmas tree lot on the edge of town. It would be nice to have one this year. We have enough lights and decorations, I'm fairly sure."

Mike agreed. He said, "I'm looking forward to my first day tomorrow. Doc Skinner said he would be with me, you know, to help if I need it since the office is new to me."

"I think he's a nice man. That's good he will do that. I also bet he's going to be at a loss of what to do with himself. I mean, he's been the vet for years."

Mike said, "I think so too. I'm going to make sure that he feels welcome to come anytime just in case he gets lonesome or feels useless in his retirement."

Shelly leaned over and kissed him. "That's my wonderful husband."

Chapter Fifty-Three

Edna Cooper and Vernon Ward were sitting in his living room talking about Christmas. Vernon said, "I want to get Jennifer something special, just haven't decided yet. I was thinking about giving Kenny a bicycle. What do you think?"

Edna said, "I think a bicycle for Kenny is a perfect idea for his gift. I can go with you to pick it out." She thought for a minute. "I think Jennifer might like a gift certificate to a clothing store."

Vernon said, "I've always liked to give a gift, not money. But I think you're probably right."

Edna asked, "Are you going to put up a tree this year?"

Vernon said, "As you know, in the past I haven't bothered because there wasn't a lot of celebrating going on. I enjoyed being at your house on Christmas. You always have a beautiful tree. But this year is different with Jennifer and Kenny in town." He looked at Edna and asked, "what would you like for Santa to bring you little lady?"

She smiled. "All I want is for you to stay healthy and to keep being my friend." She reached over and took his hand. "You are a special man, Vernon Ward." They sat quietly, looking at the fire crackling in the fireplace. When it turned to embers, Edna said, "I better get home. You need your rest." She leaned over and kissed him on the cheek. "You call me if you need me, OK?"

He called out, "Edna!" She was startled for a second. He smiled and said, "You told me to call if I need you." They laughed. He watched her walked to her porch and turn out the porch light. When he got into bed, he thought, *I know I need her. I also know I love her.* He slept well.

Chapter Fifty-Four

On Monday, after leaving work, Thorne stopped by Mike and Shelly's house to check on the dog. Shelly answered the door. "Hey, Thorne. Come on in. Mike is in the vet room. You can go on back."

Thorne walked past Jill in her playpen, waved at her, and spoke a child-like hello. In the vet room, Mike said, "Thorne, good to see you. The dog is doing much better. He's something. He seems very docile and wants a lot of attention, which I've given him, of course. Have you had any luck finding the owners?"

Thorne said, "I've had such a busy day, I haven't had time to pursue it. So, no word from anyone?"

Mike said, "Not yet. I put a poster up in the clinic. Shelly took a photo and printed it out on the copier. I added the necessary information. I also put one up at the Green Hornet. That Nellie is quite a lady."

Thorne shook his head. "Yes, she sure is. I believe she's Carly's best friend. She is a caring soul, and sometimes I wonder if she doesn't have a sixth sense or something." They laughed. Thorne walked over to the dog, who was wagging his tail. Thorne said, "It looks like he's smiling."

Mike said, "I think he is. He knows you are the one who saved him on that dreadful night."

"A lot of folks around here go to the Green Hornet, so that might be the best bet on finding his owners. Let me know if anyone claims him." They said their goodbyes and Thorne drove home.

Chapter Fifty-Five

Carly and Thorne ate breakfast Tuesday morning. After Thorne left for work, Carly checked her phone calendar and found that her doctor's appointment was at 11:00 this morning instead of 1 o'clock. Carly was ready to leave for her obstetrician's appointment when her doorbell rang. She answered it. "Hey, Shelly. Come in."

Shelly picked up Jill from the stroller and went inside. She said, "It's colder than I thought. I'm glad I bundled up Jill."

Carly took their coats. "Come in. I've got a few minutes before I need to leave for my OB appointment. Have a seat."

Shelly said, "I won't be but a minute. I just wanted to ask who you had for an obstetrician. I can have my records transferred from Raleigh."

Carly wrote the name, address, and phone number of Dr. Whitmore and gave it to Shelly, who thanked her.

Carly asked, "When is your baby due?"

"Sometime in mid-May. Yours?"

Carly said, "I hope to find that out today."

Shelly said, "Also, Mike and I were talking about getting a real tree for Christmas this year. Is there a place around here that sells real trees?"

Carly said, "Yes, in fact, Thorne and I talked about it too. Mr. Archie Greenfield puts up a sales lot on the edge of town the first or second week of this month. We could plan to go together this weekend if you would like."

Shelly said, "Mike closes the vet office on Wednesday afternoon. Maybe we could go then."

Carly said, "That would be nice. Do you think he can put two trees on his truck? We only want a small one."

Shelly said, "I'm sure he can. We don't want a very large tree. For one thing, we don't have that many decorations." She got up. "I better let you get going."

Carly got their coats out of the closet. "I'll talk to Thorne tonight. I'll see you Wednesday. I'll walk down to your house."

Shelly said, "Don't walk, we will drop by and pick you up. See you then." She put Jill in the stroller and returned home.

* * *

After the doctor finished her exam, she informed Carly that her baby will be due July 16, give or take a week or so. She explained that first babies often come early but most of the time they are born later than the given due date. Carly left the office and went by the diner to give Nellie the news.

Nellie wasn't busy at that time. She reassured Carly that all would be fine and that she would help her.

Carly said, "You know, Nellie. I think you will be the baby's grandma. Grandma Nellie. What do you think?" Carly thought she saw tears in Nellie's eyes.

Nellie didn't speak, she just hugged Carly tighter than usual. "I would be so proud, Carly. But you better talk to Thorne first."

Carly said, "No worry there. I better get home." They said their goodbyes and Carly drove home.

When Thorne got home that evening, Dinkle was outside, and Carly was preparing spaghetti for supper. He entered the kitchen, walked over, and kissed Carly. "Something smells mighty good."

Carly smiled. "Are you talking about me?"

Thorne said, "That too." He looked in the pot on the stove. "Yum, spaghetti. One of my favorites." He sat at the table so they could talk while Carly cooked the noodles.

Carly poured the noodles in the colander. Dinkle came through the doggie door and greeted Thorne. Carly asked, "Will you close the doggie door for me?"

Thorne walked over after rubbing Dinkle's head and closed the door. Carly announced, "You're going to be a daddy on July 16, give or take a week or two!"

Thorne smiled widely and hugged her. Dinkle stood looking at them. Thorne said, "I see you haven't told Dinkle, or have you?"

Carly laughed. "I think she's calculating how long it is before she's not the main princess around here." They laughed.

Thorne told her about his day while they ate supper. Carly said, "Oh, I almost forgot. Shelly came by today before I left for my appointment. I gave her Dr. Whitmore's information since she needs to transfer her records. Also, Wednesday I'm going with her and Mike to pick out a Christmas tree. I know you are busy at work, so I figured that would help. Then you and I can decorate it together this weekend."

Thorne said, "Sounds good. It seems like they are going to be good neighbors. While you're with them, get an update on the dog and explain how busy I am."

After supper, they talked about names for the baby but couldn't decide on anything. Carly put Dinkle in her kennel. They called it a night.

Chapter Fifty-Six

Kenny got home from school and called his mom at her work. She answered, "Knott Engineering."

Kenny said, "Hey, Mom, I know you're at work, but I was wondering if you could go to Bucky's house and meet his parents? Me and Bucky—I mean Bucky and I want to camp in his backyard this weekend."

Jennifer said, "I can do that. I'll talk to you when I get home." They said goodbye and hung up.

Kenny called Bucky and asked him if it was OK for his mom to come over the meet his parents after she got off work. Bucky asked his mom, and she said yes.

It was only two blocks to Bucky's house, but Jennifer drove as it was too cold to walk. Kenny knocked on the door and Bucky answered. "Hey, man, come in. Hey, Ms. Owens."

Jennifer said, "Hello, Bucky. Is your mom or dad home?"

Bucky said, "Yes, Mam." He led them to the kitchen. Bucky's mom was cooking supper. He said to his mom, "Mom, Kenny and his mom are here."

Peggy Winthrop turned from the sink, dried her hands. "Welcome. I'm Peggy. It's nice to meet you. Have a seat," she motioned to the table.

Jennifer sat down. Kenny followed Bucky to his room. Jennifer said, "Nice to meet you too. I'm Jennifer. Kenny has been wanting me to meet you, which is something I like to do before Kenny spends time at a friend's house."

Peggy said, "You're smart. These days, you can't be too careful. I feel the same way. Would you and Kenny like to stay for supper?"

"No, thank you. Is it OK if the boys camp out in your backyard this weekend?"

Peggy said, "Yes. I'm so glad Bucky found a friend and one that lives so close too. He's welcome anytime. My husband, Darren, will be here to chaperone."

Jennifer said, "I hope Bucky will come to our house sometimes too." She assumed that Peggy knew that Kenny's dad wasn't in the picture.

They said their goodbyes and drove home. Kenny was excited.

Chapter Fifty-Seven

Wednesday afternoon, after shopping for live Christmas trees, Mike took Carly and Thorne's Christmas tree to their house and put it on the front porch. He asked Carly, "Are you sure you don't want me to take it inside?"

"No, Thorne will do that. I need to get the stand and decorations from the attic. We'll decorate it this weekend. I really appreciate your doing this. It was a fun way to start the holiday." Then she said, "I forgot to ask about the dog. I got excited about picking out the tree. Still no owner?"

Mike answered, "No, no one recognizes him. I stopped by the diner and Nellie said the same thing. We are considering keeping him. He and Jill have become best buddies. Tell Thorne, it was good he found him. I think we're going to call him Jack."

Carly said, "That's great news. I'll tell Thorne. Thanks again for your help with the tree." Mike said goodbye, Shelly waved.

At home, Carly opened the doggie door for Dinkle. She then called Donna Brewer in West Virginia. Donna answered.

Carly began, "Hey, Donna. Hope you're doing good."

Donna said, "Yes, I'm being kept young these days by my sister's grandchildren. They are full of energy. I hope all is good with you."

Carly said, "I'm calling about two things. First, we've met the people who rented your house, the new vet in town, his wife, and their little girl. I don't think you have anything to worry about concerning your property. They are very nice and friendly. She's going to have a baby in May. Which brings me to my second reason for calling. Thorne and I are going to have a baby too."

Donna said, "Oh, Carly, that's wonderful. Like I said, children keep you young."

They chatted a little more and hung up.

Carly's phone rang and she answered.

Bonnie said, "Hey, Carly."

"Hey, Bonnie. I was just thinking about calling you. I went to the doctor yesterday for an exam and found out that our baby is due in mid-July."

Bonnie said, "Are you going to find out if it's a boy or a girl?"

"I haven't discussed it with Thorne, I doubt we will. We'll be happy and love it no matter."

Bonnie said, "I certainly understand that. How have you been feeling? Are you still nauseated?"

"No, thank goodness. I am going to have to buy maternity clothes soon. My pants are getting to feel uncomfortable. How are things with you and Josh, and the kids?"

She heard Bonnie light a cigarette. "We're all doing fine. I've been a little upset lately. You remember I told you that my dad was in the early stages of dementia?"

"Yes, I remember."

Bonnie continued, "My brother is the executor. He and my sister, Kate, are close. They talk about all this to each other. They consider me too negative or something, I don't really know. Anyway, my brother said that there were three choices for Dad's care: 24-hour at home, a memory care senior center, or staying with Kate. I voted for the senior center, as there are professionals there to take care of him as he gets worse. Anyway, I'm rambling."

Carly said, "That's awful, Bonnie. I'm so sorry."

Bonnie lit another cigarette. "I cried a few tears and then felt relieved. I think I'm over it. You can't let what you can't control ruin your life. It's just the way it goes."

Carly said, "What do your kids think?"

Bonnie said, "They have differing opinions. Melanie was the most upset because she went to see him the most and did so much for him. I didn't mean to get carried away on this. I'm so happy about the baby's due date. I'll tell Josh when he gets home. Give Thorne a hug for me."

Carly said, "I will. Maybe everything will work out for the best." They said their goodbyes and hung up.

Chapter Fifty-Eight

Thursday during breakfast, Carly tells Thorne that Mike and Shelly are going to keep the dog, Jack. Mike said that Jill and the dog have become best friends.

Thorne replied, "That's good. I think it will be good for them to have a dog living out here in the country."

Carly continued. "I'm going to Peabody's Fashion and Apparel store to buy some maternity clothes. I think I will stop by and let Ms. Maggie know about the baby."

Thorne said, "That's a good way to announce it to the town." He got up, put his dishes in the sink. He kissed Carly and said, "Be careful and tell Ms. Maggie I said hello. Oh, and make sure you tell her that I still can't tell her about the case." They both laughed.

When Carly arrives at Peabody's, the only and oldest clothing store in Lillington, Jessie Adcock greeted her. Carly says, "Hello, Ms. Adcock. I'm Carly Davenport, used to be Carly Jansen."

Ms. Adcock said, "Oh my, it is so nice to see you. I remember your mother. She used to buy all her clothes from me. She was such a sweet lady."

"Yes, Mam, she was and a wonderful mother." Carly looked around and said, "I just found out that I'm going to be a mother and my pants are fitting a little snug, so I want to get some maternity outfits."

Ms. Adcock said, "What wonderful news. I know your mother would love to be here." Carly nodded. Ms. Adcock led her to the section of the store with the maternity clothes. "You just take your time. The fitting room is right there through that curtain. I'll be at the register if you have any questions."

"Yes, Mam, thank you." She found three outfits that she liked, bought them, and left.

She parked in front of the drugstore and entered. Ms. Maggie said, "Hello, Carly. It's so good to see you."

Carly says, "I just came by to tell you some good news." Ms. Maggie perked up at that. "Thorne and I are going to have a baby."

Ms. Maggie clasps her hands together, "My, my, that is so sweet. You're going to be a wonderful mom. When is the baby due?"

Carly said, "Around mid-July. I just wanted you to know. I just bought maternity outfits at Peabody's, so Ms. Adcock knows. You take care. I gotta get home."

Chapter Fifty-Nine

That night, after eating pizza for supper, Kenny packed up the things he needed for camping Friday night at Bucky Winthrop's house. His mom would drop off his things at Bucky's house on her way to work. He felt excited. He would ride the school bus to Bucky's.

* * *

When Jennifer arrived home after work on Friday, she called Peggy Winthrop's house to be sure Kenny arrived from school. Peggy answered and said, "Yes, they are outside getting their tent set up. Don't you worry. I think they're going to be fine." Jennifer thanked her and they hung up.

Minutes later, her doorbell rang. She opened the door, there stood her soon-to-be ex-husband. She said, "Frank?"

He took off his cap. "Yes, it's me. Can I come in? I really need to talk to you."

Jennifer hesitated, then stepped back and let him in. They stood in the hallway for a minute, each not knowing what to say. Frank asked, "Is Kenny here?"

Jennifer answered, "No, he's spending the night with a friend."

"How's he doing?"

Jennifer turned and walked into the living room. "He's getting adjusted."

"That's good to hear. How have you been?"

Jennifer bluntly asked, "get to the point Frank. Why are you here?"

He sat in the chair and looked up at her. "Jenn, I know what I did was wrong, and I know it hurt you. I've done a lot of thinking. I was stupid, plain stupid. That relationship with Emily was nothing to me."

Jennifer continued standing. Frank cleared his throat and took a deep breath. "I'm here to ask you to please forgive me, please. We've been happy for so many years. My life is nothing without you. I've come to ask you to

167

please give me another chance. I'll do everything differently. I'll understand if it takes some time for you to trust me again. But, trust me, you will see. I've learned my lesson. Will you, Jenn, please give me another chance?"

Jennifer sat on the edge of the sofa and looked at him. "Frank, I'm sorry you drove all this way for nothing. I only had one heart and you broke it. It can't be repaired, especially by you. Kenny doesn't need the rollercoaster either. I'm sorry but I have made my decision." She stood and walked to the door.

Frank got up slowly, twirled his cap in his hands. He looked at her and said, "Will you promise that if you do change your mind, you will call me? I'll take care of everything. Just think about it. That's all I'm asking." He wanted to put his arms around her and hold her tightly until she changed her mind, but he could see that that would be useless.

She opened the door and Frank left. When she turned from the door, the tears started. She had made up her mind, but the pain was still there.

While driving, a deer ran out onto the road. Frank slammed on the brakes. "Damn, that was too close for comfort." His cell phone had fallen to the floorboard on the passenger side. He pulled the car over on the shoulder, put his car in park, and leaned down to retrieve the phone. He wanted to call Jennifer to give her one more chance to change her mind but knew it was no use. He dialed Emily's number instead. No answer.

Before putting the car in drive, he saw a car approaching, so he waited. The car slowed, *to see if I'm having a problem,* he thought. The car pulled up beside his car. Frank rolled down his window. He didn't react fast enough when he saw the gun.

Chapter Sixty

Beth Logan entered the drugstore. Ms. Maggie had just finished putting her ceramic Christmas tree on the table in front of the store and walked back to the counter where Beth joined her.

Ms. Maggie said, "I've been thinking. We ought to start our own newspaper column—you know, the latest real news in town," emphasizing the word real.

Beth laughed and said, "That would go over like a lead balloon." She looked at the tree. "Nice as usual."

Ms. Maggie said, "Did you know that Carly, the investigator's wife, is pregnant?"

Beth said, "No, Logan hasn't said anything."

"I don't think they've told many people yet." She put her dust cloth under the counter. A couple of customers came into the store.

Beth said, "I don't have any updates. I just wanted to see if you did." She walked to the door, waved a hand, and mouthed, "See you later," and left the store.

* * *

After the breakfast crowd left Saturday morning, Nellie put out the decorations at the Green Hornet. Snowflakes on the windows, a small artificial tree on the checkout counter. She wondered why snowflakes when it never snows here at Christmas. *Must be everyone's hope*, she thought. She reminisced about the days when Ed Madry went all out decorating the place. She missed him. Sometimes the tiredness and sadness came over her and she just let the feelings and thoughts come. They would pass, she knew.

A customer came in for a late breakfast or early lunch. She welcomed him and when she looked up, she saw that it was Mr. Page, Ed's attorney. She said,

"Mr. Page, how nice to see you! Please sit wherever you like. How are things with you?"

Mr. Page had been the attorney that delivered the surprising news to Nellie that Ed had left her the diner in his Will.

Mr. Page sat at a table near the kitchen. "Fine, I can't complain. Good to see that you're still in business. I was coming through on my way back to Dunn and remembered you promised me the best food I've ever had."

Nellie laughed and brought him a menu. "Yes, sir, and I'm good at keeping my promises. You look over the menu. What can I get you to drink?"

He ordered sweet tea and a lettuce, bacon, and tomato sandwich with onion rings.

Nellie brought his food. "When Ed was here, he would go all out with decorating for Christmas. He loved this time of year."

"I liked Ed. He was one of the good guys." He took an onion ring, dipped it in ketchup, and said, "These onion rings are delicious."

Nellie said, "Yes, sir, fresh onion battered and fried; no frozen food from a bag around here." He finished his food, left a large tip on the table, and paid. Nellie thanked him and said, "You have a very merry Christmas, Mr. Page."

"Same to you." He turned at the door, "You were right, best food I've ever had." He left. Nellie felt proud.

Chapter Sixty-One

Dinkle watched as Thorne ascended into the sky. He knew there was nothing to fear because Carly used to do it all the time when they first moved there. After finding the box of decorations, Thorne came back down the attic stairs and Dinkle said, *Be careful.* Thorne knew these things.

Carly put a CD in the player of her favorite Christmas songs. She had made the CD years ago and always played it when putting up the decorations. Thorne hung the string of lights on the tree and they both put on the ornaments.

As Carly picked each ornament out of the box, she would reminisce about it. "I remember this one I gave to my mom when I was in school. I made it with popsicle sticks." The next one, "My mom made lots of these bead angels, all colors." She picked out more of the bead angels and hung them. "I bought this crochet angel from a little old lady at a flea market. I know it took her hours to make these. I remember that she was charging only two dollars, so I bought three and paid her ten dollars." There were several bell-shaped ornaments. "My mom collected these. Her friends would give her a different one each year."

There were ornaments from her college friends. Thorne was impressed by her sentimentality. Carly said, "It's not easy figuring out what to give people for a gift. I did come up with one thing that might be good, especially for Bonnie and Josh, and Janice and Joey."

Thorne asked, "What's that?"

Carly said, "A very pretty tree ornament with our names and the year on it. It would be a keepsake. I also want to email a gift certificate for Bonnie's favorite online quilt shop."

Thorne said, "I like both those ideas. Where do you get these special ornaments?"

"I found them online. They will print what we want on them, and they have different choices to choose from." They sat with Dinkle on the sofa, Carly leaning on Thorne with his arms wrapped around her and enjoyed resting while watching the Christmas tree lights in the dark.

Chapter Sixty-Two

Late Sunday morning, Kenny returned home from camping with Bucky. He comes in and starts talking excitedly. "Hey, Mom. We had a great time. Bucky is really neat."

Jennifer looks at him. "Looks like you didn't get a lot of sleep."

Kenny says, "Of course not, we told scary stories and talked about all kinds of things. His mom and dad are cool. They just asked that we keep it down, no loud noise to disturb the neighbors."

Jennifer said, "I'm glad you enjoyed yourself. Do you want to take a shower and change your clothes? I thought we would go see Papa later this afternoon."

"Cool," he said and ran off to his room. After showering, he came to the kitchen and saw the overflowing plate of peanut butter oatmeal chocolate cookies his mom had made. "My favorite! Thanks, Mom."

"Would you like a sandwich?" He shook his head in no as he chewed his cookie.

Jennifer and Kenny arrived at Papa's in the early afternoon. Kenny told him all about his new friend, their camping experience.

Papa said, "That's sound good. I'm glad you have found a friend and one who lives close by. It's nice to have a friend in life. You say his name is Bucky?"

Kenny shook his head. "Bucky Winthrop. His mom and dad are nice."

Papa asked Kenny, "Isn't school out for the holidays pretty soon?"

Kenny answered, "Yes sir, starting Wednesday until after New Year's."

Papa stood up and said to him, "Come with me, I think I have something that might interest you."

Kenny followed him to his bedroom; Jennifer was close behind. Propped against the foot of the bed was a brand-new ten-speed bicycle, hand gears and all. His papa pointed, "Merry Christmas, my boy."

Kenny walked slowly to the bike. "For me?"

"Who else? Edna was going to get a big red bow to put on it, but she hasn't got around to it yet."

Kenny hugged his papa. "Thank you so much. Thank you. It's super. I need it too. Bucky already has a bike, and I was wishing for one. How did you know?"

"Papa knows lots of things. Why don't you take it outside for a spin? See if it works."

Kenny smiled, pushed the bike down the hall and out the front door.

Jennifer watched as he rode the bike down the driveway. "Wow, Dad, that is one happy kid!"

"What every boy needs. I figured with him being out of school, he can get to enjoy it."

"Thanks, Dad. You're the best." She hugged him. "Could you help us put the bike in the car? If we lived closer, he could ride it."

Kenny rode his bike to the porch. "It's great! Wow! I've never had a bike!"

Jennifer said, "We need to get home. You and Papa can put the bike in the car and when we get home since it's still daylight, maybe you would like to ride it to Bucky's house and show him."

They loaded the bike. When they got home, Kenny rode away to Bucky's.

* * *

That afternoon, Carly went online and ordered the Christmas ornaments for Joey, Janice, Bonnie, and Josh. She requested that they be gift-wrapped with a personal message. She also bought a gift certificate from Bonnie's favorite online quilting fabric store and had it sent to her with a personal message.

She always gave Nellie the same thing, her favorite bath towel sets. She had no idea what to get Thorne for Christmas. Dinkle looked up at her and Carly read her expression as *don't worry, you'll figure out the perfect thing.* She rubbed her head several times and said, "You're right, Sunshine. I'm sure I will."

She wanted Thorne's gift to be special. Then it came to her. I'll order us a special ornament together, to commemorate our marriage, our first Christmas today. Then when the baby comes, I'll get one for that very special occasion. Yes, start a real treasure of heirlooms. She walked to her office and saw Thorne deep in concentration, so she didn't disturb him and went to make herself a cup of tea.

Chapter Sixty-Three

Monday morning, after dressing in his pressed deputy's uniform and spit-shined shoes, Deputy Goss put on his hat and walked to his patrol car. He was listening to talk radio, driving the speed limit when he saw what looked like an abandoned car on the side of the road. He pulled off the road, got out, and walked to the car. The driver's head was bent forward and down. Goss could tell that the man was dead. He called to tell the chief.

Chief Logan answer, "Logan here."

Goss, short of breath, began, "Chief, this is Deputy Goss." The chief thought, *No kidding.* "I'm out here off Junction Road and I was on my way in and saw a car parked on the side of the road, you know, like abandoned looking. I pulled over to check it out. The driver looks dead to me."

Chief irritatingly says, "Goss, did you think to call 911?"

Goss answered, "I thought you'd wanna know ASAP. I'll call 'em now." He cut off, called 911 and gave them the location.

He went back to his patrol car, cranked it, and turned on the heat to wait for the ambulance. After checking the driver, one of the EMTs walked over to the patrol car. Goss rolled down his window a few inches. The EMT said, "Deputy, you need to call the coroner. I don't believe there's anything we can do for the guy."

Goss thanked him and called the chief to let him know that the EMT said to call the coroner. The chief asked, "Did you call the coroner, Goss?"

"Well, no, sir. I'll do that now."

Chief Logan said, "Yes, do that, Goss," and hung up.

Goss called Tom Sledge, the coroner, and woke him up. Sledge answered, "Coroner's office."

Deputy Goss said, "Hello, Mr. Sledge, this is Deputy Goss. You need to come. We have a dead man, according to the EMT."

Sledge sat up on the side of his bed, rubbed his face. "OK. Might you be able to give me a location?"

Goss said, "Oh, yes, sir. We're about five miles out Junction Road. You'll see it."

Sledge said, "I'll be right there." They hung up.

Goss called the chief, "Yes, deputy."

Goss said, "I called the coroner and he's on his way."

The chief said, "Good job. I'll see you when you get to the office. Oh, and Goss, be sure to get his name and any other information from the coroner."

"Will do," answered Goss. They hung up.

When Goss arrived back at the station, he walked to the chief's office. "I have the information, Chief." He handed him the driver's license.

The chief read it, Frank Evans, from Belmont. Wonder what he was doing in these parts. He placed the license on his desk and picked up his phone and called directory assistance for the number for Frank Evans in Belmont, North Carolina. *I'm sorry, the number you are trying to reach has been disconnected and is no longer in service.* "Goss!" Goss came to the chief's office. "Get me Investigator Davenport on the phone."

Thorne answered. "Davenport Investigations."

"Thorne, this is Chief Logan."

"Yes, Chief, what can I do for you?"

"I'm afraid we have a bit of a problem. I don't believe this will be as complicated as the last time. I need you to see if you can locate the next of kin for a man. He was found in his car on the side of the road this morning. He had been shot and killed. I have his name and address. I called directory assistance, but they said the number had been disconnected."

Thorne said, "Sure, Chief. What is the name and address?" The chief read it to him. Thorne said, "I'll look into it and get back to you."

"Good man. I appreciate it." They hung up.

Thorne looked at his watch. It was early enough that he could make the trip to Belmont. He called Carly, she answered.

Thorne began, "Hey, my beautiful wife." He heard her say something to Dinkle. "The chief called me just now and I've got to go to Belmont. It's on the outskirts of Charlotte so I will be gone most of the day."

Carly said, "What a way to start the week."

"Yeah. I should get it resolved today, so we can spend some time together before the holiday."

Carly said, "I would like that. Be safe. I love you." They hung up.

Thorne put the address in his GPS. About three hours later, he arrived in Belmont at the address on the license of Frank Evans. Moderate homes, neat lawns, and Christmas decorations were seen. He parked his car and walked to the door. A woman in her twenties, long brown hair, dressed in jeans and a pullover, opened the door.

Thorne began, "Hello, Mam. My name is Thorne Davenport. I'm a private investigator. Is this the home of Frank Evans?"

The woman looked puzzled. "No, it isn't. I don't know anyone by that name."

He asked, "Do you rent or own the home?"

"We rent. We've never been able to buy a house. We just moved here in November."

Thorne asked, "Would you tell me the name of your realtor?"

"Why yes, it's Belmont Realty, on Main Street." Thorne thanked her and drove to the real estate office.

When he entered, the receptionist at the front desk greeted him. "Good morning. May I help you?"

Thorne said, "Good morning. I'm looking for some information on a man that used to rent a house from your company."

Her phone rang but before answering, she pointed to a desk on the other side of the room. "You need to see Ms. Perkins." She answered her phone.

Thorne walked over and Ms. Perkins looked up from her desk. "Good morning. How may I help you?" She motioned for him to have a seat.

Thorne handed her a business card and sat in the chair across from her desk. "I'm a private investigator, Thorne Davenport. I am trying to see if you have a forwarding address for one of your former tenants. I went by his known address and someone else lives there now. The woman who answered the door said that you manage the property."

Ms. Jenkins turned to her laptop, then to Thorne. "What is that address?" He told her. "Yes, that is one of our rental properties. Who is the previous tenant you are trying to locate?"

"Frank Evans."

She hit a few keys. "Ah, found it. Yes, Frank and his wife rented that house from us for over five years. They have a son, Kenny, I believe his name is."

Thorne asked, "Do you have a forwarding address for them?"

Ms. Perkins pursed her lips. "For him, yes. In September, Mr. Evans came by our office and gave a 30-day notice. He said that his wife had left him and taken their son. He wanted to find a smaller place to live."

Thorne made notes in his notepad. "Do you have that address and, by chance, do you know where the wife and son moved to?"

Ms. Perkins answered, "I wouldn't know where the wife, Jennifer, that was her name; I wouldn't know where she moved to. I did rent Mr. Evans a smaller place, a three-room duplex on Second Avenue, 107 Second Avenue. He was always on time paying his rent, so it was no problem."

Thorne made notes and said, "You have been a great help. I really appreciate it." He started to get up, but Ms. Perkins started explaining.

"You know, I was so surprised when Mr. Evans told me that. Jennifer seemed like such a nice lady, and their son, Kenny, was such a well-mannered young man. I don't know what happened, of course. I just hate to see young people quit trying. Seems to be the way of life these days."

"I agree. You never really know what people's private lives are like." He thanked her and left.

He put the address in his GPS, arrived at the small duplex. The neighborhood looked run down, the duplex was on a small lot, only sparse grass in the yard. Thorne walked along the cracked steppingstones to the door and knocked. No answer. A moment later, a little girl came out of the adjacent apartment, pushing her tricycle. Thorne said, "Hi there."

The little girl, who looked about five years old, looked up at him. "Wow, you are big!"

Thorne smiled, "And you are little and cute."

The door opened and the girl's mother saw that her daughter was talking to a stranger. She opened the screen door. "Missy, what have I told you about talking to strangers? Get back in this house, right now." The little girl, Missy, lowered her head, took a side glance at Thorne, and waved. When she was inside, the mother asked, "Can I help you?"

Thorne answered. "Do you know the man that lives on this side?" He pointed to the left side of the house. "Do you know if he will be back soon?"

"I've met him, don't know him, really. He goes to work, comes home, that's it, mostly. Funny thing, he didn't come home Friday, and, come to think of it, he hasn't been home all weekend."

Thorne asked, "Do you know where he worked?"

"Sorry, no. I believe he was a builder, you know, a construction guy."

Thorne thanked her and walked back to his car and wrote a few notes in his notepad. He would be home in time for supper, so he called Carly to let her know.

Thorne arrived back at the police station just after 4 o'clock. Deputy Goss said hello. "You can go on back to see the chief."

Chief Logan stood up, reached to shake hands. "Good to see you again, Thorne. Have you solved the case?" They smiled and Thorne sat in the wooden chair across from the chief's desk.

"I have found out some helpful information." He took out his notepad. "The woman who now lives at the address on Mr. Evans' license said that she had moved there in September. She gave me her realtor's name and I paid them a visit. The lady there, Ms. Perkins, was familiar with Frank Evans and his family. They had rented from them for several years. She said that Frank came in September, gave a month's notice, and rented a smaller place."

"The reason being, his wife, Jennifer, had left him, along with their son, Kenny. They didn't know where the wife had moved to. However, they did give me the new location for Frank, a small duplex in town. There, no one was home, but the occupant on the other side of the duplex said that all he did was go to work and come home, except that he hadn't been home all weekend."

The chief sat forward in his chair. "Kenny? The son's name is Kenny?"

Thorne nodded. "That's what the realtor said."

The chief wrinkled his brow. "Huh, a few weeks ago, I recall an incident at the school. Seems a couple of boys got into a scuffle and the assistant principal called me. One of the boys' names was Kenny. His mother came in shortly after I arrived, and her name was Jennifer." He looked at Thorne. "I don't believe this is a coincidence."

"No sir, I agree."

The chief continued. "You might check with Templeton. More than likely, they rented a place from him."

Thorne looked at his watch. "I believe their office closes in a few minutes. I'll check first thing in the morning." He got up.

The chief said, "Good work. I'll see you tomorrow."

Thorne drove home to be with Dinkle, oh yes, and of course, most of all his wife and mother-to-be.

Chapter Sixty-Four

Tuesday morning over breakfast, Thorne said, "Today may be rough. I'm going to see the realtor about where Frank Evans' wife is living. The chief believes he met them when the son had some sort of altercation at school. If all this is confirmed, I guess the chief and I will pay a visit to the wife. That will not be any fun."

Carly said, "Why do you have to go? Can't the chief do that by himself?"

"Well, there's the matter of who killed the man. My investigation is far from over. Maybe she can give me some information to get me started in the right direction."

"I see." Carly got up and stacked the dishes next to the sink. "I don't have any plans for today. I'll probably work on my book. It's too cold outside and I want to stay in my PJs and take it easy."

Thorne walked up to her and put his arms around her. "That sounds a perfect day for my wife and mother-to-be." They kissed.

Carly said, "Hope you find out everything you need. Be careful." She followed him to the door.

Thorne said, "I always am." He put on his shoulder holster that held his .38 Ruger, and his jacket.

Dinkle was watching and listening at Thorne's feet. She lifted her paw to Thorne's pants' leg. Carly said, "She wants you to be safe too." Thorne rubbed Dinkle on the head. "Don't worry, girl, I'll be back real soon. You watch after your mama."

He left. Carly poured herself another cup of tea and she and Dinkle had a restful, quiet day.

* * *

Thorne arrived at Mr. Templeton's office not long after he had opened. Stacy was taking his coffee when Thorne walked in. She turned, "Hey, Mr. Davenport."

Thorne walked up to her. "Since you're here to see Mr. Templeton, you can deliver his coffee, if you don't mind."

"I'd be glad to." He walked to Templeton's office. Stacy continued decorating the office for Christmas, a small artificial tree in one corner of the room, a little holly with candles on the corner table, and a wreath on the door.

At Templeton's office door, he tried to put on the air of a waiter, "Sir, your coffee." He set the cup on Mr. Templeton's desk. "Will there be anything else?" They laughed.

Mr. Templeton took the cup and said, "I know a restaurant looking for a good waiter. A little humor to start the day. Nothing wrong with that. Thanks. Have a seat." Thorne sat. "What can I help you with?"

"I'm investigating a case for the chief. I assume you know about the man killed this past weekend."

"Yes, I heard about that."

"Well, so far, I've been able to find out that he was from a little town near Charlotte, a place called Belmont. Seems he and his wife separated and the chief thinks that she may have moved to Lillington. I was hoping you might know about that."

Mr. Templeton asked, "What was her name?"

"Jennifer Owens. She has a son, Kenny."

Mr. Templeton didn't hesitate. "Why, yes. In October, I believe it was, Stacy can check, her father who lives here in town and has for many years, came in to get a house for his daughter and her son. He didn't give any explanation, just that they were moving here."

Thorne asked, "What was her father's name?"

"Ward, Vernon Ward. Mr. Ward has lived here for years. He bought his house from the previous realtor, Mr. Baker. Nice man, I believe in his sixties. He seemed to be concerned about his daughter and genuinely interested in helping her. He paid the deposit and first month's rent on a house. They moved in at the end of October. In fact, he brought them by to meet us."

Thorne said, "I would like that address if you don't mind."

"No problem. See Stacy on your way out and she'll give it to you. It's on Park Avenue, but I can't recall the number."

Thorne got up, thanked Mr. Templeton. Stacy handed him the address on his way out. He thanked her and left.

* * *

It was lunchtime when Thorne arrived at the police station. Deputy Goss greeted him. "The chief's just getting ready to go to lunch. Let me tell him you're here." At that time, the chief walked into the front room and saw Thorne. "Just going to get a bite to eat, wanna join me?" He grabbed his hat.

Thorne said, "Sure." They walked over to the corner café. The waiter welcomed them and said, "The usual, Chief?" The chief nodded. "What about you, sir?"

Thorne looked at the menu on the wall. "I'll take a fried bologna sandwich, French fries, and sweet tea."

Waiter said, "Take a seat, I'll have it for you in a jiffy."

Chief Logan took off his hat and coat. Thorne didn't, as usual. That was one disadvantage to a shoulder holster. Although he had a permit and license, he wasn't particularly fond of flaunting it.

The chief asked, "What's the latest?"

"More than I thought. To summarize, you were correct. Frank Evans' wife and son live here now. Her father, Vernon Ward, saw Mr. Templeton about a place for them to rent. I got the address." The waiter brought their food and they began eating. "Did you get a chance to call the coroner?"

The chief swallowed, "Yeah, but he hasn't quite finished. He said it should be later today. I'll call him back this afternoon if he doesn't call me first, which I doubt he will. He never does."

Thorne said, "Now that we know the next of kin, you will need to notify her. I would like to go with you. Maybe she can fill me in on things to help me with my investigation. I know it's not the best time to ask questions, but anything might help."

"Sure, no problem. I'd just as soon have the company anyway and you can start the conversation. Are you going to be in town or at your office in Dunn?"

Thorne didn't hesitate. "I'm going to be around here. Just call my cell and let me know the plan."

They paid for their meal. The chief walked back to the police station and Thorne to his car.

When the chief got back to his office, Deputy Goss said, "Chief, the coroner called. I told him that you were at lunch. He wants you to call him back."

"Thanks, Goss." He took off his coat and hat, walked back to his office, and returned the call to Tom Sledge.

"Coroner's office, Sledge speaking."

"This is Chief Logan. What have you found?"

Sledge answered, "About what?"

The chief was glad he was on the phone and not there in person. *What a dufus!* "What do you think? I'm calling for the autopsy report on Frank Evans."

"Oh yeah, right. He had a gunshot on his forehead. I got the bullet but I'm sure it's too mangled to be of any use."

Chief said, "Let me worry about that. What else?"

"I'd say he's been dead a couple of days, maybe a little longer. Nothing else, really. He was in good condition, did manual labor from what I could tell. Of course, I took photos and fingerprints, like I always do."

Chief said, "Good work. I'll be by and pick up the report in a little while."

"OK. See you then." The coroner hung up. The chief slowly and quietly put the phone back in its cradle, trying to control his frustration. *If we don't get a new coroner, I might just quit my job.* He called Thorne's cell phone and told him that the report was ready.

Thorne asked, "Do you want me to pick you up?"

The chief said, "Since this is official business, we better go in my patrol car."

Thorne said, "Right. I'll be there in about ten minutes."

They arrived at the coroner's house. Sledge answered the door. "Yes?"

The chief wanted to stomp and hit the man. Thorne could see that, so he spoke up. "Mr. Sledge, we're here to get the autopsy report on Frank Evans."

"Oh, yes, that's right. Forgive me, my mind fails me sometimes. Come on in." They walked into the hallway. Sledge walked over to his desk, picked up the folder and brought it back to the chief. "Here it is."

"Thanks, Sledge. Did you keep the bullet?"

"Yes sir, it's in the little evidence bag in the folder. You'll see it."

They thanked him and left. The chief just shook his head when they got back in his car. "Sometimes, just sometimes." Thorne knew very well what he was referring to. He himself wondered about Sledge.

On the way back to the police station, the chief said, "It's late. I'm not sure what we will run into when we notify the wife. Also, tomorrow is the last day of school until after the holidays. From what the assistant principal says, Kenny is doing much better. He's made a friend and staying out of trouble. I think it might be better to wait until tomorrow to notify Jennifer Evans."

"I agree," said Thorne. "She will be at work, I guess. Do you think we ought to wait until she gets home tomorrow?"

"Sounds like a plan."

They arrived back at the police station. Thorne said, "I'll see you tomorrow, Chief. Call me if anything changes."

"Will do."

Chapter Sixty-Five

When Kenny got home from school on Wednesday, he asked his mom if he could ride his bike to Bucky's house. "Are you sure his mom doesn't mind?"

"He said he asked her last night, and she said it was OK."

"Alright, you be home before dark." He left. A little while later, she went to the kitchen to fix herself supper. The doorbell rang. She looked out the window and lost all color in her face, her knees felt weak. She opened the door. The police chief and another man stood there. "What happened? Is it Kenny? My dad?" Tears came to her eyes.

The chief said, "No Mam, we just need to talk with you."

Jennifer opened the door wider for them to enter. Neither took off their coasts. The chief removed his hat. "Please come into the living room. Have a seat."

The chief said, "I take it Kenny's not home?"

She answered, "No, he rode his bike to his friend's house. He'll be back before dark."

Thorne began. "Let me introduce myself. I'm Thorne Davenport, a private investigator. Can you tell me when you last saw your husband?"

"Frank? Why? What are you investigating?"

Thorne leaned forward. "If you could please just answer, I'll get to all that."

Jennifer sat back, crossed her legs. "I saw him this past Friday. He came by the house but didn't stay long."

Thorne said, "I understand you are divorcing him?"

"That's right. What is this all about?"

Thorne continued. "What was his purpose for the visit?"

She said, "He wanted us to get back together, for me to forgive him and give him another chance."

"Forgive him? For what?"

She hesitated, uncrossed her legs, and sat forward in her chair. "He had an affair. I know because he told me. I guess his conscious got the best of him and he had to confess. At first, I was heartbroken, but I realized that there could never be any more trust in the relationship, not on my part."

Thorne said, "I see. So, when he asked you to try again, you said no?"

"That's right. I made up my mind. To try again would be foolish. Kenny and I are adjusting fine. I think Frank realized that it is truly over, and I don't think he will be back. Why do you ask about him?"

Thorne asked, "Do you know who he had an affair with?"

"Yes, it was a married woman who lives next door to a house Frank was repairing or remodeling or something, I'm not sure. Her name is Emily Duncan. I don't know anything about her and don't want to. Now, can you tell me why all these questions?"

"Do you know Emily's husband's name?"

"No, just her name, Emily Duncan. Again, why all these questions about Frank?"

Thorne looked at the chief, who began. "My deputy was on his way to work Monday morning and spotted your husband's car on the side of the road. When the deputy checked it out, he saw that the man had been shot and killed."

"Shot! Frank? You must be mistaken. Who would want to kill Frank?" Her hands started shaking.

The chief said, "We will need you to identify the body, since you are the next of kin. Maybe tomorrow?"

"Do I have to? Don't you already know who he is?"

"It's a necessary formality, I'm afraid. Tomorrow if you can."

"I'll call my dad. He can come with me if that's OK."

"That's fine."

Thorne and the chief got up. Thorne handed her his business card. "If you think of anything to help, you can call me at the number on the card."

She numbly took the card and followed them to the door. She was in a daze. Her mind would not focus. So many questions running through her mind, no answers. She didn't know what to do first. Softly aloud, she said, *"I'll call my dad, no, I'll wait until Kenny gets home, no Kenny and I will go to my dad's before I tell him. Oh god, what do I do? How do I tell Kenny? Who would hurt Frank? Would this not have happened if I had not said such a final no?"* Kenny would be home any minute. She called her dad. When he answered, she said, "Dad, Frank's dead. Somebody shot him." Tears filled her eyes.

Vernon Ward said, "Say again."

"The police chief and a detective just left. They said somebody shot Frank. He was found in his car on the side of the road on Monday morning."

Her dad asked, "Where's Kenny?"

"He's rode his bike to Bucky's house. He should be home any minute."

"I'll come over."

"No Dad, it's late. I just had to tell you. I'm not sure I'll tell Kenny tonight or wait until tomorrow. It's going to devastate him. It'll be fine, don't worry. I'm just shocked at all this. I can't believe it."

Her dad said, "Neither can I. I mean, I believe you, but it's just hard to take in. Are you sure you don't want me to come over?"

"I'm sure. We'll come to see you tomorrow and I can tell Kenny then. Is that OK?"

"You know it is. You know how much I care about you and Kenny. You get here when you can. I'll have lunch fixed. Now you try to rest. I'll see you tomorrow or call anytime."

"Thanks, Dad. We'll see you then."

Kenny came through the door like a whirlwind. "Mom," he called. He went to the kitchen. "Since there's no school, Bucky and I made some great plans. I'm starved. What's for supper?"

Jennifer gathered her thoughts. "I just made myself a sandwich with some chips. There's the sliced ham in the refrigerator." Kenny prepared and ate his sandwich, then went to his room.

Jennifer could not sleep. She was trying to figure out what was going on and how she was going to explain it to Kenny.

Chapter Sixty-Six

Wednesday, while Thorne was at work, Carly bundled up and walked down the street to visit Shelly. Shelly answered the door. "Come in, come in. It is cold out there! Is everything all right?"

"Yes, I just thought I would see if you're up for a visit." She took off her coat. "If you're busy, I understand."

Shelly laughed. "I'm always busy. Come in here and stay awhile." They went to the living room where Jill was in her playpen. "Keeping the house straight and playing with Jill takes up all my time. Now, with Jack, it can get interesting. He's a wonderful dog. He follows Jill everywhere. When she's playing in her playpen, he lays down beside it, like he's keeping watch over her. I think he's going to make a great watchdog for her."

Carly said, "That's how Dinkle is with me. You need to come meet Dinkle. I wonder how Jack and Dinkle will get along."

Shelly said, "They would probably smell each other for a while, then decide they could be friends. Then, again, you never know. We'll probably get to find out at some point. Would you like some coffee?"

"No, I'm fine."

Shelly said, "I know you like tea. I'm afraid I never could get in the habit of drinking tea. So much preparation and all."

Carly said, "I got the habit in college. My friends drank coffee to help keep them awake to study. I found that it makes me too jittery."

Shelly asked, "How are you feeling? This is your first baby, right?"

"Yes. I was nauseated for a few weeks. That was no fun. I've been fine since that stopped. Do you know if you're going to have a boy or a girl?"

"No. we like to just wait until the baby is born. You?"

"We feel the same. You know, sometimes I feel a little nervous about it all."

Shelly said, "I understand that. During my first pregnancy, I had all kinds of thoughts, worries about the birth, being a mom, could I do it right, just everything. I think that's normal."

Carly changed the subject. "Where are you and Mike from?"

"I grew up near Boone. I couldn't wait to move from there because it was so cold. The snow every year made activities impossible. When I graduated from high school, my parents insisted that I go to college. I went to North Carolina State, just general classes. I had no idea of a profession that I wanted. That's where I met Mike. He grew up in Raleigh and, although he was used to the big city life, he prefers to be in the country. Mike loves animals and was going to school to be a vet. We married and nine months later, Jill was born. After his education, he worked in a veterinary clinic in Raleigh and when he saw the ad for this job, he got so excited. So, here we are."

"I'm glad you moved here. The people I know in the town are much older. I grew up in Lillington. I went to college, majored in journalism. I've always wanted to be a writer and, in fact, I'm working on my first novel."

"Wow, that sounds exciting. I'm sure I wouldn't have the imagination to do that. What's it about?"

Carly summarized a little of the story. Jill started fussing and Shelly went over and picked her up out of her playpen. "She needs a diaper change. I'll be right back."

Carly said, "I better get home. You come to see me sometimes, OK?"

Shelly walked her to the door. "I will and you feel free to visit anytime. I'm always here."

Chapter Sixty-Seven

Thursday, before going to his office, Thorne searched for property in the name of Emily Duncan in Belmont. He found a listing with both her name and her husband's, Carl Duncan. He made notes. He then did a criminal background search on the two. There was nothing on the wife. However, the husband was a different story altogether. He wrote on his notepad.

Assault and battery four times; assault with a deadly weapon; illegal weapon charge; DUI; three months in jail for a misdemeanor hit and run.

He sat back in his chair. *Interesting*, he thought. He got up and went to the kitchen and poured another cup of coffee. It came to him, his old buddy from the Richmond police force, Al Covington, who had left the force at about the same time and opened his private investigation office near Charlotte. He googled and found out that he was in Gastonia, which is only fifteen miles from Belmont. *He might just know this guy*, he thought and gave him a call.

A deep gruff sounding voice answered, "Covington Investigations."

Thorne began. "How is everything in the metropolitan city of Gastonia?"

Al, "Big Al," as he was called by some, laughed, and said, "Are you trying to disguise your voice, Mr. Davenport? I would know your voice anywhere."

Thorne said, "I should have known. You have always been the best. How's business?"

"Can't complain. My belly ain't complaining, got a roof over my head, my car is paid for. How about you?"

"Same here. Al, I'm calling for a reason. I've got this case that involves some folks out your way. Not sure how it all fits together but wanted to see if you could give me a heads up."

"Shoot, not literally, you understand. Go ahead. What's up?"

Thorne asked, "Do you happen to know people in Belmont by the name of Emily and Carl Duncan?"

"Boy, do I. A real piece of work, that guy. He has the whole community of Belmont fooled. Have you had a chance to look into his past?"

"As a matter of fact, I have. I found problems, but they were years ago. How do you know him?"

Al answered, "Mainly because he hired me a while back to tale his wife because he suspected her of having an affair. He pays well but wants everything hush-hush. Seems he has this high opinion of himself and doesn't want anyone in the town to know the real him."

"With what I saw, I can understand that. Was the wife having an affair?"

"Oh yeah. Seems this fellow, a construction guy working on a house next door to the Duncan's, was the one. One day she goes over to the work site and the next thing I see is her bringing what looked like sandwiches and a thermos of water or coffee. Don't know. She didn't stick around, but her take-out services became more frequent. This one fellow is always the one who returns the thermos; everything else goes in the trash. This went on for a week or so."

"On a Friday, I saw the husband, Carl, put a suitcase in his car, so I figured he was going away for the weekend and, sure enough, Emily and the construction worker thought the same. I, of course, took photos, and reported my findings to the husband. What's this got to do with what you're working on?"

Thorne said, "It's a bit too much to get into over the phone. I was planning to drive to Belmont today or tomorrow to talk with the wife, Emily, hopefully."

Al said, "You better plan it when Carl's not there. He's somebody I wouldn't trust. He's liable to have you arrested. Also, if he's involved in anything suspicious, you'll have a hard time, if not impossible, getting anything done about it. The whole police force, town council, lawyers, and judges are in his pocket. I only know one cop who isn't fooled by him, a good, serious, honest, law-abiding guy, the whole nine yards. His name is Dale Stone, just in case you need somebody to trust around here. Good man, that one. And about Duncan, he's the chief loan officer at the Belmont Bank, a deacon in the Baptist church, and donates to all kinds of fund raisers and charities."

Thorne said, "Since it's still early, I think I'll try to see Emily Duncan today. Hopefully, Carl is at the bank."

Al said, "Listen, how about I meet you today? I don't have anything pending."

"That would be helpful. I should be there around lunchtime. Where do you want to meet?"

Al gave him the address of a small diner. "See you then." They hung up. Thorne called Carly.

He said, "I'm going to drive to Belmont today. I'm meeting an old partner of mine from the police force in Richmond. I called him this morning and I think he can help with this case. Turns out, he is familiar with the people that may be involved."

Carly asked, "What's his name?"

"Al Covington. People call him Big Al. He fits the name. He's a huge guy, low gruff voice, black as the walls of a well-used fireplace, and looks like a football linebacker. He's one of the good guys and one I trust to have my back. He left the force a little after me and opened his own PI firm in Gastonia. It'll be good to see him again."

Carly said, "If you have time, could you stop by the drugstore for me?" She told him what she needed. "I'll see you tonight. Be safe." As always, Thorne told her that he loved her. They hung up.

Chapter Sixty-Eight

Jennifer and Kenny arrived at her father's house after lunch Thursday. They greeted each other with hugs. Vernon knew they were here for her to tell Kenny about his dad. They sat in the living room.

Vernon began. "Kenny, sounds like you've got a good friend."

Kenny answered, "I sure do, Papa. His name is Bucky. It's kind of funny. We started out as enemies in a way, but he apologized and, well, we're good friends. What's so great is that he only lives a couple of streets over from our house. We went camping last weekend. It was fun."

Papa said, "Well maybe I can meet him sometime. Do you think he would like to go fishing?"

Kenny shrugged, "I don't think he's ever been. His dad is more like a businessman. His parents are nice to me."

Papa looked at Jennifer, then Kenny. With a serious expression on his face, he leaned forward in his chair, clasped his hands together. He said, "Kenny, sometimes terrible things happen and lots of time we can't understand why. I know a while back, it seemed you were upset and all, I assume about your mom leaving your dad." Kenny shook his head, yes. "First, let me tell you that I'm real proud of you and the way you have adjusted to your new life here. I'm also proud to have you for my grandson. Your mother wants to explain things to you, and I hope you will listen and think before you respond too hastily."

Kenny looked at his mom. "What is it, Mom?"

Jennifer began. "I never explained to you the reason I left your dad. I didn't think you were old enough to understand, really. But now, hopefully, you can understand. Your dad and I were happy when we married and having you in our lives made it more wonderful. Over the years, your dad and I, I guess, took each other for granted, stopped being special to each other. One day, your dad came to me and told me that he had made a terrible mistake. He had met a woman near where he was working."

Jennifer paused, took a deep breath. "It seems she was very tempting to your father, and he didn't resist, and they were together on several occasions. When a married person has an affair, it's called adultery." Kenny had a blank expression. "I was crushed, my heart broke. I knew that I could never trust your dad again. Once someone breaks a trust, it takes a long time to get that trust back and sometimes it never comes back. That's how it was with me. I would always wonder where he was, who he was with. Anyway, that's why we left and moved here."

Silence filled the room for minutes. Kenny spoke, "I think I get it, Mom."

Jennifer, although feeling relieved, dreaded the next part. "That's not the whole story, Kenny." She looked at her dad.

Papa said, "Would you like some water, or tea? Edna made a pitcher of sweet tea." Jennifer and Kenny both shook their head, no. Papa said, "Go ahead, Jenn. I didn't mean to interrupt."

Jennifer continued. "Last Friday, when you were at Bucky's house for your camping weekend, your dad came to our house. He wanted me to give him a second chance. I knew there was no hope and I said no. He left. Yesterday after I got home from work, and you were at Bucky's house, two men came to see me. The chief of police, and a private investigator." She saw Kenny's expression change. "I was told that your dad's car was found on the side of a road. He had been shot and he was dead." She put her hand on Kenny's shoulder. "I'm so sorry, sweetie."

Kenny looked at her. "And you're just telling me this now?"

"I didn't believe it myself at first. I didn't know how to tell you. I just found out last night. Papa wanted to be with us when I told you. That's why I waited until today."

Kenny slumped back on the sofa, his arms hanging by his side. He leaned his head back and took a deep breath. Papa came over and sat beside him. "Kenny, I know how you must feel. It is understandable that you will have lots of different feelings about everything. Will you promise me just one thing?" Kenny lifted his head. "Will you promise me that you will talk about how you feel and not hold it inside? Both your mom and I will understand, no matter what it is. Do you promise me that?"

Kenny had tears in his eyes. "I guess." He then thought about how his papa had cried when his wife died. That gave him the freedom, so he cried.

Jennifer said reassuringly, "I'm sure the police and the detective will find out who did this, Kenny."

Papa said, "They will. It may take a little while. We'll wait and see."

Chapter Sixty-Nine

Big Al and Thorne arrived at the café at the same time. Al drove a 2014 dark gray Range Rover. They greeted each other and went inside.

Al said, "I've eaten here several times, food's pretty good."

"It's good to see you, man. You're looking fit, as always."

"Working out, trying to eat right, you know, longevity stuff. How's life treating you, Thorne?"

When they sat at a corner table, the young waitress came over and took their order. Al ordered two of the lunch specials, Thorne ordered one. Both had sweet tea.

Thorne said, "I got married in September. How we met is a long story, but all is good. In fact, we're expecting a baby this summer, July sometime."

"Wow, congratulations, man!" Their food was brought to the table.

Thorne said, "Thanks. What about you?"

Al took a bite of food and a gulp of tea. "Me and my wife, we split right before I left Richmond. Hadn't been able to find anybody that can put up with me since then." He wiped his mouth with his napkin. "I've been thinking about your case. I checked on any handgun registrations for Carl Duncan. He has a couple of handguns." He looked at Thorne. "I assume you're packing."

"Yep. Hopefully, there won't be any trouble with just a conversation."

Al said, "Better safe than sorry, my man." Thorne shook his head in agreement. "Since you say Carl Duncan has the entire town in his pocket, how would I go about getting any resolution if it turns out he is guilty?"

Al answered. "I've thought about that. I've had a few occasions that I needed some backup. Like I told you, there's one cop in Belmont, an all-around tough but good guy. His name is Dale Stone. He's young but has had quite a bit of experience. I thought about calling him if you think you're going to need backup."

"That's good to know." Thorne swallowed a bite of food. They finished their meal. Thorne said, "It's on me, no argument." He paid.

Al said, "Follow me. We can leave your car parked nearby. Besides, if Carl is at home, he will recognize me. That may help."

Thorne agreed and followed Al to the parking lot of a church down the street from the Duncan residence. He got in Al's Range Rover. "Nice car." Al drove. His enormous hands made the steering wheel look like a toy. As they neared the Duncan house, Thorne noticed the house next door under construction. He asked, "That's the house they were building when you were investigating?"

"Yep. It's been a while. Looks like they've made progress." Al pulled in the Duncan's driveway. They got out and walked to the door.

Emily Duncan opened the door slightly. "Yes, may I help you?"

Thorne said, "I'm Investigator Davenport. I'd like to ask you a few questions about your husband."

"My husband? What on earth would you want to know?"

Thorne introduced Al Covington. "Could we come in, Ms. Duncan?"

"Oh, no, my husband wouldn't like that. What is it you want to know? I'm sure whatever it is, it doesn't involve Carl."

Thorne continued, "That's why we need a few answers. It would help us straighten out some details." Thorne could tell she was about to close the door and he said, "Ms. Duncan, are you aware that your husband knew about your affair with Frank Owens?"

Her face lost all color. Her lips trembled slightly. "Who'd you say you were again?"

"Investigators. We're looking into a murder, and we think your husband may be involved." Thorne thought she was going to faint. He continued, "Can you tell me where your husband was last weekend?"

She regained her composure. "Why he went to a banking conference in the Research Triangle area? He does that sometimes, that is, goes to conferences about his work. He's an important man in this town, you understand. He would never commit a crime, my lord no."

Thorne persisted, "Not even out of jealousy and revenge?"

She put her hand on the door. "I think you better leave. He'll be home any minute and if he sees you here, I'll have a lot of questions to answer. You've got the wrong man, I assure you."

She was about to shut the door, and Al spoke up. "Ms. Duncan, I'm the PI who your husband hired to find out about your affair, so I know that it is a fact.

We'll come back when your husband's home and question him then. We'll also bring a police officer with us."

She shut the door. The investigators walked back to the car. Thorne said, "My gut tells me that this guy may not be the guy, but he is definitely involved somehow."

"My gut agrees. It must be the lunch we had." They laughed and drove back to Thorne's car. "What's the plan?"

Thorne said, "I need to think. You got any ideas?"

Al said, "We could go to his office at the bank. He wouldn't dare put up a fuss there."

"I think you and I ought to partner up in business. Good idea. Let's go. We can just leave my car here, unless you think there is a better place in town."

"It's fine here." Al drove them to the Belmont Bank.

Thorne said, "I feel like I'm getting ready to rob the place."

Al said, "Partner, aye? Not in crime, old buddy." They laughed again. It felt like old times for both. Al thought and said, "You know, he knows me. Why don't you go in first, so he won't run and hide? I'll come in after a few minutes."

Thorne got out and went inside the bank. He told the desk clerk his name and that he was there to see Mr. Duncan. She asked him to have a seat and she would let him know. Thorne took a seat in the lobby, watching Carl Duncan in his glass walled office. The clerk called his name and said he could see Mr. Duncan now. Thorne walked back to his office.

Carl Duncan stood and shook hands with Thorne. "How may I be of service?" He motioned for Thorne to have a seat.

Thorne began, "Mr. Duncan, I'm Thorne Davenport, a private investigator. I need to ask you a few questions."

Duncan sat up straight in his chair. "What about?"

Thorne said, "Sir, could you tell me where you were this past weekend, in particular, Friday night?"

"How, may I ask, is that any of your business?"

"I'm investigating a case in which I believe you may be involved."

"A case? Me? Involved? What kind of case?"

At that time, Al Covington entered Duncan's office. The expression on Duncan's face paled a bit. He didn't stand. "Mr. Covington, are you a part of this charade?"

Al walked over, took a seat, barely fitting in the chair. "Afraid so. Not much to it really, just a few answers and we'll be on our way. We know you are a busy man."

Duncan looked a bit unsettled. "Alright then, what is the question?"

Thorne repeated. "Where were you last weekend, Friday and Saturday, specifically?"

Duncan rubbed his chin with his index finger. "Let's see, last weekend. Oh yes, I was in Raleigh at a banker's convention. I stayed at the Hyatt Regency. You can verify that, I'm sure."

Thorne said, "We will. You were there the whole time?"

"Yes, of course. I ate at several restaurants in the area, attended the meetings, otherwise I was in the hotel."

Al spoke up, "You have two handguns registered in your name, is that right?"

"Of course. Every law-abiding man in this county who believes in the constitution has at least one. Why do you ask?"

Thorne answered, "The case I'm working on involves a man killed with a .22 caliber handgun."

Duncan asked, "What, man? Where did this happen? Who was he?"

Thorne watched Duncan's face carefully. "His name was Frank Evans." Sure enough, although Duncan tried to disguise it, Thorne saw that the name rang a bell.

Al spoke up. "He's the man who was having an affair with your wife. Remember that?"

Duncan appeared more uncomfortable. He looked out through his glass walls to be sure no one was close by. He cleared his throat. "Yes, you know I'm aware of his name. You found it out for me."

Thorne asked, "Would it be possible for us to take a look at your handguns?"

Al said, "We can get a subpoena, you know."

Duncan laughed, "In this town? I don't believe so, gentleman. Besides, that won't be necessary. If you'll come by the house this evening, I'll give them to you."

Thorne said, "The .22 is the only one we need."

Duncan said, "Everyone knows I would never break the law, much less kill anyone."

Thorne said, "That's not exactly true according to the criminal background check I did."

Duncan's face got beet red, the veins in his neck bulged. He flattened his hands on his desk and stood. "You gentleman can find your way out, I'm sure. Don't come back to my office with such nonsense." They left.

Thorne asked Al, "What do you think?"

Al said, "I'm not sure. My gut says he knows something, but I'm not sure he's the killer."

Thorne said, "I got that impression. I don't think he has the guts."

Al looked at Thorne, "Maybe we ought to eat together more often. Our guts, at least, are on the same track."

Thorne said, "Just like in Richmond."

"Yep, I remember."

"Listen, the holidays are around the corner. If you don't have any plans, why don't you spend Christmas Day with Carly and me? I have to warn you, though, she has the most ferocious guard dog you've ever seen."

"You know how scared I am of dogs."

Thorne laughed, "Oh yeah. I remember a few times in Richmond, when you tried to climb on the roof of the car."

Al laughed. "I'll bring him a bone."

"First of all, it's a female, and the only thing she eats is Alpo Filet mignon. Seriously, the invitation stands, think about it."

Al said, "I will and thanks."

Al drove Thorne back to his car. "Keep me posted about your case. I'll see what I can dig up further on this end."

Thorne said, "Good deal. I will. It's been great seeing you again, Al."

"Same here, man. Take care."

Chapter Seventy

Before going home, Thorne stopped by Barton's Drugstore for things that Carly had asked him to pick up. He walked into the store and was surprised not to see Ms. Maggie behind the counter. He walked over, then looked around the store. Then he heard a low moan coming from behind the counter. Ms. Maggie was slowly trying to get up off the floor.

Thorne rushed around the counter to her. "Ms. Maggie, what happened? Are you alright?"

Ms. Maggie, shaking and weak, said, "It was pure, awful, so scary. I was afraid for my life, I tell you."

"Don't try to talk just now. Let me call an ambulance." He reached into his pocket for his cell phone and called them with the necessary information. "Are you hurt? Do you remember what happened?"

She slowly sat up with Thorne's help and leaned against the counter with her hand on her head. "I believe I hit my head."

"Ms. Maggie, tell me what happened? Was anyone else in the store?"

"Oh yes. A robber. I tell you it was a robber." Her breaths were short and shallow. "Can you help me stand?" she asked.

Thorne helped her to her feet. She looked like she had seen a ghost for real. "A robber? A man? Did you know the person?"

"No, never seen him. Yes, a man." He came through the door, pointed a big gun at me and said something like, "Make a sound and you're dead. I didn't make a sound. When he turned toward the back of the store, I knelt, and I think I went down too fast and lost my balance." She rubbed her head. "I may have hit my head on something."

"You just stay right here, Ms. Maggie. I'm going to check out the rest of the store. The ambulance will be here shortly."

"No worry. You be careful. He may be back there with that gun."

Thorne pulled his Ruger from his shoulder holster and made his way to the back of the store. *The pharmacy*, he thought. *Drugs*. He spotted the pharmacist sitting on the floor, stiff as a corpse. He made his way around to him. He was in shock, but alive. Thorne didn't see any sign of injury. He took his cell phone and dialed 911 again to advise that there were two victims at the drugstore.

The pharmacist slowly raised his hand and pointed. Thorne saw a .22 pistol by the side of his leg. When he looked over, he saw that a man, or a boy, dressed in jeans, tennis shoes, wearing a hooded sweatshirt was sprawled on the floor. Thorne walked over. The guy was dead. Thorne went back to the pharmacist. "Sir, can you hear me?" He nodded. "The ambulance is on the way. Are you hurt?" The pharmacist shook his head no. Thorne called the police department.

"Police Department, Deputy Goss speaking."

Thorne said, "Goss, put the chief on the phone."

Deputy went to the chief, "I think it's an emergency, chief. Detective Thorne is on the line."

"Thorne, what's the problem?"

"Chief, I'm at the drugstore. I've called the ambulance. Ms. Maggie and the pharmacist aren't hurt, just dazed and shocked. However, there is a dead man, the guy was trying to get drugs. I believe the pharmacist shot the robber and he's dead."

Chief said, "I'll call the coroner and be right there." He then called Sledge.

"Coroner's office, Sledge speaking."

The chief didn't have time to dilly-dally around with the coroner's nonsense. "You have a dead body at Barton's Drugstore."

Sledge said, "Is Ms.—" The chief hung up in the middle of his words.

Chief Logan walked into the drugstore. Ms. Maggie was sitting on her stool behind the counter. He walked up to her. "Ms. Maggie, are you alright?"

"Scared half out of my wits is all. You need to check on Steve."

The chief asked, "Steve?"

"The new pharmacist. Steve Edwards."

The ambulance arrived and the EMTs entered. They did a brief exam of Ms. Maggie and Steve Edwards. They escorted both to the ambulance and left.

The chief and Thorne met in the aisle. As they waited for the coroner, Thorne filled the chief in on what he saw. "Looks like this is one case that won't cost your City Council anything."

Chief smiled. "I believe you're right. Open and shut, for sure. You know, we've had quite a bit of an increase in various crimes. Seems like they are getting more violent."

Thorne said, "That's probably why the pharmacist had a weapon. He knew the drug problem was growing and, working in his profession, he could be a target."

"I agree."

The coroner arrived, examined the robber, who was sprawled on the floor. "Yep, he's dead, not long ago either, maybe half an hour or a little more, I'd say."

Thorne thought, *If I had been minutes earlier, things could have been quite different.* He said to the chief, "I better get home to Carly. I'm late as it is. I'll fill you in on my progress of the Evans' case tomorrow if that's OK with you."

"Fine, fine. You get home and take care of things. I'm glad you were the one who came in on the scene rather than another citizen who wouldn't have known what procedure to follow. Have a good night."

* * *

When Thorne arrived home, Carly met him at the door. She had already put Dinkle in her kennel for the night. "Sorry, I'm late. You won't believe my day." He took off his jacket and shoulder holster and hung them in the closet.

Carly said, "I've been thinking. Your job would make a good book. Maybe I'll write that after I've finished Bonnie's story. Can I get you something?"

They went into the kitchen. "I ate a good lunch. I'll just have a snack. It has been one busy day." He then remembered. "Oh man, I forgot to get your things from the drugstore!"

"I should have called and reminded you."

"No, that's not why. I went to the drugstore. When I went inside, I didn't see anyone. I found Ms. Maggie on the floor behind the counter. She had passed out and hit her head, is what she said."

Carly interrupted, "Is she OK? What happened?"

"The EMTs took her to the hospital to be sure, but I think she just panicked. Seems a man came in to rob the store for drugs. She said he pointed a gun at her. Then I found the pharmacist, Steve Edwards. He was sitting on the floor in shock. He had shot and killed the guy who was going to rob him."

Carly was quiet a minute, then said, "Oh my god, Thorne, you could have been there when that happened. You could have been hurt or killed." She walked to him and hugged him and began to cry. "I don't know what I would do if something happened to you."

He held her, rubbed her hair. "No worry, I'm fine. I'm big enough to take care of myself. Tell you what, why don't you go sit on the sofa and I'll make you some chamomile tea. You don't need stress. I hate I have to tell you some of things that I do."

She said, "I like to know about your job, your life, everything about you."

Thorne returned with the tea. "It was good to see Al today. He hasn't changed at all. Oh, and I invited him to visit us on Christmas day. He doesn't have any family, so I thought it might be good."

Carly said, "I hope he can come. I would like to meet him." She yawned. "I'm going to bed early. You?"

"Yeah, I'm pretty beat."

Carly finished her tea and put Dinkle in her kennel.

Thorne said, "We'll talk about it more tomorrow, OK?"

She agreed and they called it a night.

Chapter Seventy-One

Stacy was at her desk when Arthur Templeton entered with a smile on his face, carrying a bouquet of roses. He walked over to her desk. "Good morning Mam, these are special delivery from a newly and finally divorced gentleman who request your company for a special celebration this weekend."

Stacy took the flowers. "What in the world? Have you lost your mind?"

"Oh no, my dear. My divorce is final. I want us to celebrate this long-awaited day!"

"What did you have in mind?"

"I want it to be a surprise. I'll pick you up this evening at 7:00. Pack one fancy outfit, the rest casual. You'll love it, I promise."

Stacy looked to be sure no one was entering the office. She leaned up and kissed him on the lips. They embraced for a moment. "I'm looking forward to, I think. The roses are gorgeous. Thank you." She found a vase, filled it with water and arranged the roses and sat it on her desk.

Mr. Templeton said, "I'll see you at 7 o'clock."

* * *

Friday mid-morning, Beth entered the drugstore. "My word, Maggie. Logan told me! Are you alright?"

"I'm fine. It was the scariest thing I have ever seen. You know, nothing like that used to happen around here. Things are getting scarier every day, it seems. You just can't feel safe anywhere."

Beth said, "I know. Logan says the same thing. He's even considering not running for re-election because of it. He likes the town the way it used to be."

Ms. Maggie said, "Don't we all."

Beth said, "I gotta run. I just had to come by and make sure you are OK."

"I'm fine." Beth left the store.

Carly had lunch at the Green Hornet. She hadn't seen Nellie in a while. She told Nellie about the drama at the drugstore. Nellie just shook her head. "It's a sad day, these days, things are getting worse all the time. I feel for the young ones who will never know how it used to be." She then heard what she had said. "Oh, I'm sorry Carly. I didn't mean to worry you about your baby. Sometimes things just come out. Forgive me?"

Carly smiled. "Nellie, you are my best friend. I could never take anything you say as being hurtful. Don't think another thing about it. I mean it." She walked over and hugged Nellie. "You are going to be sure my baby knows all about the ways thing used to be. Right?"

Nellie smiled. "You are one special person, Ms. Carly—I mean, Ms. Davenport." Carly finished her lunch and left the diner. She thought about checking on Ms. Maggie but felt tired and went home and took a nap on the sofa with Dinkle.

Chapter Seventy-Two

Dale Stone exited the diner. He saw Al Covington. "Big Al, my man! How the heck are you?"

They shook hands. "Good to see you, Dale. I've been good. I was just talking about you yesterday with an old buddy of mine."

Dale laughed. "Hope you didn't tell him anything bad."

"I gave him all the dirt I could think of. Listen, Dale, we might be calling on you soon. We have a very high standing individual, if you know what I mean, who is suspected of being involved in a crime."

"I'm here for you, man. Just call. You have my number."

Al said, "I knew I could count on you. Have a good holiday. Later." They went their separate ways.

Al called Thorne. When he answered, he asked, "Anything new?"

"Afraid not."

Al said, "Oh yeah, I was headed out of the police station and ran into Dale. I gave him a heads up on the situation."

"That's good. I hope to meet him."

Chapter Seventy-Three

Friday night, Templeton picked up Stacy in a limousine.

Stacy exclaimed, "Wow, this is a surprise! You mind telling me what gave you this idea? Where are we going?"

"You'll see. I think you will be more than pleased. I have made all the reservations."

Later, they pulled into the parking lot at the Hyatt Regency. The driver opened the door and carried their luggage inside and they checked in. Stacy entered the room. "This is beautiful! This must have cost a pretty penny."

Templeton said, "Not for you to worry about. We deserve this. We've been secretive about our relationship too long. You've been so patient. It's time the world knows how I feel about you."

The next day, they walked along the city streets decked out with decorations for the holiday. People were bustling with their shopping bags full of gifts. They saw a deli and stopped in for lunch. When they arrived back at the hotel, they rested for a while.

Shelly dressed for the special night. She wore a strapless black dress with sequins all over that ended at the top of her thighs, black pantyhose, and black heels. Her hair was twisted in a fashionably flared bun. Her makeup was impeccable. When she entered the room and Arthur saw her, it took his breath away. He just stared without speaking. He had on a tuxedo that enhanced everything about him. They just gazed at each other. He finally said, "I've never seen anything as beautiful as you."

He held his bent arm out, she took it, and they left the hotel in the limousine. When they arrived, Stacy thought that the restaurant didn't look all that prestigious, but when they entered, she couldn't believe it. She felt like a country girl coming to Hollywood. They were escorted to a private room. Candles and vases of roses on the white satin tablecloth-covered table, thick carpet, chandelier over the table, and soft Spanish guitar music coming through the speakers on the ceiling.

Arthur pulled out her chair and he sat across the table. The waiters came and went throughout the course of their meal, bringing small amounts of diverse types of cuisine. They were still quiet. After they had the final course of the meal, Arthur got up and walked over to Stacy's chair. He knelt on his knee and held out a small jewelry box, opened it. It held the largest diamond Stacy had ever seen.

"My dear Stacy, you have been my everything for so long. I have waited patiently, but no more. I am asking you to be my wife."

Stacy's heart was beating faster, tears in her eyes, she looked in Arthur's eyes. "You know I will."

He placed the ring on her finger, they kissed and had a glass of champagne. The music changed to a waltz. They danced until closing time.

Chapter Seventy-Four

That weekend, Jennifer and Kenny visited Papa to help him put up a tree. Edna was there.

Jennifer said, "This is going to be a wonderful Christmas. It's been so long since we've been able to be with you, Dad."

"I know. I'm so happy ya'll are here."

Edna said, "Vernon hasn't put up a tree in quite a while. Since he has you two here, things are much more festive feeling. Listen, I'm going to fix a dinner on Christmas Eve. I definitely want ya'll to come."

Kenny piped up, "I'll be here, for sure." They all laughed.

Papa and Jennifer looked at each other, thinking the same thing. *He's taking everything a lot better than I thought.*

When they arrived back home, Kenny asked, "Mom, can I—"

Jennifer interrupted, "May I."

He continued, "May I ride my bike to Bucky's? I won't be gone long."

"Sure honey. Just be home before dark."

Bucky was in his room playing video games when Kenny arrived. They played a couple of games together. Bucky said, "I hate this cold weather. I like it when we can get outside more."

Kenny said, "Me too. When it gets warmer, I want you to go with me to my papa's house and go fishing. It is the coolest thing. Have you ever been fishing?"

"No. My dad is too busy. I would like to go with you and your papa. I'll ask my mom if she knows how to cook fish." They put up the controls. Bucky asked, "Do you and your mom celebrate Christmas?"

"Not too much before we moved here. This year is going to be different. My papa and his friend, Edna, are having us over. They have decorated and everything. My papa gave me the bike, like I told you, but I saw another present under the tree when I was there earlier today. I can't imagine what it is."

Bucky asked, "What about your dad? Do you ever see him?"

Kenny shrugged. "It's not a good thing." He cleared his throat. "Last week, I found out my dad had been killed. My mom told me that the police chief and a detective came to the house and told her. They are investigating to find out who did it. So, I won't be seeing my dad anymore."

Bucky said, "Oh man, that sucks. Sorry, dude. Let's play one more, OK?"

Kenny said, "It's almost dark and I promised my mom I would be home before dark. Maybe I'll come over tomorrow." He left and rode his bike back to his house.

Chapter Seventy-Five

Carly got the two packages that had come in the mail that afternoon. She handed the smaller one to Thorne. "You wanna open it? It's our gift to us."

"I like that idea. We give ourselves a present. Never heard of that before."

Carly said, "I do it all the time, birthdays, Christmas, anytime that it seems like a good idea."

Thorne laughed, "You mean good excuse." He opened the small box and took out the special ornament that Carly had ordered. "Nice." He handed it to Carly. "You want to do the honors?"

She took it, the engraving was precise and elegant. She was pleased. She then pointed to the bigger box on the floor. "It's from Bonnie and Josh."

Thorne said, "Don't you want to wait until Christmas morning?"

"Look, I'm patient about a lot of things, but this, no way."

Thorne said, "If I open it, I get to keep it all to myself."

"I don't think so." They laughed. Thorne got out his pocketknife and carefully opened the box. When she saw the contents, she exclaimed, "Oh, my lord! I can't believe this! I thought the other quilt was the most special thing I've ever seen, but this? This is truly a treasure. Look at the applique, all hand stitched, each piece."

Thorne stood up and held up the quilt to see the full design. Carly said, "Let me get my phone and take a picture." After she took pictures, she said, "This is perfect for the sofa. I'll put the knitted Afghan on the foot of the bed. I sure will enjoy napping under this. I've got to call Bonnie right now."

She dialed the number. Bonnie answered. She hardly gave her time to say hello.

"It's the most gorgeous treasure I've ever seen! You shouldn't have. It is too special!"

Bonnie broke in, "Hold on. First, it's not too special for you and Thorne. I don't like to sell my applique as it takes so long to finish, and a stranger wouldn't appreciate it like family. I've given my kids special quilts in the past."

"Well, Thorne and I thank you so very, very much. I'm going to put it on the sofa for when I take a nap, which is most days now."

Bonnie said, "We haven't opened your gift yet. Josh makes me wait until Christmas because he knows it drives me crazy. I used to be the most excited person this time of year, but it's been a long time. We don't do anything too special at home. Melanie has a get together at her house and Renee and I go over there. Sara and her family go also. Of course, Jeremy, living in Colorado and having their four kids, it's hard for them to travel during Christmas. I wish Josh would go but I understand him better than he realizes. Renee gives everybody some of her potholders she makes all year. I don't know about my dad this year."

"Speaking of Dad, my sister can't keep him after all. I heard that my brother met with a man at a senior facility and also interviewed a 24-hour home care agency. The facility had no vacancy, and I believe my brother is looking into other things. I heard all this second hand. It upsets me that I don't get any information. At least my dad won't be gone away from everything and everybody he knows." Bonnie lit a cigarette. "Listen to me, getting all carried away as usual. I didn't mean to go on and on."

Carly said, "No problem. I really hope things work out for the best with your dad. I just wanted to say thank you. Have a good time with your family and we'll talk soon. Tell Josh Merry Christmas for us." They hung up.

Carly summarized the conversation to Thorne. "I'm gonna call Joey and Janice." She dialed.

Joey answered, "Hello."

"Hi, Joey, this is Carly."

"I know who you are. How is everything? Ya'll ready for Christmas?"

"Oh, yes. We have our decorations up and have already started opening gifts. I wanted to thank you and Janice for the sheets and towels. They are nice and most useful."

Joey said, "We got your package but haven't opened it yet. Janice is a stickler for waiting until Christmas morning. But I'll go ahead and thank you. I know it will be special."

They talked a few more minutes, then Janice came on the phone. "You shouldn't have, Carly. We didn't expect you to get us a gift."

Carly said, "I hope you like it. It's difficult to know what to get everyone."

"I agree. I hope ya'll have a wonderful holiday. We hope to see you soon. Merry Christmas."

Carly said, "Same to ya'll."

After they hung up, Carly told Thorne about the conversation. She said, "I think I'll have some tea. How about you?" While she made the tea, she said, "I've been thinking about a title for my book. I have decided on *Through It All*, I'm also going to publish in under the name of *Deborah*, first name, because I've always liked that name. And *Reardon* as the last name, because it's a good Irish name and the will power and determination of Bonnie to keep going seems to fit. What do you think?"

He thought. "I don't get the use of another name, but I like the title."

They spent the rest of the evening in the living room, Dinkle beside Thorne on the sofa, with only the Christmas tree lights on.

* * *

Jennifer and Kenny had Christmas dinner with Papa and Edna. They gave Papa two flannel shirts, his favorite, and to Edna, they gave a much-needed apron.

Jennifer received a Timex watch. Her dad said, "It lights up in the dark if you press the button. I know how you wake up and have to get out of bed to see the time." Kenny opened his gift from Papa. It was his very own checker set. Papa said, "You can teach your friend to play." They all hugged and thanked each other.

* * *

Ms. Maggie, Doc Skinner, Mr. Matthews, Chief Logan and his wife Beth, Deputy Goss, Mike and Shelly and Jill, and people in the surrounding area came to the Green Hornet Grill for Christmas dinner, most everyone brought a covered dish to add to the meal.

Everyone had a nice Christmas.

By New Years, all the decorations had been taken down. There were firecracker sounds, otherwise, a quiet town.

Chapter Seventy-Six

Not long after the new year, Police Officer Dale Stone answered his phone. "Stone."

The officer on the phone said, "Officer Stone, I have got a guy that we've been trying to interrogate. He refuses to say anything. He says he will only talk to you. Can you swing by the station and see what he has to say?"

"Sure. I'll be there in fifteen."

Officer Stone was escorted to the interrogation room. When he walked in, he recognized the guy from when he arrested him for possession with the intent to sell drugs. He sat in the chair across from the guy. "They say you wanted to see me?"

"Yeah. I got something to tell. I know something real big. Ya'll need to know it."

Stone said, "That sounds good. What is it?"

"I ain't no fool, man. You gotta promise me something, like, out of this hole."

Stone said, "I'm afraid I don't have the authority to do that."

"Yes, you do. You know who does. You can talk to them. Tell them I know something big but I ain't spilling the beans unless I get out of here."

Stone considered his options. He knew there wasn't enough evidence to get this guy to serve real time, but he wanted to know the big something he was talking about. He finally said, "I tell you what, I'll call the D.A. and tell him what you said. I'll be back after I make the call."

"Fine man, I can wait."

Stone went into the hall, called the district attorney's office, and relayed the situation. The D.A. said, "Tell him anything to get him to talk. It won't matter, but it might be helpful down the road."

Stone said, "I'm not going to lie to the guy. He sounds adamant about not talking unless he walks."

The D.A. was quiet for a moment. "You can't lie? I've heard that about you. How'd you get this far in life anyhow?" Stone didn't answer. The D.A. finally said, "Tell you what, I'll come down there and do the lying and you can get the story he has to tell."

Stone said, "If that's what you want to do."

"I'll see you in about ten minutes."

Stone went back into the interrogation room. "I called the D.A.'s office. He's on his way here to speak with you."

"All I want is promises, in writing. You wait till you hear what I gotta say. It's going to be shocking, to say the least."

Dale thought, *In writing; this ought to be interesting.*

The D.A. arrived, went into the interrogation room. "I'm the district attorney. I hear you want a deal because you have something big to tell us. Is that right?"

"Sure is. I want it in writing too, or I ain't saying nothing."

The D.A. pulled a folded paper from his coat pocket. "I figured as much. I have it here. Read it and I think you can start talking."

The guy read it. "This says if what I have to say ends up helping ya'll, then I'll get a deal."

The D.A. said, "That's correct. You can't just come up with any story and expect to walk out of here. We have to verify what you say is true."

"Fine then. OK. Tell that other officer to come in here and I'll tell him."

The D.A. left the room. He told Stone that the guy was ready to talk. Stone wondered what the promise had been.

Stone entered. He turned on the recorder, identified himself and the prisoner. "I'm ready to listen. I need to record what you say. First, I need to read you your rights." *Better safe than sorry,* he thought. "You have the right—"

"Yeah, yeah, I know all that stuff. I agree, no attorney needed. I just want out of this joint. Recording is good, that way you won't quote me wrong."

"OK, let's have it."

The guy began. "A while back, can't remember the day, but I got a call from this person, sounds like a man. He always calls me when he needs something. Mostly small stuff, you know. This time it was something not so small. He wanted me to do away with somebody. At first, I was scared. I told him, no way. But he promised a boatload of money, so I said what the heck. Then I got the details a little later.”

Stone asked, “Who was the somebody you were to do away with?”

“Just some guy. I don’t know anything about him. I was to follow him and when the time was right, take him out.”

“How were you to accomplish this?”

“With a pistol, of course. You know, that’s the quickest way, no hassle, no struggle, just bam, you’re dead.”

“So, did you follow the guy? And where did you get the gun?”

“Yeah, I followed him. I waited for a good opportunity, you know, don’t get caught and all. When I got the opportunity, I shot him. Bam, it was over, just like that. Damn fool never saw it coming.”

Stone was quiet for a moment. *Talk about an idiot. This guy just confessed to murder. Go figure. He won’t be going anywhere soon.*

Stone asked, “Where did you get the gun?”

“From the man who called me. He left it where he said he would.”

“What did you do with the gun afterwards?”

“I threw it in the river. That’s what everybody does, right?”

“So, you don’t remember where you picked up the gun?”

The guy said, “No, I told you, I don’t remember details like that.”

Stone asked, “Have you ever seen this man who hires you?”

“No way. I just take a call and do the job.”

“Do you know the name of the person you shot?”

“Heck no, that was weeks ago. My brain just don’t keep stuff like that in it. All I know is that I shot a man.” He changed his position and said, “Can I get out of here now?”

Stone stood, took his handcuffs off his belt, walked over to the guy. “You are under arrest for suspicion of murder. You have the right to remain silent—”

The man jerked, “Do what? You told me I’d be out of here if I talked. Now let me go. I know my rights!”

“I’m afraid that won’t be possible.” He took the prisoner to the duty officer at the desk and said, “Book him, charge is suspicion of murder. He confessed, on tape.”

Dale went to see the chief of police. “Morning, Chief.”

Chief said, “Yes, Stone, what can I do for you?”

"Just wanted to ask if you have had any dead bodies turn up around town, say, in the past month."

"No, in fact, other than old man Somers, everybody's still alive, as far as I know."

Stone shook his head. "No problem, just needed to clear up something. Thanks, Chief."

Dale thought, *Yep, just like I thought, a big mouth who watches too much television.*

* * *

Dale Stone searched in his notepad for Al Covington's number.

Al answered, "Covington Investigations."

"Al, Dale Stone here."

"Happy new year, Dale. Hope you are starting the year off right."

"For sure. I don't know if this is important or, for that matter, even true."

"Do tell, my man."

Stone said, "I'll come to your office, or we can meet here. Whatever works for you."

Al thought and asked, "You on duty?"

"Yep, until 7 p.m."

"I'll come there. Where do you want to meet?"

"The café is around the corner from the station, if that's OK."

"Fine, I'll see you in 30 minutes." Big Al couldn't imagine what was so urgent. He put on his coat and drove to the café. He walked over to where Dale was sitting. "If these booths get any smaller, I'll have to stand up to eat." He slid across from Dale. "What cha got?"

The waitress comes over. They both order coffee, and Al ordered two donuts.

Dale said, "I recently brought in a guy for drug charges." He told Al the whole story. "Confessing to murder to get out of jail? Do you believe this guy? He didn't have any facts, nothing to nail down anything specific. Just made me wonder if by chance it might have to do with your case."

Al shook his head. "In my line of work, and yours too, we run into some real characters. But I think this guy may be at the top of the list. Dale, I appreciate you keeping me in the loop if anything else comes out. It would sure

219

be nice to have a name. I guess since the guy only talks on the phone, he wouldn't be able to identify him."

"Yeah, I thought about that. Who knows, maybe he'll agree to another get-out-of-jail free card and tell us the rest of the story, if there is anything else to tell."

"We can only hope." They finished their coffee and left.

Al drove to his office. He needed to call Thorne. Thorne answered on the third ring.

Al said, "Had a chat with Stone this morning. I'm beginning to believe the world is full of idiots. You won't believe the tale this guy cooked up."

Thorne laughed. "You know I believe everything you say, Al."

Al went over the details of the situation.

"You're right, I don't believe it. I guess, like they say, an idiot is born every minute." Thorne shook his head in disbelief. "I got the cell phone out of the evidence room, Frank Evans' phone. I checked the last number dialed. It was to Emily Duncan's cell phone."

Al asked, "How long did they talk?"

"That's just it, the call only lasted a few seconds, maybe a voice message. I'll need to get her cell phone to check that out."

Al said, "There's more to this than meets the eye."

"I agree. We'll talk tomorrow. Have a good night." They hung up.

Thorne turned to Carly, who looked curious. "That was Al. Seems a man that the cops arrested for drugs right before Christmas wanted a get-out-of-jail free pass if he told something important. Ends up, the guy sat right there and confessed to the murder in front of the police officer who was questioning him and recording it. Both Al and Stone are sure he was making up the whole story. He had no details. It was more like something he had seen on television."

Carly said, "That's one for the record book, don't you think?"

Thorne laughed. "Only Big Al can come up with this stuff."

"That sounds like a good story, though unbelievable, for one of my future novels." She put Dinkle in her kennel. They called it a night.

Chapter Seventy-Seven

On her way to her doctor's appointment, Carly stopped by to see how Nellie was doing. Nellie was preparing the chicken salad, people's favorite. She called, "Come on in, Carly."

"I just stopped by to see how you're doing. Did you have a good Christmas?"

"Yes, I sure did. The usual people and people from the surrounding area came. We had more food than everybody could eat. It was a happy time. Just like all the years, these people are like my family. Of course, we all missed Ed. How about you and Thorne?"

"We did. Mainly quietly enjoying the Christmas tree lights. I just stopped by to check on you. I'm on my way to my OB appointment, my regular checkup."

"Hope it goes well. Stop again when you can stay longer."

"I will."

Carly arrived a few minutes early for her appointment. After the examination, the Dr. Winthrop told her she could dress, and she would return shortly. She came back into the exam room, "Well, my girl, you are going to have twins."

"Me? Twins?" She couldn't tell if she wanted to cry, shout, scream, run or what. "I was worrying about having one, now I'm doubly worried."

Dr. Winthrop says, "Often it's easier with two. They keep each other occupied when they get older. You'll be fine, I'm sure. I want to see you back in six weeks. You can make the appointment at the front desk."

"Thank you, doctor." She made her appointment and went to her car. Before cranking it, she wanted to call somebody, but decided this was news better told in person. She couldn't tell Nellie first, it had to be Thorne, so she didn't stop at the diner. The day dragged on. It seemed forever for Thorne to get home.

Thorne came in the door, took off his coat and shoulder holster. When he stepped into the living room, she raised her arms in the air and said, "yay! We're going to have twins!"

Thorne wondered for a second if she was having some kind of attack or hallucination. Then he realized what she said. "What? Us? Twins? You're not kidding?"

"No. Dr. Whitmore did her exam today and confirmed it."

They hugged and Dinkle barked. The excitement was too much for Dinkle. Thorne said, "My goodness, instant family."

Carly said, "I can't wait to tell Nellie. I almost stopped at the diner on my way home, but I knew you would want to be the first to know."

"This is going to take some planning. I mean, the house isn't big enough for a big family."

Carly said, "No rush. You realize it takes them quite a while to get old enough to have separate rooms. Babies don't take up that much room. I'll convert my office into the babies' room. We just have to buy twice as much of everything."

They went to bed that night, but neither went to sleep for a long time.

Chapter Seventy-Eight

The next morning, Thorne called Al Covington. He answered on the first ring. "Covington Detective Agency."

Thorne said, "Al, I think I have it figured out. Do you think Dale could meet us this morning? It would be a good idea to have the district attorney there as well. It's time to get a subpoena for the .22 pistol, Emily's cell phone, as well as the GPS tracker in her car."

Al laughed. "Did you sleep at all last night?"

"Not much. So, what do you think?"

"I'm sure I can arrange that. What time will you be here?"

"In about three hours. Since it's close to lunch, do you want to meet at the café again?"

"You know me, I'm always hungry. I'll get things set up and see you then."

Thorne arrived at the café, went inside and at the side table sat all three men. He walked over and said hello. The waitress took their order. Al ordered enough for all of them. Al made the introductions. They made small talk until their food arrived.

Thorne filled the district attorney in on the past events. "As you can see, we need to get a subpoena for the gun, her cell phone, and the GPS in her car."

The D.A. wiped his mouth with his napkin. "I'm sure you fellows know what you're doing. My question is, do you realize who you are messing with?"

Al said, "We realize that Emily Duncan is married to the biggest fake that ever hit this town. It's a murder, premeditated, cold, and I don't think she has any conscience."

Thorne said, "When we talked to her the first time, the only thing she seemed to be concerned about was her husband's reputation and how he would react to us being there."

Al shook his head. "I'm ready to throw a grenade at their pretense." He looked at the D.A. "Carl Duncan has a past criminal record, which I know is of no benefit in proving this case, but it stands to reason that he is living a lie to everyone in town. His money talks big."

The D.A. said, "Alright. Sounds like I don't have a choice." He looked at Dale. "Are you up to serving this subpoena on Emily Duncan, if I get one?"

"No problem. Let me know when and where."

The D.A. said, "I'll call Al with the particulars. He can let you know. We'll all meet at the Duncan residence, hopefully this afternoon." They all understood. The D.A. left the diner.

* * *

The district attorney entered the judge's office and told the secretary he was here to see the judge.

"Have a seat, sir. I'll tell him you are here."

After about thirty minutes, the secretary told him that the judge would see him.

"Hello, judge. Thanks for seeing me." He didn't sit down.

"Well, get on with it. What is it you want?"

"I need a subpoena. It is for a .22 handgun, a cell phone, and a GPS. It's regarding a murder case."

The judge sat back in his chair. "Who might this person of interest be?"

"Carl Duncan's wife, Emily Duncan."

The judge laughed. "OK, what's the joke? You are kidding, right?"

"No, sir, afraid not. I know everyone has a high opinion of these people. Checking these items would help alleviate her as a suspect."

"And ruin their reputation? Put a mark on their name? No way. No way. I will not allow it. We have a few people with spotless reputations, and I refuse to tarnish such citizens as Carl and Emily Duncan."

The D.A. sat in the chair. "Judge, this is needed. We have enough evidence to substantiate this subpoena. Elections are coming up and I'm sure you wouldn't want the people in our town to think you would cover up a murder. Would you?"

The judge said, "Of course not. You know how these things work. You better be damn sure you have this right."

"We do. The evidence is strong, and this will prove or disprove what we believe. You won't regret this, judge."

The judge leaned back in his chair, rubbing his chin. He leaned forward, putting his arms on his desk. "OK, you better hope I don't regret this. You make sure of that."

The D.A. said, "Yes, sir. I understand. I don't believe you will be sorry. Thank you for your time." He left the judge's office.

* * *

Al, Dale, and Thorne had pie and ice cream for dessert. They talked about things other than the case. Thorne told about Carly expecting twins. Thorne asked Dale, "Are you married?"

Dale answered, "No, I see a couple of friends, but nothing as serious as marriage on the horizon."

They all ordered a cup of coffee. Al's phone rang. "Yep. OK. We'll meet you there." He hung up and told Thorne and Dale, "It's on. He got the subpoena. We'll meet him at the Duncan house at 1:30. We can all go in my car."

Dale said, "That's OK. You two ride together. I better take the police car. It's official business."

Thorne spoke, "I'll wait. You guys go ahead."

* * *

Emily Duncan answered the door. "Oh, my goodness. What is all the fuss?"

The D.A. spoke first. "Emily Duncan?"

"Yes, of course. That's me. What is it you want?"

"May we come in?" He didn't wait for her to answer. As he was entering, he said, "Ms. Duncan, we have a subpoena signed by the judge. We are here to take possession of your cell phone, a .22 caliber handgun, and your car keys."

Emily gasped. "You need to leave now! I'm calling my husband!"

She took out her cell phone and the D.A. already had his gloves on, and he reached for the phone. "I'll take that, Mam. Now for the handgun." She stomped to the hall cabinet, mumbling to herself. Dale said, putting on his gloves, "Step back, Ms. Duncan. I'll get that." He saw the pistol in the drawer, took it out and put it in an evidence bag. Al just watched.

225

Emily started for the phone in the kitchen to call her husband. "My husband will put a stop to his nonsense. You just wait till he hears what you are doing."

Dale spoke up, "Your car keys?"

She got her purse from the kitchen bar and threw it at the police officer. He caught it. "Mam, I need you to get your keys out of your purse, please."

She huffed several times, took the purse, found the keys, and tossed them to the officer. Al was watching and thought, good catch. The D.A. spoke up, "Thank you, Mam, we'll be getting out of your hair, for now. You are not to leave town. Do you understand?"

"I understand alright. You are going to be sorry for the way you've treated me."

They left the house. The D.A. said, "I'll drive her car to town, and turn in the cell phone and gun for testing. You guys gonna be around for a while?"

Al shook his head.

Stone said, "I'm on duty, but I'll be close by."

They all left. Al rejoined Thorne outside the café. Al's phone rang. After he hung up, he looked at Thorne. "Sorry, man. That was a new case, a missing child. I gotta get on it pronto. You got this?"

Thorne said, "No problem, Al. You go do what you have to do. I'll call and give you updates. Hope you find the child and are in good shape."

Al said, "I left your number with the D.A. so he will be calling you, or possibly Dale. Let me know if anything comes up and I can help."

"Will do. Thanks. Later."

Thorne got in his car and called Carly. She answered. He said, "I just wanted to let you know that I'll be staying in Belmont tonight. This case is about to break, I do believe. Rather than drive back tomorrow, I'll be here when I need to be."

"I understand. I'll miss you terribly." Dinkle barked once. "Dinkle said she'll miss you too but has everything under control." They hung up.

Thorne checked in at the local motel. The next morning, he went to the café and had breakfast. Dale walked in. Thorne invited him to join him. Dale walked over and said, "I'm just here for a cup of coffee. Can't stay. We should be hearing something soon."

The officer's phone buzzed. After he hung up, looked at Thorne. "It's on. They have issued an arrest warrant for Emily Duncan. Let's go."

Thorne followed him and said, "On second thought, I'll wait until she is brought in. I would like to question her then."

Dale nodded. "See you in a bit."

* * *

Soon after Emily was brought in, Carl Duncan showed up at the police station, belligerent, demanding, appearing to be at his wit's end. Thorne watched his demeanor. *His self-assured confidence was waning*, he thought. When he asked to see his wife, the clerk said, "I'm sorry sir, she can't see anyone just now."

"Well, when, for god's sake?"

"I'm not sure how long it will be."

Duncan huffed. "This town, you people, all worthless, useless, do-gooders. You better know who you are messing with. I won't stand for it!" He turned and left.

Thorne entered the interrogation room and Emily had a defiant look on her face, her lips pursed, her hands clasped on the table. "Emily, you remember me, I'm sure. I'm here to ask you questions. We'd like to clear all this up. Will you answer some questions?"

She just shook her head slightly, then. "I really don't have anything to say."

Thorne turned on the recorder. "I'll be recording this." He read her rights to her. "Let me begin by telling you what we know. First, the gun we took from your house is the murder weapon. Second, your phone is the one the victim called just before he died. And third, your car's GPS shows that you drove that Friday to Belmont and back." Thorne thought he saw a tiny tear form in the corner of her eyes. "How do you explain that?"

She shook her head. "I never thought it would be found out. I mean, with my husband's reputation, the lack of law enforcement. I didn't start out to kill him. We were in love. I knew he loved me. For months, he was the only thing that mattered. My husband is never home and, when he is, he's busy, working, talking on the phone, or on his damn computer. You can't imagine how lonely I felt."

The tears came more freely. She wiped her eyes and nose. "I thought Frank and I had a future, at least in secret, since we both were stuck in a marriage. He was so understanding. He listened to everything I had to say. Then, one

227

day, out of the blue, he says it's over. Just like that, it's over. He said his wife was going to divorce him and he had to save their marriage. I never dreamed that would happen. I got depressed, then I got mad, then I got angry."

"How did you know he was going to Lillington?"

"I didn't. When I got to his house—I was going to confront him in front of his wife. What difference would it make? Anyway, when I got to his house, I saw him driving away. I followed him. And, yes, all the way to Lillington. I saw him stop at her house. I waited and when he left, I followed him some more. For some reason, he pulled to the side of the road. I pulled up beside his car. He rolled down his window. I don't think he knew it was me. When his window came down, my pistol came up and I shot him, I just shot him." She stopped crying suddenly and looked dazed.

Thorne turned off the recorder, pulled out the cassette, got up and walked out of the room. He handed the tape to the desk clerk. "I think this is all we need."

Outside, he reached into his pocket and cut off his own recorder. *You can't be too careful in cases like this.* He got in his car, feeling drained.

He dialed Al's number. The answering machine came on. "Al, it's me. Just a final word on the case. She fully confessed on tape. I guess it's a done deal. Talk later."

He called Dale, who answered on the first ring. "Dale, just wanted to let you know that she confessed, on tape. I called Al and left him a message. I appreciate your assistance in all this."

Dale said, "I'm glad it's over. No problem, I'm here anytime you need me. Are you headed back home?"

"Yeah. You take care." They hung up.

He arrived home. Carly and Dinkle met him at the door.

Epilogue

Carly and Thorne's twins were born July 12.
Girl: Julie Marie Davenport
Boy: Liam Thorne Davenport

Both babies and mother were doing well. Thorne took them home. Dinkle examined the babies thoroughly and gently. Dinkle sat and looked at Carly and then Thorne. *I think I'm going to like my new brother and sister* and wagged her tail.

THE END